JED COPE

The Village - A Vampire To Die For

Copyright © 2022 by Jed Cope

All rights reserved. No part of this publication may be reproduced, stored or transmitted in any form or by any means, electronic, mechanical, photocopying, recording, scanning, or otherwise without written permission from the publisher. It is illegal to copy this book, post it to a website, or distribute it by any other means without permission.

This novel is entirely a work of fiction. The names, characters and incidents portrayed in it are the work of the author's imagination. Any resemblance to actual persons, living or dead, events or localities is entirely coincidental.

Jed Cope asserts the moral right to be identified as the author of this work.

First edition

This book was professionally typeset on Reedsy. Find out more at reedsy.com

To you Dear Reader, you with the bold, brave and inquisitive nature, not content with the safe choice, but instead pursuing new paths, new authors and new stories...

1

There was a knock at the door.

The knock came from nowhere and Jim, who had only just closed that door behind him, felt a jolt of surprise and grabbed his chest theatrically as though someone would see him and understand the gesture.

Who could be at the door? He thought this to himself as he took a moment to restore some calm. Just as his heart rate climbed back down from the dining room table, another, insistent knock followed close on the heels of the first.

A knock.

Not the doorbell. And the knock was a rap of knuckles on the wood of the door, when there was a perfectly good knocker in the form of the brass Green Man, in the middle of the door. The doorbell was off to the side of the door and as often as not, people missed it. Certain delivery people didn't bother with either, some didn't bother with actually delivering the parcel itself either, Jim quashed that train of thought swiftly.

He'd expended far too much time on that particular delivery experience and the notorious company behind what seemed like a concerted effort at shoddy service. All the same, his mind was racing alongside his heart, like runaway horses pulling the stage coach that was Jim.

The knock.

It was a distinctive knock and Jim knew it for what it was. An ominous prelude. Something was not right here and by rights he should not open the door, he should at least be cautious. They had never put a security chain on their front door, Jim had said they didn't need to. He hadn't voiced this opinion, but he'd seen that chain as an admission. A sign that he was not enough. That they were scared. He didn't want to let that fear into their home, because once it was there, the sanctuary of their home was diminished and once that had happened they were lesser people.

He opened the front door, his curiosity getting the better of him and overriding his caution. He had just this minute walked through the door and was certain no one was behind him. They would have had to have been close behind him or they had run swiftly to close the distance and that did not bode well did it? Even as he turned the catch to open the door, he realised he was hoping for a certain someone to be at the door. Someone he had seen in passing from time to time and found himself day dreaming about, the day dreams increasing in frequency until they became a fantasy.

An impossible fantasy that he now found himself wishing to

become real, right here and right now behind the door he was about to open. He found he was holding his breath as the catch undid and he pulled the door open.

And there she was.

A ghost made real. An amalgam of women from his past, those he'd dated and those who had got away. She was more than that though. He could see that basis and the simple ingredients, but somewhere along the way she had been elevated into something more exotic and exciting, after all, this was his dream girl, so why stick with the mundanity of reality?

He knew that she wasn't real. Not the woman he had caught glimpses of every now and then. That was his imagination running away with him, using the thousands of faces he encountered during the drudgery of his daily commute. Using his theory that there were only so many combinations of features, so, if you looked hard enough you'd see familiar faces in the crowd. Sometimes they may even be faces you had seen before, after all, people were creatures of habit and routine, even in times of uncertainty when everyone's routine was thrown out of kilter. Those changes had if anything intensified his sightings. On half empty trains and quiet streets, she was still out there. Standing at a bus stop as he drove by, disappearing into a shop up ahead of him. During those times, her face would be obscured by a face mask, but he would still spot her. He would know her anywhere. Of course he would. She was his creation and she was his and his alone.

This dream woman of his though, he had only ever caught fleeting glimpses of her. Whenever he tried to focus on the spot he thought he'd seen her, she was gone. That was, if he was afforded that opportunity. Mostly he saw her as they passed each other by, usually a window separating them so she may as well have been some clever code in a realistic computer game.

He'd seen her today, of course he had. He saw her each and every day now. Where though, he could not say. She haunted his waking hours and dwelt in his sleep also.

In the doorway before Jim, she smiled a smile that promised much and his legs almost gave way as his head swam with the impossibility of it all. He stood dumbly before her, not wanting to speak or move for fear he would cause this dream to collapse in on itself and leave him bereft.

"Can I come in?" she asked.

Jim wordlessly stepped away from the doorway and ushered her in, still not wanting to speak and instead watching as she entered his home.

* * *

Shirley unlocked the front door absently, her attention taken up by the handbag that had a habit of slipping down her arm whenever she needed it to stay put. As the errant bag fell down

1

her arm and tugged at the hand that was in the process of turning the lock, she thought about Jim and how, if he saw her right now she would hear his disgruntled sigh from over her shoulder. A dull admonishment stemming from his repeated, grumpy advice on the matter of that very bag: you need to sort the contents of that thing out. It's cluttered. You lug far too much *stuff* around with you, no wonder it's a faff to carry around.

Her handbag was a totem. The meaning that it carried extended well beyond the chaos it contained. It represented Shirley's life and Jim's chagrin at the chaos that stalked her every move. Mostly, he quietly picked up after her and restored some semblance of order to their homelife as she breezed through, the breeze being more like a whirlwind. She did try, but life had a habit of getting in the way. She found that she was busy and before she knew it there would be a pile of items on her side of the bed. Thankfully, the window of their bedroom was on Jim's side of the room and her side of the bed was not visible from the bedroom doorway, so Jim did not get too fraught about that mess and it had seldom been a battleground. On this point, she knew she was kidding herself, she'd seen the look on his face when she had to hop, skip and damn near launch herself onto the bed when they turned in of a night.

He knew.

He knew her all too well, but then that was what happened when you shared a home with someone for all that time. Over twenty years of marriage and if you added the time they'd dated before that, they'd been together for nearly thirty years really. How had that time passed without her noticing? It were as though they were accelerating to the end now. Shirley had thought it would be different for them, no kids to define a period in their lives and then empty the nest and leave them with a gaping hole in their life that they could never adequately fill. That there was supposed to be their particular silver-lining, only it wasn't shaping up that way and that, Shirley thought, as she tried to open the door whilst wrestling her over-ladened bag, was bloody unfair.

With a final effort, the key in the lock turned and the door sprang inwards, hitting the wall. What a way to announce *honey! I'm home!* Jim would appreciate that and Shirley could see his eyes rolling in her mind's eye. She followed the trajectory of the door, stumbling into the hallway and kicking the door closed as she went. This time, the door clicked shut, not that Shirley noticed. Details such as these slipped her by, and they were the predominant cause of her spouse's eye rolling and over-exaggerated sighs.

The hallway was in darkness and this discovery led to a trickle of uneasiness.

Was the house in darkness as I walked to the front door? Shirley looked around the hallway as though she could discern the answer to her question from this vantage point. Her brow creased and she tried to remember whether Jim had told her he would be out tonight. She doubted it, she always knew when he was going to be out. She knew and she didn't like it. Didn't like being in the house alone. It felt so empty without Jim. The place transformed without him, almost as though it were an animal. His animal, not hers. He had never voiced similar concerns. Never said he didn't like it when she wasn't around. That he missed her. She suspected he enjoyed the occasional break from their wedded bliss, that it gave him what he would call a well-earned time out.

She dropped her handbag on the table in the hallway and rummaged around until she found her phone, it was lit as she lifted it upwards. She went to her messages to see if there was anything from Jim. An explanation for this inexplicable absence. Neither of them went out of an evening all that often. The options to do so were few and far between these days, even after the restrictions had been lifted and life had gone back to something that was supposedly normal.

Nothing.

And her breath faltered as she remembered that there were so few options for him to actually go out. Pretty much everything had been closed over the last two years, so he had had two options and he'd not broken that habit once things in the outside world had reopened and presented more options to him. Neither of them had. So, Jim could go for a drive, but his car was on the drive, and he was unlikely to go for a nocturnal stroll, not once he was home for the evening. Once he was home, he was home. The effort to leave the confines of the place was rather too much for either of them and they would slip into a routine that revolved around the evening meal and the seductive appeal of the sofa and TV.

Shirley was shocked to feel and hear her breath catch in her throat, more so as she attended to it. That was more of an involuntary sob and as this dawned on her so too did the fact that she was not only worried but worse than that, she was scared.

Something was not right.

She had never liked being home alone, but this went beyond that feeling of discomfort and into unchartered territory for Shirley. She cast her mind back to think about whether she had ever felt scared like this before. She supposed she had, but way, way back when she was a child. She vaguely remembered being ill with the flu and how a pile of clothes on a chair at the foot of her bed had moved and become something alive and frightening. She had watched the transformation with terrified fascination as the illness unbalanced her and played with her reality. The thing with that was that even though she was young, impressionable and not very well, she had still known that it wasn't real. Here and now though? There was a palpable feeling of something very wrong. She could smell an oddness to the place.

Some homes had a distinctive aroma, a combination of the smells of the people, their pets and the cleaning products they used. Many did not, or more likely, they held a subtle or bland aroma that was not worth attending to. Shirley had sometimes wondered what their home smelt like. She knew Jim's smell, or rather his array of smells and she loved him for them. Like the wonderful smell of fresh baked bread, Shirley looked forward to being greeted by the smell of her husband, there was something reassuring about that. It completed her.

1

The smell in the hallway now though, well, it wasn't precisely a smell. It smelt wrong and it smelt cold. Shirley realised that it was her instinct that was kicking in and her instinct wasn't one for long explanations. It couldn't give two hoots about a sommelier's interpretation of any smell right now, it had got all it needed and now it was telling her to get the hell out of here. To calmly turn around and leave the house and get to a safe place. It didn't even bother to emphasise that this was not a safe place right now. Maybe it should have taken the time to do that, because even now, Shirley's so-called rational mind was overruling her instinct…

You leave the house – then what do you do?

What are you going to tell people?

What are you scared of – scaredy cat!?

How old are you? You're supposed to be a grown woman! Act your age, not your shoe-size!

Pull yourself together woman!

This last was in Jim's voice and it was accompanied by that trademark eye-roll of his. He had never said anything like that to her and she doubted that he was even aware of his eye-roll. Jim quietly got on with things and didn't want to hurt or upset her. Shirley knew that, and she also knew that it was she who had given power to Jim's eye-rolls and imbued them with her own meaning. She'd taken her self-doubt and placed it right there in Jim. He'd be mortified if he knew she was doing that.

That wasn't fair on either of them and Jim was one for fair play. She'd endured enough cricket on the TV to know that.

And so it was Jim, or more precisely, a version of Jim that Shirley had created for her own purposes, that was the voice of reason. The voice that coaxed Shirley down the hallway and into the living room of their home despite her misgivings and that out of kilter feeling she had, a feeling that was very wrong and made all the more wrong as that flutter of panicked fear in her midsection coursed down and gave rise to an inexplicable pulse of pleasure. It was those sporadic pulses that caused a shiver down her spine and scrambled her thoughts. It may have been Jim's voice that she thought was encouraging her down the hallway, but mostly she was drawn by that pulse-pulse and as she moved closer to the living room door, the pulses got stronger.

As she opened the door with a trembling hand and noted the continuing absence of light, she wondered why she had not turned the light on in the hallway. That thought of hers was detached. It was another detail that somehow got lost in the chaos of the moment. If she'd attended to it, she'd have realised that the light was important, that if she'd had the presence of mind to turn the light on then things might have gone differently for her.

In the living room, the curtains were open, bathing the space in a gentle, blue light. After the comparative darkness of the hallway, Shirley's eyes saw well enough and what she saw were two figures on the sofa. Their sofa. That anyone would sit in the dark was incongruous, but two people threw her completely. It took her a while to understand that she was seeing a figure with its back to her and this figure partially obscured the second person. The second person who was seated farther away from her and slouched under the person who was sitting up and leaning over them.

Shirley did not know or comprehend what she was seeing, her mind was faltering and the images made no sense to her. She stood frozen to the spot wondering whether her feeling of dreamlike detachment had preceded this scene or was as a result of it. Her mind languorously reached for a partial explanation and only found one certainty, that was Jim laying under the other figure and that figure was moving against him slowly, gently and rhythmically. As though to punctuate this, Jim let out a low moan. That moan caused another of those pulses down between her legs and it was all she could do to stifle her own moan. Her hand shot to her mouth to stifle any sound she might make.

Shirley did not know what to do, part of her didn't want to be here. She felt like an intruder in her own home, but now this was no longer her home. She did not belong here and she certainly should not be watching these two strangers doing whatever it was they were doing on that sofa.

Strangers. This was not Jim. It certainly wasn't *her* Jim. He would not do this. He could not do this and definitely not with a man!

She felt a strange thrill as she understood a little more of the situation before her. The figure leaning over her husband was a man, she saw that now. She could see from his powerful back and his size. This man was bigger than her husband. Even seated, there was an obvious difference in size between the two men.

And then, as though Shirley had spoken her thoughts aloud and interrupted the stranger, he turned and rose up before her in a beautiful, fluid motion. She felt another wonderful flutter inside her as he turned towards her, this flutter spread throughout her and threatened to overwhelm her, she felt her legs pressing against the back of the armchair that matched the sofa and as he stepped towards her, she fell back into the welcoming comfort of the chair.

She sighed, her eyes impossibly wide.

"What...?" she managed to breath the word through her mouth, but no other words would come.

The beautiful stranger crouched down, his hands finding her wrists and gently pinning them to the arms of the chair. She found she was parting her legs as another of those pulses of pleasure sent a shiver up along her spine, inviting him closer, even as a part of her screamed. Screamed to push free and run from the house. The scream was impossibly small. She was impossibly small. She felt a strange electricity running up and down her spine now and out through her legs, it were as though her energy was being drawn from her. That she had submitted right from the outset should have terrified her, but she only felt a small portion of that fear and that fear seemed to morph into even more of that inexplicably pleasurable feeling, the pulses building in frequency and intensity.

An odd fascination compelled her and as she watched the beautiful stranger draw near, she thought she knew what had happened and what was even now was about to happen. She had been in the thrall of this creature from the moment she had stepped into the house, possibly before that, after all Jim had let it in and she thought maybe that was all that it needed.

As the powerfully built man ever so slowly leaned closer and she felt his touch, she found herself revisiting the hallway and the moment she had known there was real danger in the house. In her home. She could have turned around right then and left.

Couldn't she?

She sighed as she felt cold lips on her neck and despite the horror reaching up inside of her and sending shards of ice through her veins, she pulled her arms free of his grasp and pulled him closer. Urging him on. She wanted this. She wanted him. The man of her dreams made flesh and come to her at last.

She let out a long, low sigh as she got what she thought she had always wanted.

2

The small village of Brokmaster was off the weather beaten track. Some would say that it barely qualified as a village, but those who lived there would hold with none of that. They had a pub and the pub doubled up as a shop for essential provisions, so it was nothing as small, wee and piddling as a hamlet. Brokmaster was a village and that was all there was to it. And that was before they had gotten around to the small village shop that afforded them a generous level of amenities and convenience to boot.

Not that anyone would quibble with the assertions of the populace of Brokmaster, as few outsiders knew of the existence of the place. Unusually, the one road that connected Brokmaster to the outside world was a single track unadopted by the local authority. A farm road pockmarked with holes, grass rising out of the hump in its midst, brushing the underside of the cars that made their way carefully into and out of the village.

The postman left all the letters and parcels in a secure box at the end of this road as the Post Office did not want to risk wear and tear to their vehicles, and each day, one of the chores of John, the pub landlord was to head down to that box and bring its contents back to the Broken Dragon. During the course of the day, residents would visit The Dragon and whilst buying eggs, bread, toilet roll, milk, or a swift pint of beer, they would also take the post addressed to them and their nearby neighbours. The Dragon was not only a pub and a shop, but a post office of sorts. Sited in the centre of the village, it was the very hub of the community and in days not long past, it had also been the morgue, the incumbent landlady responsible for the care and dressing of the deceased.

Folklore dictates that villages such as Brokmaster harbour a dark secret. Regardless of this arbitrary rule, Brokmaster did not hold such a dire and ominous secret, nothing terrible cast a shadow over the people that lived there. There were small and dirty secrets though. Life easily gave rise to those sorts of things and the place was a patchwork quilt of guilt and shame and as each secret aged, another, younger secret would arise and take its place in the very fabric of the community. These were some of the ties that bound, and Brokmaster was a tight-knit community. Half of the village had family ties with one of the three families that could trace their time back in this place for well over two hundred years. There were other long termers of a similar vintage and newcomers were all those who were yet to reach three generations within the village. This latter group was a small proportion of the village population.

The inhabitants of Brokmaster said that no one ever left and if they tried to, then they would be back, one way or another, they always came back and the large, well-tended graveyard at the edge of the village, attested to this. The dry stone walls forming a border with the rolling fields beyond and providing shadow and shelter for its most permanent of residents.

The population of the country was ageing and Brokmaster mirrored this. No new houses had been built in the village since a row of local authority houses had been built after the second world war. The village may be ageing, but none of the houses lay empty and families found ways to accommodate their own. Some of the youngsters had spread their wings and tried life outside and a few had made it stick, but that came at a price. It wasn't that the people of Brokmaster were closed to the outside world, not even standoffish, it was more a question of investment. If you lived in Brokmaster then you were a part of it. You had to put something in and keep giving of yourself. Those who left were quickly forgotten and soon they were dead to the insular world of the village. Those who returned missed something that only Brokmaster could provide and they quickly worked their way back into the society of the village, the prodigal son returned and welcomed with open arms.

Few newcomers joined the village. This would predicate an awareness of the existence of Brokmaster and also a line into the village network to discover that rare moment when a dwelling may be available. Houses for sale were never advertised and social media was something that passed Brokmaster by. Of course, people in the village used social media, but they all knew better than to broadcast the existence of their village to the outside world.

The biggest secret of Brokmaster was that it existed at all.

2

From the main roads, Brokmaster was never visible, not even during the dark days of winter when the trees were laid bare. The village itself was obscured from any and every vantage point, mostly by the geography of the area. It sat in a small bowl which formed the boundaries of the village itself and this small bowl sat within another, larger bowl. Those few places that may have afforded a view or even a glimpse of the village were screened by trees so densely planted that even when they bore no leaves, remained in tight ranks so the village remained invisible.

No public footpaths went near, let alone through the village and the spot was so remote that it was a rare occasion that even a light aircraft would fly over. It were as though someone had decided they wanted to seek the quiet life and they had taken every possible measure to secure that solitude when they found the place they would choose to make a life.

Brokmaster suited its residents and they protected it accordingly.

As with many villages and places with a history that went back centuries, there were stories, myths and legends. One of the legends of this place was that it harboured old magic. Whether the magic had been brought here by the persecuted witches who had sought sanctuary here or, that the magic had drawn those people to it was a matter of debate, but that there was magic here was beyond doubt. The more sceptical of the villagers called it community spirit and a shared love of a place that had been home longer than anyone could remember, but those of a more sensitive disposition *knew*.

One thing was certain and that was that Brokmaster was special and uniquely so.

3

That Brokmaster was different and had the potential to be a special place to reside had not escaped its newest visitor. The nature of this visitation was unlike anything the villagers had experienced before and as a result, they would perhaps not call it such. The visitor had time on her side and the way she insinuated herself into the community of Brokmaster was slow and steady and approached in a painstakingly methodical way. So, concerted were these efforts that they had no discernible pattern and largely went unnoticed.

The visitor was patient at all times, but more so now she had found this spot. The remote, cut-off nature of this place suited her and she found that she had thoughts of making this place her home, not just a place to hide in plain sight.

Home.

She had not had thoughts of home for such a very long time, her life for as long as she could remember had been that of a nomad. She had felt the need to move on and keep moving and that need had become more urgent and necessary as the world turned and became more observant and connected whilst at the same time becoming more divisive and fractured. If anything, this brokenness made the world a more dangerous place for her and she was weary with the care she had been forced to take.

Now this.

And better still in the aftermath of a pandemic. An isolated community that had been locked down and away so that the isolation became overbearing and consumed all. The invisible epidemic stalked Brokmaster and somehow found a way into each and every home and into each and every inhabitant of this place. Even without infecting the body, it made itself known in their minds. The pandemic was a game changer and it had taken its toll, making the village all the more appealing for the visitor.

Yes, this place would do very well. She would become the very embodiment of that infection and she would enjoy this place in a way she had not enjoyed herself since the early days, if she had enjoyed herself that much at all, she had an idea that she had created a halcyon past to contrast with an existence that had had mundanity seep into it over the ages. She had become a creature of habit and had become bored as a result.

She watched from a distance and eyed the village of Brokmaster. This place was going to be her playground. Brokmaster would be hers and if she played it right, then she could do as she pleased. She could be creative and express herself with these people. In a place like this, she could elevate her existence from the drudgery of merely surviving to something more interesting.

Yes, that was the word. Interesting. She was going to make life interesting for these people and some of them may even thank her for it. She smiled to herself at the thought of it and observed a change within her. She was excited. Hungry, but also excited at the prospect of a new life.

The hunger was rising within her and this would not do. She could not rush this and her hunger had caused her problems in the past. She was blinded by her hunger and threw caution to the wind when she was hungry, now was the time to stay her hand and work on her patience. She eyed the village one last time and found that she was loathed to tear herself away from the place, so it was with some effort that she moved away across the fields and headed towards the roads. The roads were always a good spot for the hunt. She could sate her hunger and once satisfied, she could return to her study of the village.

That was the first stage, to observe and learn and understand the rhythms of the village. To identify the ebbs and flows and move with them. To become attuned with the place so she became a part of it. Then she would show the villagers fleeting glimpses of herself. Tiny doses of what she truly was, weaning them onto what she promised a little at a time so that when she came calling they would welcome her with open arms.

Well, she thought to herself as she came up the rise and towards woodland, they wouldn't always welcome her. That would be part of the fun. She could have some sport here. She had time to do things differently. She could use her powers more fully.

That was what she was looking forward to and what had dragged her down so, to have power and yet be so restricted in the way she wielded it. She had been oppressed for far too long and now she had this opportunity she wondered how much of her drab existence had been self-inflicted. How long had she allowed herself to live a grey and uninspired life when, with a little effort, she could have something like this?

As she walked through the trees and picked her way through the undergrowth, she let her mind wander. A ship! How could that play out? Maybe she should start with a private yacht? A modern retelling of the Mary Celeste.

Oh how exquisite! Her life was on the up and already she was dreaming about a bright and fulfilling future!

She cautioned herself. She should not get ahead of herself, and certainly not now, when she was hungry. There was an animal inside her and it would not be denied. It could barely be controlled, and if it caught her day dreaming it would rudely awaken her from those dreams of hers and she'd likely have to get as far from here as she could.

"Focus", she hissed to herself.

She could day dream later. Now it was time to feed.

4

There was a light drizzle coming down now. A certain level of precipitation that fell in between the capabilities of the intermittent and what Sally liked to call the full-fat wipers. She'd never gotten around to naming the wiper setting after that as at that point in the proceedings the rain was pelting down and there was little time for her to make light of the situation. Now though, the rain was gentle, if not a little annoying as she switched between intermittent and full-fat. The wiper blades squeaking as they cleared moisture from the windscreen so efficiently they were left with too little to lubricate their way on the next sweep, and yet, at intermittent setting the rain settled a little too much between the sweeps of the wipers that Sally's view was obscured.

Sally was just in the process of thinking that this was a little like life. That it wasn't often that things fell into a sweet spot that just bloody well worked, and even when they did, you didn't appreciate it until later when it all eventually turned to poo. Yes, that was life alright. She was just about to wax lyrical in her head about the fly and the windscreen meeting and how that was another aspect of life when something appeared in the road ahead of her.

Appeared. One moment the road was clear, the next there was a shadowy figure shimmering behind the veil of droplets on her screen. These droplets did not obscure Sally's view as much as confuse the mind receiving the sudden image of the figure. That confusion caused a delay and Sally failed to react until the figure loomed larger.

Now her mind was telling her the simple and obvious truth: she was about to hit that object and she had better do something and do it quickly.

She heard the rasp of her breath as she pulled it in, going rigid with panic she tore her eyes away from the figure and found she was looking at trees. No, she was looking directly at one big tree trunk and hoping against all hope that she was not going to hit it.

Too late.

Once her eyes had fixed on that single tree. The largest of all the trees around her at that moment, that was where she was going. There was no doubt about that. This was a simple truth: you go where you are looking. She barely registered her hands turning the wheel away from the figure in the road. Steering was a motor response now. What she did notice was that she hadn't lifted off. Her foot wasn't on the brake, it was on the accelerator.

"No!" she gasped, and she looked down at the foot that was

betraying her.

It were as though her leg was not her own. She could feel it, and yet she could not move it. She almost expected it to no longer be there, and so as she looked down at the last moment, she did not see the impact with the tree.

This might have been a saving grace had that been the end of Sally's story, her story had not yet run its course though. The crumple zones of her car had absorbed a lot of the impact and the airbags had deployed at just the right moment to cushion her from the steering wheel and the other, hard edges of the interior of the car. Nonetheless, she was hurt and she knew it. Dazed and hurt and scared.

Scared, because she was hurt, but she didn't know how badly hurt she was. Scared because she didn't know just how much trouble she was in and not knowing was terrible. Scared because suddenly she was in the dark in the middle of nowhere. Her existence had transformed from travelling a road well-travelled and only being twenty minutes from home, to not knowing whether she would see her home ever again.

She heard the driver's door of her stricken car swung open and she gasped in surprise, the gasp turned to a groan as pain swept up from the middle of her chest and more pain shot down from her head and neck. She did not move as the pain gripped her. Her eyes stayed facing forwards and the knowledge of the door opening was down to her other senses. She'd heard it and knew it for what it was. Now she could feel the chill evening air against her and despite the pain, she thought that sensation of the cooling air was a good thing.

"Stay still," said a voice that should have been reassuring, was aiming for reassuring but somehow was colder than that air that was now lapping at her side.

The air bags deflated one by one. Sally saw the finger nail puncture the steering wheel air bag last. Black and pointed and impossibly sharp. Surely a finger nail couldn't pierce an air bag? Could it?

She realised that she was shivering. Shivering with the cold. Shivering with shock. But most of all, shivering with fear. She could feel the figure's eyes on her. Cold, compassionless, they observed her as though she were pinned and ready for dissection.

"No," she said softly, "please don't…"

The figure leaned in, lips almost touching her ear and sending a shudder through her as it spoke, "is that all you have for me?"

"Wha… what?" she stuttered.

She kept her eyes facing forward, already seeing too much of the figure looming in the doorway of her car, but knowing that to look upon it would be so much worse. She could feel eyes upon her. Boring into her. They looked her up and down and as though to emphasis the gaze, that nail stroked her leg.

4

"Well, you're not all that badly hurt," said the figure, "smash like this, be a surprise if anyone walked away. And yet here we are having a pleasant chat and all you can do is moan and plead pathetically…"

"I don't…" Sally began, confusion cascading around her head.

The figure straightened, it's voice becoming almost theatrical, "where's your vim and vigour!? Where's your desire to live! Why would you give up so easily, Sally?!"

Sally turned her head at the mention of her name, thinking that this was some sort of obscene joke, that this person knew her so…

So what? What did she think the use of her name meant?

She turned her head and her eyes found something that was not altogether human and was not altogether right. The wrongness of it made her scream. She had no choice over her response, something about the creature undid her and the scream arose from her as it did.

A hand snaked out and covered her mouth, stifling the scream, "that's more like it!" the voice was at her ear again, sending a shudder through her.

Sally twisted in her seat and pushed at the figure, she wanted to get her legs free and out into the doorway in order to kick out at the thing, kick it away and then run. She twisted and writhed, but the figure was leaning in at the door and it was so, so strong.

"That's it!" said the figure as it pinned her, "yes, Sally, yes!"

Then, just below her ear, she felt impossibly cold lips and experienced another shudder closely followed by her back arching and her body going rigid as she felt two sharp teeth against her neck.

"No!" she gasped, pushing with all her might, but the figure did not give, it were as though it were a marble statue come to life.

She felt the two sharp teeth press down and pierce the flesh on her neck and her mouth opened to make a sound, to beg or to cry out, but as the teeth entered her she gasped instead. Her fists beat a tattoo against the figure as it sucked against her. Gasping and writhing against it, trying to get free, but knowing she was fighting a losing battle.

The figure shifted its weight and slipped a hand behind her head, pulling her closer and it lapped and sucked and kissed at her neck more insistently. Something changed in Sally as this happened and she sighed. She stopped hitting the figure and her fists unclenched. Inexplicably, she began stroking the figure and then pulled it into an embrace, urging it on. Moving against it as though they were two lovers.

"Danny..." sighed Sally as she gave in and gave herself over to the feeding figure, waves of pleasure sweeping through her and taking everything else away with them, her pain, her fear, her very self.

Eventually, Sally's embracing arms fell away and soon afterward that, it was finished.

The figure was no longer hungry.

As she stood up and stepped away from the open car doorway leaving a prone and lifeless Sally she thought she felt a fleeting pang. Was that sadness? The tragedy of another life taken? She doubted it, not after all these years. The pang was more likely a remembrance of what she had once been and what she had lost. It was gone as quickly as it had appeared, she pitied these creatures more than she envied them.

She walked the length of the car and dragged a finger along it's flank, sparks flaring from the gouged and ruined metal as she did so. Some of those sparks caught the fuel and as they did, they illuminated a woodland and roadside devoid of the figure that had been there only moments before.

5

"Terrible business, eh?" said John.

One of his regulars, Graham, had walked in to herald the commencement of the evening's proceedings and John, after asking what he would be having, despite his certain knowledge that it would be a pint of best, was pouring the pint as he now deployed a conversational starter.

The Broken Dragon was the hub of the community and John, as it's landlord had an ear to the bar when it came to local news. He wasn't a gossip and he avoided trouble. That was part of the skill of barkeepery, managing the space and the people in, and even beyond the pub, such that they all got along and if there were to be any nonsense, none of it occurred on the premises. John was very good at all aspects of his vocation and made it look effortless, a skill in itself, but also a trap for those who eyed the ownership and running of a pub as merely a case of drinking behind the bar as opposed to in front of it.

Graham took the hook, this was not a foregone conclusion, sometimes a drinker wanted solitude in the midst of a pub and

5

that was enough for them. On occasion they would listen to the conversations around them, but more often than not, they tuned the soundtrack out and took time to themselves.

"What terrible business would that be then, John?" asked Graham, placing a foot casually on the brass footrail, readying himself for the transmission of local news.

"The car crash up on the main road there," John pointed in the direction of a road neither of them could have seen, even if there hadn't been a pub surrounding them. The direction he pointed wasn't quite right either, but still, it made his point for him, "I'm surprised you haven't heard anything about it. Terrible business."

Graham shrugged, he hadn't heard anything about it.

"What's this about terrible business?" asked Ian as he walked into the pub, his red Labrador at his side.

"Car accident," said Graham nodding a greeting.

"What will it be?" asked John.

Ian stroked his chin thoughtfully as he eyed the ales, "I'll have a pint of that truncheon."

"A fine choice," said John pulling a pint, "got it in yesterday and I think I'll be needing to order some more by the weekend."

Ian took the pint he was handed and supped some, "that ain't half bad, mate. Anyway," he added turning back to the previous subject matter, "this terrible business?"

"Accident on the main road last night," explained John.

"Was that what it was?" asked Ian.

"Yeah, woman hit a tree," said John.

"They were still clearing it away this morning," said Ian shaking his head, "I didn't see much, but there was evidence of a fire."

John nodded, "poor girl didn't stand a chance, car went up like it was bonfire night."

The two regulars made with sounds of sympathy and all three took a moment, it was a terrible business indeed.

"Bloody hell!" shouted a newcomer as she entered the pub, "it's as quiet as a church in here, either you were just talking about me or someone's died!"

"Janet!" enthused John, "you busted us, we were just wondering whether you were going to grace us with your presence this evening and here you are as though summoned by our very conversation!"

Janet grinned bashfully, "you flatterer! I could almost believe you! Now poor me a G&T will you? A girl could die of thirst!"

5

That was the vanguard of the evening's drinkers. People came and people went. It was a quiet night for a week night by the Dragon's standards. At its peak there were around ten punters dotted around the bar and there was a pleasant hub-bub of conversation. John oversaw the proceedings ensuring no one went without drink and moving between the small groups of people in between times, asking after them and their families. He was good at prompting conversation but didn't again bring up the accident on the main road, that first conversation had sobered him and reminded him of other, bad news from his past life. Once he had been the deliverer of bad news and he'd never gotten over the reactions of the people he'd gone to visit as that messenger. Many of them knew why he was there, even as they opened their door to him, his presence was enough, it was usually worse for the ones who didn't know or refused to understand why a police officer had come knocking on their door. When they didn't react, or their reaction was off-kilter, that was the worst. That was the hardest to deal with. Seeing someone deconstructed in front of you was terrible, but at least that was understandable. The ones who refused to believe and who went into denial were lost somehow and John wondered whether they would ever be found. Having seen everything in his twenty years in the job and having picked up the pieces time and again, he knew that some never recovered and were never found, not until they followed their loved ones beyond the veil.

"...incomer then?" said Janet.

The hour was now late and there were only a few left in the Dragon. Janet had stayed the course, making her drinks last and yet having drunk enough to be in her cups. John could see she was inebriated and could also hear it, her volume crept up as she went beyond her fourth gin and tonic.

"Sorry love," John rubbed his eyes, he was tired and he'd missed the first part of what Janet had said, "an incomer?"

"Yes," said Janet, "I saw someone at the Big House earlier."

John gave a puzzled expression, he had not expected this, and it was made all the more curious that it was a subject of conversation several hours into Janet's tenure at the bar today. Why had she not lead with this? Divested herself of this interesting tidbit from the outset of the evening. Maybe she had meant to, thought John, but it had slipped her mind and events had conspired against her. Easily done, especially as you got older and more so when you added alcohol to the proceedings. John thought about his own mind slips and the trouble he got into with his other half Maxine. Maxine gave him short shrift as she asserted that all of his forgetfulness was centred on her. He never forgot a beer or drink order, he even bought toilet blocks before they ran out, but when it came to her, he just didn't care. He could hear her saying it now. She'd said it so often that he was beginning to doubt himself now, or maybe it was a self-fulfilling prophesy, John having understood that this was one that he could never win, going along with it for a quieter life.

"John! John!" Janet flicked her hand in John's face and clicked her fingers, "Earth to John!"

"OK, Jan! Enough of that!" he made a show of swatting her

hand away, but was careful not to make contact, didn't want to escalate matters and he knew that Janet was harmless, but sometimes loud and quite frankly, a bit much at times.

Janet laughed, "you looked like you'd zoned out, honey!"

"In your company? Never!" John grinned.

"Flatterer!" Janet returned the grin and then held her empty glass and jiggled it to and fro.

"One more?" asked John.

Janet nodded, but they both knew that it was unlikely to be just the one more. *One more* was drinking parlance and sat alongside various other colloquialisms that referred to a singular, additional drink when several were likely to be taken. This language added something to the proceedings and somehow managed expectations that were conducive to a better night out. One more also allowed John to manage expectations in a very literal sense when that was called for and it was time to wrap things up for one customer or all. Sometimes John really did mean it as just the one more.

Pouring Janet her next drink gave John a little more time to think about the Big House. The Big House was called the Big House for one, very obvious reason, it was big but it also loomed large in the village. That house had a presence to it that went beyond its size. It was said that the stone for the Big House had been shipped from the heartlands of the dark, satanic mills. John had visited those Northern hinterlands and could well believe it. The stone there was grey, but it's time in the midst of the Industrial Revolution had rendered it black. When people jokingly said it was grim up North, John instantly thought of that blackened stone.

The thing was, the Big House hadn't been anywhere near the dark, satanic mills or anything of that nature and John doubted that the stone had come along already impregnated by decades or even centuries of grime, unless it had been reclaimed from an earlier structure and picked apart stone by stone and reconstructed here in Brokmaster, but that was far-fetched and if that had been the case then surely that aspect of its history would be known in the village, instead little was known of the Big House nor of its occupants.

That lack of knowledge of house and inhabitants was unusual for this village or any other village for that matter. The Big House was and always had been an enigma. It sat in plain sight and no one ever remarked upon it. The very idea of stealth bombers could have been derived from that structure, it was there and yet it defied attention. This was part of what had wrong footed John, he knew the Big House was there, but at the same time there was a strange kind of absence associated with the place. The absence had come to the fore and he'd had a hard time trying to replace it with anything of substance.

There was something a bit wrong about the Big House and John had never really questioned it, which was wrong in itself. A house that big demanded attention and speculation and rumour and the filling in of the gaps. There was always someone who knew something and when they didn't they filled the gap in any case, it was then the job of someone more knowledgeable to come along and provide a more accurate entry. Wickivillage had been around centuries before the internet ever existed.

By rights, the Big House should have been the residence of the Lord of the Manor, but there was no such thing here. Brokmaster was not part of a large estate. Neither was the Big House a former rectory, some of which were impressive piles built for the fourth born son of a Lord, the first born inheriting the estate and probably going into politics, the second taking a commission in the army, the third going into the profession of law. Presumably any further sons made their own way in the world, unencumbered with any familial expectations.

Neither had this house been bought by anyone rich and famous or turned over to the provision of courses for busy execs on their way up the corporate ladder. The Big House was a complete mystery and John thought he should at least know who lived there, but was coming up with a blank.

All of this and more was scurrying about in John's mind and he was almost at a loss as to what to say. Almost. This was a thread that he wanted to pull though, and he knew how to make conversation.

"Someone else at the Big House, you say?"

Janet's eyes clouded for a moment, "yes, there's that old lady lived there for an age, isn't there…?" she clicked her fingers as though that would summon more information as to the single, old inhabitant of the Big House.

"Mrs Morris?" called Don from his table.

"That's the one!" said a beaming Janet.

John had an itch, didn't know whether it was that the name was wrong or something bigger than that. An old lady living at the Big House seemed right, or at least that there had been an old lady living there. There were a lot of old ladies, out survive us all would old ladies and they said that the population was ageing, so there were more and more of them. Yes, an old lady belonged in the Big House because if anything was as anonymous as a ruddy big house, it was an old lady. John knew this from bitter experience, if there was an old lady in the vicinity of an incident then they had no hope in hell of finding her unless she chose to come forward.

"Was there anyone here when the incident happened, sir?"

"Yes, yes there was officer."

"And what did they look like?"

"Look like?" that was when the trouble started, when they asked the question back at you.

"Yes, sir. What did this person look like?"

"Well she looked like an old lady." This was when the trouble made itself known and from here there was nothing but the

5

cul de sac of Old Lady.

"Any distinguishing features?"

"Well, she was old."

"Anything you can add to that, sir?"

"She had grey hair?"

"How about clothes?"

"Erm... old lady clothes..."

"Do you remember the colour of the clothes?"

"A pastel of some sort, you know... green or blue or something."

Yes, an old lady fit perfectly in the Big House and that unremarkable inhabitant could live the life of a hermit in the midst of a village, especially if she had everything delivered to the house and didn't take with mixing with the villagers. John knew that that happened. That for some inexplicable reason, people would move to a village and isolate themselves entirely from the community. Maybe this new arrival would be different and their presence would unravel the mystery of the Big House. John wondered whether the Big House would become more visible if this occurred. That some light and warmth might not bring life to the old building yet and bring it out of its shell.

"So, did you meet this new person then?" asked John.

Janet eyed him over her glass and took a moment to reply, "Oh! The incomer!"

"Yes, did you meet him?" persisted John.

"Her," corrected Janet.

"A lady was it?" called Don.

"Too young for you, you old soak!" Janet called back.

John nodded, "maybe a granddaughter then?"

"Yes, that would fit wouldn't it?" said Janet as she considered this.

John nodded agreement.

"Funny thing though, she looked like she was off the set of a costume drama, there was something quite eerie about her…" Janet's face clouded over with confusion and some small measure of concern.

"Really?" John's forehead creased at this comment of Janet's.

"Yes, but you know how youngsters dress. Probably clothes from a charity shop or something, a resurgence of the New Romantics, goth or punk for all I know."

5

"Sounds like you saw a bloody ghost, Jan!" called Don.

"Bugger off you cheeky git!" retorted Janet.

Typical banter and all good fun, but John saw that cloud pass Janet's face again and he could have sworn she gave a small shudder…

6

The Big House had been empty for some while, that was why John could not recall it's owner or occupant. As to the matter of its ownership, that had been dealt with some time ago and there was no question of anyone turning up to claim the house as theirs. No one with a legitimate claim anyway.

They say fortune favours the brave, it also favours those who have existed for an age and have time on their side and nothing better to do than to go through the effects of those who have passed. Those that have passed thanks to the age old being paying them a terminal visit.

This particular visit had been to an elderly gentleman in Shepherds Bush. He had lived a modest life in a house in the area. That he owned the entire house and lived there alone was unusual. Property prices in the area were exorbitant and most of the houses had been made into flats that were still beyond the financial reach of the average buyer.

She didn't like to prey upon the elderly. They were dry and

flavourless, most of their life had already left them. It was like eating the wings from an old bird, a lot of effort without much reward however you dressed it up. The elderly though were a necessity as they were easy pickings. No one really cared how an old person died when their passing was an increasing inevitability, so as long as she didn't get carried away and kept their death within the realms of natural causes then she could snack as she pleased with very little consequence.

This particular gentlemen was of consequence though and the cause of a stroke of luck. She knew you made your own luck and by the law of averages she would find treasure. In this case, lying on top of his stout mahogany desk, as though it were laid out for her, were the deeds of the Big House along with various title papers and effects that meant that is was a moment's work for the Big House to fall into her possession. She knew in that moment that something special was happening, that a door had opened to her, but she couldn't know that this was the universe providing. That the path she was being shown would be such a rich seam.

She still did not dare to hope that the Big House and the village of Brokmaster was all that it seemed and that was as simple as it got...

Hers.

Caution had been her mantra and it had served her well and already she could feel her letting go. She was excited and eager. The kill on the main road was all very well if she was passing through, but her hunger had gotten the better of her and she had hunted too close to home and then today, she had been seen. Really seen. Not a glimpse or a suggestion of an image, she had been seen and now she knew that she wanted to be.

She wanted to *be* here.

She wanted to *live* here.

She was sick of the running and looking over her shoulder. She wanted more than that. She deserved more. Humankind had spread and infested the world until there was room for little else. She was better than the existence that she had been forced into, better than her prey.

Settling anywhere for any meaningful span of time had for so long been beyond even her wildest dreams. Had she been getting old, or perhaps her diet of the elderly had slowed her and made her dull?

Well this was going to be different! She was only now making up her mind on that. She would give this modern world a try and she would live in it and sample it and take it for all it was worth.

Decision made, she would have to go shopping for something suitable to wear in this new home of hers and this time, she was not going to make a mess in her own back yard. She would go further afield and she would pick something suitable for country living.

6

* * *

"Seen anyone else at the Big House?" John would ask Janet from time to time over the next few weeks.

Janet would shake her head and that cloud would pass over her. As days turned to weeks she began to think that she had seen a ghost after all.

Don spoke to John about it a few days after that first conversation, picking a time when Janet wasn't around, not wanting to rub her nose in it or upset her, "that house is as dead as the grave," was all he had said.

John had flinched at Don's unfortunate choice of words, but nodded in agreement, he'd made a point of walking past the Big House and actually looking at it not once, but three times. He found that he was approaching it from different angles and trying to catch it out. Daring it to move, to give up some of its secrets, but it remained steadfast and would not budge.

Still, John didn't think Janet was making it up, nor was she seeing things. She may have liked her G&Ts from time to time, but in her day she had been a boss of some sort of investment firm and the high and mighty had come to her, not the other way around.

As the weeks passed they all let the sighting go and let the Big House lapse back into its state of invisibility…

7

"See the lady up at the Big House?" Don directed his question in the direction of the bar where John was stood pouring himself a lager top.

"Piss off, Don!" Janet hissed right back at him, her voice like a whip crack.

Don looked hurt and Janet completely missed this as she sat at the bar with her back to him.

"Now, now, Jan," warned John.

Janet caught the tone and nodded almost imperceptibly at the landlord and turned in the direction of his gaze: Don.

Now that she saw that Don was upset and that he hadn't been making her the butt of a joke, she formed an O with her mouth.

Don nodded, "there was a van earlier."

"A removal van?" asked John.

7

"No, it was only a transit van and a bit fancy really."

John smiled, you sure it wasn't the undertakers, mate?"

Don's face lit up, "I knew I'd seen that sort of van before!"

"Now he's pulling our leg, Janet," John rolled his eyes theatrically.

"No! I swear! There was this prim and proper lady got out and went in the house. Walked in as though she owned the gaff she did."

"Maybe she did," John shrugged.

He wasn't convinced.

* * *

Time.

Time was on her side. Only now, she did not need to play her usual games. There were other games to be played. Old habits died hard though and she wasn't going to pass up any opportunities as and when they came along. Besides, she liked to go abroad and take in the sights and sounds of the world. She liked to watch and to wait whilst the world went by, ignorant of her presence. Cocooning themselves in the mistaken belief that they were safe and that monsters did not exist. She saw plenty of monsters as she observed the world of people, if truth be told, they were all monsters, but they liked to deny this. They liked to pretend that they were special and they alone were not capable of the monstrous. She watched as they deluded themselves and lived a lie. She had the best seat in the house and the outside world fascinated her.

Too long had she sat outside of everything, only ever reaching in for a bite to eat. She had treated the world like her own private larder and over time she had retreated inside of herself and become diminished. Times were a-changing and she already felt invigorated at the new life she had embarked upon. The village of Brokmaster had just gotten that bit more interesting and she was looking forward to playing with her new neighbours as she settled into her new home and her new life.

She was now a busy lady of means and it was in keeping with this new persona of hers that she would keep herself to herself. She would pick her time and emerge from the house eventually, but what was the rush? Keeping herself to herself suited her just fine and added to the air of mystery that she was weaving.

Smoke and mirrors.

Always the smoke and mirrors. Nothing was ever as it seemed and that suited her just fine, that it suited everyone else just fine was the recipe for her success and longevity. Yes, her kind lived for a very long time. There were tales of immortality, but she didn't think that was right. All things must end. But this was splitting hairs when it came to the meagre life span of a human, in comparison to them, she was forever.

Forever, that word and others like it caused her pain. Yes, she had time and time was on her side, but this was a sword with two edges. Time also wore her down and took its toll. She felt its weight upon her and although she had never entertained the possibility of a date with Death herself, she could see her allure.

And she was careful. This she had had instilled in her. She was rare and precious and she had to take care. She was one and they were many. They killed that which they did not understand. She had seen this played out so many times it was a wonder anything special survived in this world, but survive it did. In spite of the worst efforts of man, and the occasional woman of course, but women seemed less prone to destruction unless it was of her fellow women. Yes, this was a cruel world and she walked it with care.

Could she be killed? She considered this from time to time. It must be possible and she had felt the passing of one of her kind when Death took them, but so rare were those instances that she questioned that they had ever happened. They were few, but they endured.

Why had she never sought out any of her kind? This was a question she rarely dwelt upon, accepting that she was solitary in nature. That none of her kind had found her bore this out. Even with the crushing bleakness of loneliness, she had never seriously considered paying a house call on one of her own. There was danger there. True danger. As things were, there was a balance and the arrangement worked, there was no point in upsetting the apple cart.

So here she was, addressing her loneliness, clambering upwards and dragging herself out of the dark well that she had been digging deeper and deeper for as long as she could remember. That this episode in her life had run in parallel with an interesting period in the history of humankind was counter intuitive. Humans had grown in knowledge, power and numbers and she had retreated from the world. Only now was she venturing forth into this bold new world of theirs, but would she make it stick? Or was this an experimental phase that would see her prove herself right in digging that well and staying well clear of the world and all of its pain and misery?

She smiled bitterly to herself and felt the lips on her new face respond, this extended the smile itself. How strange and contrary the world was and how amusing that she was just as strange and at least as contrary. She had sought to avoid all the pain and misery in the world and had found only pain and misery. She had mined her own rich seam of darkness.

Well things were going to change!

Yes, she must kill in order to survive, but why had she been so despondent about it? Why had she judged herself so harshly? She'd avoided the judgemental gaze of the world but felt its judgement all the same. Was she really evil?

How stupid she had been! What a waste of time her languishing had been! For when she sat and she watched this world that she was a part of she saw no counterpoint to her supposed evil. That opposing force of good only existed in her mind. She had created it and used it as a stick to beat herself with.

Humans were more cruel and vindictive than she ever was. She acted out of necessity and even when she had to act, she made the best of that moment and she gave each and every one of her meals what they wanted out of the transaction. She had stopped herself from falling into judgement of herself right there. She was about to call her meals victims. When a lioness brought down a gazelle, was he a victim? Prey, yes. Meal, certainly.

She nodded to herself, her reinvention had begun. She was as much a victim as any of the rest of them. She had been built this way. She was a part of an imperfect world and had been made to feel like she was at fault, but no more! She was going to try things a different way. Her way.

She stood and she laughed. Threw her head back and brayed at the ceiling. The sensation was new and strangely wonderful. This was the new *her*. She'd laughed because she had caught herself referring to her as a her. She had reclaimed a part of herself that had been long lost. Until now, she had been a product of her environment and belonged to it and to them. She had taken on the attributes of those she stalked and prayed upon. She was one moment a *she,* and in the next a *he.* She was a confusion of identities caught under labels that had never fit or suited her.

Now she felt empowered and strong and she was excited for

what the future may hold. She was choosing to live again.

This was a good day and it would be the first of a whole host of good days.

She turned on her heel and left the front room of the Big House. She had things to do and places to be.

8

As part of his morning routine, John liked to grab some of the older, undelivered post and take a walk around the village. It was an excuse to leave the confines of the pub and stretch his legs. There had been a time when, other than driving down the lane to fetch the post or driving to the cash and carry, he had spent his days and nights hemmed in by the four walls of the pub and as much as he loved that place, he realised that he was getting stir crazy. The deficiency of vitamin D thanks to a lack of sunlight did not help matters.

The final straw had been when he'd stood outside the Dragon, smoking a cigarette and taking five. He stared back at the open doorway and found himself resenting its pull. Knowing that he would have to return to the bar shortly and that even these few minutes could be truncated if a regular were to come passing by. Some of his punters thought nothing of interrupting his break and cajoling him back into the pub. He'd not once moaned or complained, but that didn't mean that it didn't get to him.

He missed walking. Walking had been such a big part of his

working day once upon a time, in another world and another life. So, he'd made a concerted effort to get out and walk ever since. The post was just the excuse he needed and he had other chores he could do if there were a couple of low post days. He'd even resorted to buying items they didn't really need from the village shop, going the long way around to the shop itself and finding another loop on the way back. The direct route was a matter of yards and not much better than the hop, skip and jump to the smoking shelter outside the pub.

Today, as he walked past the Big House thinking about the fact that he had never once had post for the place, something caught his eye. Brokmaster was not a large village and it did not sprawl, so it was relatively easy to cast his eye upon the majority of the houses if he was so minded. Granted, there were a few lanes and spurs with a house or three hidden away and hedges that obscured places so they could easily be overlooked or forgotten. That he was walking past the Big House and something caught his eye was not a complete coincidence. Talk of the place had piqued his interest and if nothing else, he wanted to make it a familiar spot and find a way to override its stealthy demeanour and make it less interesting. Less *other*.

The thing that caught his eye was movement and he was attracted to that movement in a place that he still considered to be vacant and would be until he saw this fabled new owner that there had been talk of. He resisted the urge to react in an obvious and noticeable manner, even after years of working on this, it was not habit. He didn't like giving away that he was interested and in a case such as this, peering in at the windows of a house was Peeping Tom territory and Sod's Law would inevitably leap into action, someone would drive past and catch John in an act that he was not engaged in, but the evidence of their eyes would be enough to accuse, convict and hang him.

Something had moved beyond the window he was passing. He slowed, but avoided the meerkat reaction that this inspired. He kept the window in his peripheral vision, hoping that there would be more movement, that he would see that there was indeed someone living in the Big House. Or, he would have to dismiss the moment as an illusion of movement caused by a reflection on the glass of the window. The latter would be a disappointment to him, the Big House held mystery and John was intrigued.

If he didn't stop now then he was going to go beyond the limits of his vision and he didn't want to miss this chance. Something had moved, he was sure of it. He had a decision to make, give it up, or become a conspicuous rubber necker. A nosey neighbour. A potential nuisance. There was a fine line between looking out for people and becoming a problem, and that line wasn't up to John, that line was drawn by anyone who may be in the house or who may witness his behaviour.

"Sod it," he muttered under his breath, and he turned so he was full on to the window.

As he turned towards the Big House, his blood ran cold and he shivered. He had thought it was a simple case of someone standing in the depths of that front room, perhaps leaving the room, or getting up from a seat. He could see nothing, and that was part of the problem. The room was impossibly dark. It wasn't that the window was tinted or the sun was shining against it making it difficult to see through, it was that the light didn't seem to permeate the room itself and the darkness in that room seemed alive.

John stood almost transfixed. He felt as though he had eyes upon him. He wasn't being watched as much as appraised and those appraising eyes, obscured in the darkness of that room were hungry. This is how a mouse feels when a cat has it's paw on its tail, thought John. But it was worse than that. There was something evil about that darkness. John could feel its pull and it terrified him.

As he stood there, looking into the room of the Big House, with it looking back at him and into him, his sight began to narrow. The process was gradual and almost subtle. The light of the world surrounding him dimmed and faded as though it were no longer important. His vision became a tunnel and the further along the tunnel he went, the darker it became. The darkness beckoned and John felt himself leaning towards it, just a breath away from falling and falling and being sucked into an oblivion that would feed on him for an eternity. The finality of death would be a blessing when compared to this.

He heard a small child whimper and wondered where the sound was coming from, unaware that the sound had come from his own lips. The world around him was now superfluous and all he wanted was the promise that was the darkness before him. His jaw went slack and his bladder let go, he barely

8

registered the feeling of liquid warmth on his thigh as he was now beyond caring or shame.

"John..."

A far away voice.

"John!"

A familiarity in the voice and a vague feeling that it had been calling him for some while now.

"Someone help me!"

Panic, but not his own.

"John! John! Please! John!"

The voice pleading and urgent.

Staring down the corridor and wondering why his legs won't take him further down. A hand on his shoulder, pulling shaking...

Then the darkness rushes at him insanely fast, and he braces himself for what will come next...

9

"…funny turn."

"…blanket…"

"He seems to be coming around."

John heard voices from far away at first, then snatches of words, it were as though he were an old fashioned radio, the volume eased up and then the dial tuned in properly so he could receive the whole show.

He opened his eyes to bright light and the moon face of Maggie, a recently retired school teacher who had worked for a private school further out in the sticks than Brokmaster, if that were even possible.

"How are you feeling?" she asked him, concern etched on her face.

"Fine," was his automatic response.

9

He was going to ask what had happened when he was distracted by a nudging at his leg and near his crotch, his face crumpled in confused consternation.

"Trixie!" said Maggie sternly, "stop that!"

Her shaggy, off white terrier was sniffing around John's nether regions as dogs had a wont to do, but then John felt the cold, wet urine soaked into his underpants and trousers and against the flesh of his thigh. The shock of realisation made his eyes go wide, he was mortified. He looked down at the dog and was relieved to see that someone had placed a blanket on him, covering his modesty and saving some great degree of embarrassment. He expected that Maggie knew he had wet himself, but the blanket spared them both any awkwardness.

He was just wondering how the blanket had materialised when he felt a second body near him, as though responding to his awareness, the second person crouched down and spoke.

"How are you feeling?"

He turned in the direction of the voice. The voice was pleasant, but clipped. A professional voice. A voice that said something of money and standing. There was something authoritative and commanding about it. The voice could have been that of a consultant on a hospital ward and John felt like that was where he was right now. There was also something cold and detached about it.

John did not recognise the voice and when he focused on the

owner of the voice, he did not recognise her either. Her face he supposed, was beautiful, or it may have been, in another life. That same edge, that same coldness, was present here. The set of the mouth was a part of it, then there was the harsh, calculating gaze. There was a lack of warmth here and if a smile were ever to grace this face, John knew that it would not reach those eyes, even if it did make the effort to go that far, those eyes would not accommodate it.

John imagined that this was someone who was so used to getting their own way they didn't even consider any of the other options. She got things done and that was all that mattered. That she was here and asking that he was alright was already pushing the bounds of his expectations. He wondered whether it was she who had provided the blanket and he was already scanning around for a vehicle parked nearby as he answered her, he expected a Range Rover and couldn't think of a second alternative.

"Fine, I think," he propped himself up on his elbows by way of further answer, "I must have blacked out."

He felt Maggie give him a look, possibly judging him unfairly, it wasn't uncommon for publicans to partake regularly of their stock and John liked a drink as much as the next man. Drinking with his regulars was all part of the job as far as he was concerned. They would be surprised to discover that his well charged glass was rarely entirely beer and that he managed to nurse the same drink for an inordinate length of time. Some things were about show and John believed in looking the part.

9

The lady crouching beside him right now certainly looked the part. Dressed for the country, she looked like she belonged more than he did. Maggie passed muster because she had that terrier of hers. Trixie was currently chewing on a corner of the thick blanket. A tartan blanket that would not look out of place in a Range Rover, but John could see no four by four at the kerbside, so that part of his deductive reasoning had fallen down. He was losing his touch as well as losing his consciousness.

"No dizziness? Nothing broken?" asked the stranger.

John felt the need to demonstrate that he was in fact fine. He felt compelled to heed these words and take conspicuous action. He sat up, taking care not to let the blanket fall away beyond his waist and limbered up. First his right arm and then his left. He drew his legs towards him and was thankful that he had no pains or even aches. He must have gone down like a sack of spuds on the hard pavement, so he would not be surprised to discover bruises when he got home and cleaned himself up.

"No, I'm good, thanks."

"So, it wasn't your…" Maggie was nodding at John as though he would know what she meant, he wasn't sure why she wouldn't just come out and say it.

He shrugged and gave her a puzzled face, he couldn't work out what she was alluding to and he hoped she didn't mean his mythical drink problem.

"Heart beating normally is it?" asked the stranger.

John noticed Maggie wince and then the penny dropped, it was barely a year since she had put her hubby in the ground. Dave had been fit as a fiddle and strong as an ox. A tradesman who doubled as village caretaker, doing odd jobs and bigger than odd jobs around the village as and when they were needed, better still doing jobs that no one had spotted needed or wanted doing. He was a good bloke was Dave and everyone was shocked when he passed, none so much as Maggie, she had gone to sleep on a day that was no different to any other day and awoken to a cold body beside her.

John felt awful for putting Maggie through this and didn't know how to make amends. He didn't want to make a fuss and make it worse, and he didn't want a fuss being made over him anyhow. His mind was already made up as he found his feet, thankful that he had no trouble getting up and that his head was sound, no sudden dizziness at the upwards movement. He also managed to bring the blanket upward with him. He held it there in front of him, slightly awkward, but far less so as he would have been without it.

"I..." he began, not knowing quite what to say.

"I'm just glad you're OK," said Maggie, now making to continue her walk with Trixie.

"Thank you," he said first nodding at Maggie and then the stranger, "thanks, Maggie."

He said this a second time, having turned his attention back at her and she used this as her cue to move on.

"Just you take care of yourself," was her parting shot, "come on Trixie!"

John glanced down at the dog to see her sniffing at the damp patch on the pavement. He couldn't help sighing at the ignominy of it all.

"You can keep the blanket," said the stranger.

She was standing now. Straight and to attention, there was something military about her bearing, alert and proud.

"Oh, right. Thanks," said John.

And with that, she turned on her heel and marched to the side of the Big House and John supposed, around to the back.

By the time he'd mustered his wits and moved, there was no sign of her. He had meant to call after her and tell her he would launder and return the blanket, but there was no one to say anything to. Strange he thought. He could have sworn that he hadn't been standing there for any time at all. He supposed that marching of hers was quicker than it looked.

Stranger still was the feeling he had as he quickly walked away and back to the pub, keen to get indoors and cleaned up. Two things vied with him as he walked away. One was that the Big House felt even more empty in spite of him seeing the stranger walk towards it and presumably go inside. The other was that feeling of being watched intently.

As he unlocked the back door of the pub and stepped inside, he realised that he had not asked her name. And Don was right, that van at the side of the Big House looked exactly like the sort of van an undertaker used to transport bodies.

10

She watched the man walk away.

She knew who he was. She knew them all. It was surprising how much could be gleaned if one was patient and learned the art of seeing. Not looking. Looking was easy, that was merely turning one's head to direct their gaze. Seeing was making a deliberate effort to take everything in and more importantly, do something with it. She had a very deliberate gaze and it had served her well.

Isobel had lost count of the number of dull, unseeing eyes that had filed past her in this life of hers, and that was even before she had rendered them truly sightless, forever. There was a sadness and a magic in their final moments. Most of them lived more in their final moments than they had in the years proceeding. So many of them lost their way, caught up in things that in the final analysis, were meaningless.

Was she any better? What had she become over these past decades? A hermit obsessed with where her next meal was coming from. There was more to this life than that. She smiled to herself, the self-imposed exile that had seen her set apart from the world meant that she had so much to learn and that in itself added to the excitement.

Walking amongst these strange creatures for the first time in over a century instead of remaining separated and watching them and studying them from a distance, yes that was going to be an adventure, and a welcome change.

"Did you have to do that?" she said quietly, almost as though she were speaking to herself.

"I did nothing," said a dry, rasping voice.

"Well, can you be a little more careful when you decide to do nothing, please?"

"I will do as I see fit, and I will do as I please," the voice now sounded even more unpleasant and disturbing.

"We've been through all of this…" said Isobel, she sounded like a petulant teenager now.

"No, you've been through all of this," retorted the strange dry voice from the darkness of the front room.

Isobel sighed, a weaponised and meaningful sigh, "You're hungry. I will find you food tonight. In the meantime, don't antagonise the locals."

"Whyever not?"

10

Isobel thought for a moment, "this is..." she was going to say home, but she thought that wouldn't cut it, "...a safe place for us. We can stay here a while."

There was no spoken reply, but that was good enough for Isobel. Any objection would have been voiced. Tonight she would go on the hunt, hunger pangs affected them both, and things could go seriously awry if the hunger was not sated at the earliest opportunity.

She looked out of the window again and wondered how she had felt to be out in the world in such a tangible way. Interacting with people for no other reason than the interaction itself. She had helped the man, brought him a blanket, asked how he was. She thought she might have touched him and he had not recoiled. She raised her hand and turned it this way and that, inspecting it, a sense of wonder at the sight of it. It had been too long, why had she left it this long?

She felt an itch near the back of her neck, but knew it wasn't a physical itch, it was a mental itch and it was a warning. There was good reason for her having avoided all of this, but it had been such a long time ago and she had chosen to ignore history and the lessons that it provided. Her urge to be out in the world again and try to be one of them was too great.

She thought she might enjoy herself this time, and it might even work out. If she was careful. If *they* were careful.

* * *

"Had a funny turn did we, John?"

John went for a poker face and hoped he hadn't missed by too big a margin. How the hell did anyone know about that!? He had to remind himself that this was a village and information travelled quicker around a village than it did along fibre optic broadband cabling. Maggie would have mentioned something to someone else in the village and that person would have told a few people and they would have told a few people a piece. Soon enough it would be broadcast at the school gates and in the shop, and now it was here, in the Dragon.

He'd had time to get over it, but he hadn't taken time to think about what he'd say if he was confronted with the news, or the news distorted via gossip into who knew what. John had learnt that straight out denials were one of the worst responses imaginable. If a person denied something then the fuzzy logic applied to that denial was that it was most certainly true – why else would a person deny it? Innocent until proven guilty did not apply to gossip.

Ad hoc responses usually worked best for John, if he'd rehearsed a response, he'd likely have overthought it and at the very least, he'd not come over convincingly.

"Age," was his answer now, "apparently this happens in your thirties, Chris."

"You're alright now though?" asked Chris, genuine concern etched on his face.

"Yeah, fit as a fiddle," John shrugged and as he did, he remembered the darkness. Being drawn down that corridor into a darkness that harboured something loathsome and terrifying. That had been the precursor to his so called funny turn.

"You alright, mate?" asked Chris, now the concern was in his voice.

John brightened and smiled, "yeah. Sorry, Chris. Miles away for a moment then." He saw that Chris's pint glass was nearly empty, "another one? On me this one."

Chris grinned and handed over his glass, "you sure that funny turn of yours hasn't had any lasting effects?" he winked as John took the glass and refilled it.

"Best take advantage while you can," John handed the pint to Chris and returned the wink.

John weathered a few more comments about his bout of unconsciousness, but nothing more was made of it, despite the discomfort he felt at the episode. He was losing it. Never a superstitious sort, sceptical of those who were overly spiritual, something in the Big House had really spooked him. However much he tried to put his loss of consciousness down to overdoing it or a bug, he couldn't shake the feeling that he had been in the grip of something truly awful and had been lucky to escape relatively unscathed, barring the afront to his dignity.

He had laundered the blanket already and partially tumble dried it. He'd left it on a radiator to finish drying, not wanting to shrink or damage it in any way. He was conflicted when it came to the prospect of returning the blanket to its owner. He had to, it was not his blanket and keeping it felt like a casual act of theft, and he wanted to, not only because the blanket absolutely must be returned to its owner, but also because he was curious and any excuse to go back to the Big House was an opportunity to take another look and possibly learn a little more. The new arrival in the village also intrigued him. There was something about her. There was a lot about her. She had an air and bearing, some would call it gravitas. There was more to it though.

John realised that she might just scare him, that the conflict he felt was fear. Irrational fear after the dream that proceeded his funny turn. He couldn't quite put it all together because he refused to accept that he was behaving like a frightened child, that he was genuinely scared by his experience outside the Big House. He saw his slight fear of the woman as a case of her being tainted by association: she lived in the scary house, so she much be scary.

John felt ashamed at his feelings towards the house and towards the woman and this was compounded by the shame he felt at having wet himself. He wanted to go back with the blanket to somehow make amends and put that sorry episode behind him, if that was at all possible.

10

Did he want the lady of the house to invite him in and give him the grand tour, thus dispelling his crazy and irrational fears? As he thought on this, his insides churned and complained. That window. Would he even dare look into that window, let alone walk into the room that held that darkness and something much, much worse than the darkness itself..?

11

Isobel had wondered whether she was really hungry. She was in that mild limbo state where she was neither one thing nor another. By rights, she should have been unsettled and out of sorts, but this new state of hers suited her well enough.

She marvelled at how easily she had slipped back into being in this physical form. She had worried that she would feel awkward and manifest this awkwardness with clumsiness. She hadn't had to learn to walk all over again and had barely thought about how she was moving her new body around in the world, she had merely filled the body with herself and carried on as normal. Normal being a relative state of course.

Thinking about how to be was no different to how it had always been. There was always a degree of thinking, some of it going on in the back ground and unheeded, some of it more conspicuous. Most of the thinking concerned those around her and what she may want from them. No, not much had changed really, except that she thought she might actually be enjoying herself.

11

That night, she had driven the van from the village and kept going until she had found the large, sprawling town she'd looked up on her laptop. She congratulated herself on her observational skills as she drove. The only thing that had taken a little time to master was the gear changes, but once she had the biting point sussed she was driving smooth as silk. She'd even taken a moment to look over the buttons and switches and worked out what they all did. It was really quite simple if you took a moment to attend to it.

When the young men in the Ford cut her up, she was at first surprised and then the surprise was surpassed by anger. That she experienced several other examples of bad driving on her way into the town, built upon this anger and a frustration at not understanding why people had to drive so badly and rudely. What was even in it for them?

What had begun as an enjoyable experience had deteriorated into something that was only to be tolerated. Other people had ruined her good mood, so when the cocky man in a BMW came the wrong way down the car park and swooped into the car parking space she was patiently awaiting the elderly lady in her Kia to vacate, Isobel lost it and she barely remembered getting out of the van to go and see the man and establish exactly why he thought it was a good idea to steal her parking space.

She tapped on the driver's side window. He completely ignored her despite the deliberate taps accompanied by her staring eyes. She tapped on the window again. He continued staring at his mobile phone. She nodded her head and made a decision, as she walked off, the man looked up and slipped his phone in his jacket pocket. He watched the haughty bitch climb into her van and park it in a space diagonally opposite the space he had taken. His space.

See? He thought to himself, not so difficult is it, you snooty cow.

He got out of his car and sauntered off, chuckling to himself at the cheek of some people. He muttered under his breath as he left the car park, "one nil, love. One nil!"

It was Friday night and busy in the centre of town. People would be milling around in the pubs and bars despite the ongoing threat of a virus that would not let go, that made the known variants of flu seem meek and mild. The BMW driver was looking forward to a few pints with his mates and then they'd go on the pull. He took the most direct route into town, cutting through an alley that zig-zagged towards the main stretch, meeting a side lane which opened out onto the high street, he was aiming for The Lamp on the corner of that lane.

Part way along the alley someone stepped out of the shadows, looking for all the world like they had peeled themselves from the wall itself. His heart leapt for a moment, but then he calmed. This was likely to be one of the chefs from the curry house kitchens. The alley went along the back of a series of shops, cafés and restaurants and this was a popular spot for fag breaks.

Only, the figure didn't look like they were relaxing and having

11

a smoke. They had taken up a position in the middle of the alley and even in the grey-blue semi-darkness, he could see they had taken up what he could only describe as a fighting stance. Resting, but somehow alert.

He was relieved when he saw that it was only that silly posh woman who had gotten her knickers in a twist when he'd parked his car in what she stupidly thought was her parking space. Her lot thought they bloody well owned the place. Daddy had probably donated the land to the local council. Stupid bitch.

"Remember me?" she said when he was a few steps in front of her.

"Should I?" like he was going to give her the satisfaction of acknowledging her.

"Yes, you really should," she even sounded posh, she shouldn't be out in town on a Friday night. This place wasn't for her. As for being down this alley on an obvious wind-up? Well, she'd think again about that one. She was lucky that he was on the clock and headed to see his mates. This was his bit for charity. Another night? When he wasn't in such a good mood? She'd be in a lot of trouble. Some people really didn't have a lot of common sense.

He side-stepped her, intending to go past. Smirking as he knew he would wind her up no end as he left her to stew in her own piss.

"Oof!"

He staggered back a couple of half steps. Winded and bent slightly at the waist. He shook his head looking at the spot where he'd hit something hard and unmoveable. There was nothing there. It had felt like the flat of a hand on his chest, only that was impossible. The only obstacle before him in the alley was this bird and she just was not capable. She wasn't small, but she wasn't big either and she certainly wasn't going to present a problem to someone like him.

He thought about giving her some mouth. Saying something to both put her in her place and wind her up, but the words did not present themselves. He was too pissed off by this inexplicable development. He decided to be the better man and walk away. If it meant walking through the idiotic woman then so be it.

He walked forth with purpose and he aimed right at her. She could bloody well move out of his way. He tensed his shoulders and upped his step, not caring if she moved or not, almost willing her to stay put so he could knock her flat on her back and teach her a lesson.

It didn't quite work out like that. Whatever did happen, happened so quickly it took his brain some time to catch up. All he did know was that he was the one lying on his back and when he raised his head to look back up the alley she was there, and he was quite a way back down the alley, and his back hurt like a bastard.

He pushed himself up to his feet and without thinking he

11

marched at her, "what the f..." he began spitting the words at her, covering fire for his imminent attack.

Then he was up against the wall and pinned. Pinned so hard as to be flattened against the wall. This did not compute. None of it did. He should have been in The Lamp by now, instead he'd been lain out by some bird and now he was in a spot of bother. It took him a further few seconds to realise that it was her that was halting his progress.

"Remember me now?" she said calmly.

It was the calm that was really unnerving. She wasn't even trying. No strain in that voice. No heavy, laboured breathing. He was trying to push his way off the wall, but he may as well be cavity wall insulation for all the good it was doing him.

"Yes," his voice showed strain and he was finding it difficult to breath, such was the restriction that he was under.

"And what do you have to say for yourself?"

"Sorry," his own voice annoyed him. He sounded like a little school boy. Pathetic. Weak.

"Why are you sorry?" and she sounded like the teacher.

He had hated school and been glad when he could leave. He hadn't punched the bloody maths teacher. He'd wanted to, but his mate Carl had done it and well deserved it was too. Carl was a legend.

"I took your space. I saw that old biddy was backing out and blocking you, so I nipped in and took it. I shouldn't have. Sorry." He wasn't quite sure why he capitulated, and it angered him that he had, but if it sorted this little lot out then he supposed it had to be done and besides, no one had to know. He'd be a couple of beers in soon enough and listening to his mate's tall tales of womanising and derring-do. Most of it was absolute bull, but it was entertaining all the same.

"There, that wasn't so hard was it?"

She released him and smiled a cold smile. The way she so casually freed him was humiliating and should have scared the crap out of him, but his humiliation had helped build his anger and he was barely in control now.

He nodded at her, eyes blazing, then he stepped past her, barely missing her with his shoulder and stormed off.

"Bitch!" he spat over his shoulder once he was a few steps away and hitting his stride.

There was a bang as his back hit the floor. No, it wasn't his back, which hurt bad enough driving all the air from his lungs and sending him dizzy as he fought for breath, it was the back of his head and that hurt like a bugger. What the hell had just hit him and taken him down?!

He looked up as he felt, more than saw a shadow crossing his prone body.

11

Her.

She stepped over him, so she was stood astride him. He wanted to kick her right there and then. Boot her right between the legs and take her down and punch her again and again until all of this stopped. All of this had to stop right now!

Only the thought didn't travel to his leg and the kick never happened. Instead he lay there as she lowered herself down on top of him. She moved slowly and carefully, like a lover would have done, but he knew there was no love here, far from it.

She crouched over him and he felt her on top of him. Was he physically pinned? He didn't think so, and yet he didn't feel able to move. She stroked the side of his face as she brought her own close to his.

"You're a naughty boy aren't you? Just can't help yourself. Never amount to much with that temper of yours. *Unfortunately, Micky does not apply himself. The way he is headed, prison is a strong possibility in his future.*"

Micky's eyes went comically wide. How did she know about his final school report? He'd never seen this woman before.

"Oh Micky, Micky, Micky..."

She began with words of disappointment, but then the tone of her voice became excited and rapturous and he felt a thrill of excitement as he remembered Tina saying his name just like that and how good it had been that night. Both of them drunk, but not too drunk to perform and to enjoy themselves, all their inhibitions a distant memory. She'd asked him to slip a finger in her arse that night and when she came it was bloody intense, he'd worried they'd have the neighbours over asking if there'd been a murder...

And then there was a strong hand covering his mouth, that woman's mouth on his neck, passionate and insistent. He could feel her teeth and they were pressing against him, puncturing the skin of his neck and entering him. Going deep. Then she was sucking hungrily against him. Sucking and making a strange mewling sound as she squirmed against him. He was hard. She'd made him hard, and even though they were both fully clothed, what she was doing and the way she was moving was too much for him and he could feel that familiar feeling as he passed the point of no return and was going to lose control. Harder and harder she sucked and he could feel her going too far. She was going too far. His back arching and his arms beating a tattoo on the concrete of the ground, they lay locked together for some time until he eventually lay still and she finished her ministrations.

12

She hadn't thought that she was all that hungry, but having gotten angry and encountered the bullish Micky, she found that she was still hungry even having fed and fed well, she had yet to find suitable sustenance to bring back to the Big House. These sorts of forays for take away meals were few and far between, but needs absolutely must when they were required. Her own hunger would not be denied, the infrequent hunger of her companion that had reared up and opened its hideous maw was a force of dark nature.

She had to give it to Micky, he certainly knew how to make a girl happy and now that he had provided her with exactly what she had wanted, her anger was a dim and distant memory, an irrelevance that had her wondering how she had ever become so keyed up, buzzing with a violent energy which Micky had kindly allowed her to dissipate during their encounter down the dark alley.

Isobel cautioned herself to be more careful, it would not do to slip. Ever. She regularly cautioned herself, knowing that it was best to remind herself of the risks she faced and the gauntlet she ran whenever she was abroad. Now was a time for further caution as she was changed and there was no telling what effects this change of hers would have on the way she operated and even behaved. Besides, she wanted this to stick. She wanted to *be* Isobel for a good while yet, so she didn't want to become lax and complacent and ruin it all, especially now, before it had even begun.

Sauntering towards the town centre itself, she took the time to enjoy the very act of sauntering. Here she was, out in the world and not just hidden in plain sight, she was *conspicuous!* She stood out in a way that made her strangely invisible. She was a walking contradiction and best of all, she felt good!

"'Right, luv!"

"Behave Mark!"

"Why!? She's well fit! An' she knows it!"

The two lads had both checked her out as they approached, the lairy one turned to check another aspect of her as they passed. She smiled to herself, she had chosen well when she had found Isobel. There was fun to be had here and a different sort of fun to that which she had become so accustomed to so that it all started to feel so *samey*. Falling into a routine was a death of sorts and she had had to break out of it.

Well here was her opportunity. Here she was on her first proper foray into the world in this form. She entered the bar and

12

paused once she was a few steps inside, taking it all in. Taking it in in a way almost incomprehensible to the people she was checking out and assessing.

The novelty here was that she was also being checked out. Her. Well, Isobel anyway. She wasn't subject to the changes that each and every gaze made to her, here she just *was*. Such a refreshing change not to be moulded and manipulated and affected to such an extent she began to forget herself and who she was. Now she could forgo that, or at least most of it anyway. There were always forms of projection and expectations and preconceptions, but in this form, she could relax. More so because she could gently encourage people to see her how she wanted to be seen, sexy, alluring, dangerous, but somehow safe. Operating in a blind spot which allowed her to get people exactly where she wanted them, which in this case, was all the way home.

Walking to the bar, she made a point of smiling at a woman sat in one of the dark booths that had seating for four. The woman was sat next to a man. They were a couple and Isobel could tell they had been together for quite a while. Grown comfortable together. Too comfortable, and now they were looking for a little something more. Seeking something to reignite the spark in their relationship. They just didn't know what it was that they were looking for.

Well, now they had found it.

At the bar, she deployed another, winning smile and flirted with the barman while he poured her a straight whiskey. She would allow herself sips from the glass. She turned from the bar and looked around, became agitated. Looked at her watch. Frowned. She caught the eye of the same woman she'd singled out as she walked to the bar, then she walked over to the booth.

"Do you mind if I sit down?" she asked, eyeing the empty seats opposite the couple.

"Not at all," the woman smiled as she said this.

Isobel plonked herself down and sighed, "bastard has stood me up! Again! This is the last time! I hate being in bars on my own. Especially on a Friday night!"

It was an age old sob story and she could see both the man and the woman softening as she told it. All to the good and all part of her plan. They both smiled sympathetically, but didn't say anything, what was there to say? Her boyfriend was obviously in the habit of letting her down. They were likely already judging her. Why did she put up with someone like that? People were their own worst enemies at times and she was likely following a destructive pattern that she may never break out of. Little did they know, they were the ones following a pattern, a pattern of Isobel's making.

"Sorry," she said with a deep sigh, "neither of you need this on your night out. Some random interrupting your date and… bursting… into… tears!"

Isobel was pleased to note that she could put on some very convincing waterworks. She was ad libbing, but she had a wealth of experience, so she knew exactly which buttons to press. Where she was really winging it was with this new physicality of hers. She hadn't tested her body at all, nor practiced any scenes. That was a bit of a concern to her. She'd taken unnecessary risks without realising it. She hadn't thought things through as fully as she should have and she'd made assumptions as a result. Assuming that she could rely on her experience and the well-practiced routines that she easily fell into. That and her knowledge of people and her quick wits. She was better than all of those around her. That wasn't arrogance, it was fact. She saw more and she knew more. She was quicker on the uptake and she was stronger.

What they had though was sheer numbers and that random factor that some called luck. Isobel was very aware that even with her best efforts, one day her luck would run out. She made her own luck and this had worked until now, but everyone had a bad day at the office. She'd already had a few. Sometimes things went against you and all you could do was tough it out and find the nearest exit.

As it was, she didn't think the quality of her tears mattered all that much. The tears were a crude and simple signal. She wanted a reaction. She couldn't really mess this bit up, not unless she missed the mark by a country mile and made people uncomfortable as her efforts to cry descended into an awkward show of something that was not only not crying but somehow not socially acceptable.

The woman reached out and touched her hand gently and carefully. Isobel looked up from her tears and tried for a brave smile, this let the woman know that she was OK with being touched. That her hand was cool to the touch was not all that unusual, Isobel was well aware of the old adage, *cold hands, warm heart.* Not that it applied here, to her.

The woman added her other hand and squeezed Isobel's reassuringly.

The man stood up, "I'll get us all a drink shall I?"

Isobel tried for a smile again, "that would be nice. A Jameson's please."

What was nice was that the woman had to get up and move out of the way in order for the man to go to the bar. She took the opportunity to seat herself by the needy Isobel, just as Isobel knew she would.

Now she had an arm around Isobel and was telling her that it was going to be alright. She combined this reassurance with careful platitudes, not quite joining Isobel in referring to her feckless and fictitious boyfriend as a bastard, but making sure that she knew that she deserved better and so the inference was that she could do better than the sort of bastard that stood women up at a busy bar.

The woman's partner had taken the opportunity to visit the men's room and he wasn't in a rush to come back. Isobel had seem him almost flinch when she referred to their night out as a date night. This couple had, as they were fond of saying, grown apart. A lazy reference to the way so many people stopped making an effort, and didn't even attempt to maintain their relationship whilst taking it for granted that things would be alright, despite the neglect. That was like imagining a house plant would survive without ever being watered. Even a cactus would die eventually if it was shown no attention at all. Some of the dreams and beliefs that people adopted were mystifying to Isobel, but she recognised that they did some of her work for her. She needed those fissures that people allowed to open up within themselves, it was those gaps that she exploited with such aplomb.

The woman's hug and close proximity spoke to Isobel. She could feel the woman opening up to her, that she was enjoying the closeness and warmth that she had been deprived of for so long. The woman was likely surprised at her own responses to Isobel, but not so surprised that she stopped and withdrew.

Isobel breathed a word of thanks and sobbed for good effect. She moved a hand out and placed it on the woman's knee, returning that squeeze of reassurance to emphasise her thanks, that she then left her hand there meant something more than thank you. In response, the woman tensed just for a brief moment and then relaxed, she relaxed deliberately, welcoming Isobel's touch. That was when Isobel knew she had her, any resistance after this point would not bring the result the woman desired. Escape was a diminishing option, even now.

"You're too kind," Isobel leant into the woman's embrace and nuzzled her, "you're such a nice person and I don't even know your name?"

She was moving her head ever so slowly around, speaking quietly so the woman had to lean in closer in an attempt to understand what she was saying.

"Charlotte," said the woman, "and my boyfriend is Nick."

Isobel raised her head so she was eye to eye with Charlotte, this also gave her the opportunity to scan the room. Nick was at the bar, he'd been served, but was talking to two women who were sat on tall stools, a good spot to watch people and to do exactly what they were doing now. That they had allowed Nick to engage in conversation with them was an encouraging development both for Nick and for Isobel.

"Charlotte's a beautiful name," she smiled through her tears, "it suits you."

They shared a moment, Charlotte returning the smile. Isobel doubted that she had been complimented in years. Isobel leant in, resting her head against Charlotte, her mouth near her ear.

"Thank you, Charlotte," she breathed the words into the woman's ear and felt her respond, her breath momentarily ragged.

Charlotte wanted to speak, but hesitated, not trusting her voice to cooperate.

Instead Isobel spoke again, "I'm Isobel," she drew just a little closer, "and I really like you."

12

She slid her hand up Charlotte's thigh, not far, but enough to send a shock of sensation along her leg and leave her in no doubt as to what she meant.

"I…" croaked Charlotte.

Isobel had to supress a smile, instead she placed a gentle kiss on Charlotte's neck.

"Yes?" she asked, brushing her upper lip against Charlotte's ear.

"Well, Nick…"

And that told Isobel all she needed to know about Charlotte and Nick and the way this night would go.

Charlotte sought the warmth of Isobel's touch. She craved intimacy. The embrace they were locked in right now was reminding Charlotte what she had been missing out on and she wanted more. Charlotte also wanted to please Nick, after all, it was his intimacy that she craved most of all.

As for Nick, he had obviously told Charlotte about one of his fantasies. Maybe it was a passing comment, but Isobel thought it was more than that, she thought that Nick was willing to risk his relationship with Charlotte in the pursuit of a cheap thrill. That he'd watched online as other men enjoyed the attentions of two women and he wanted a piece of that for himself. That the online stories that were acted out for eager voyeurs were not real had escaped him. He had seen enough of these videos to begin to mistake these as evidence that many men were getting what they wanted and yet he wasn't.

Well, let him get what he thinks he wants, thought Isobel to herself as she gently kissed and nibbled Charlotte's neck and stroked her thigh. In the end, it never turned out as they expected. Two was company and three was a crowd. The dynamic was imbalanced and what tended to happen was that two of the three focused on each other and the third felt left out, and from there jealousy and insecurity invariably reared their ugly heads and ruined any chance of the encounter working out.

Isobel smiled to herself, tonight would work out very differently from Nick's expectations, very differently indeed.

"Are you sure you want this," Isobel whispered in Charlotte's ear, she then withdrew so she was face to face with her again, "really? Because I want you Charlotte. I really want you."

She stared deeply into Charlotte's eyes and slipped her hand further up her thigh, rucking up her skirt as she did so. Charlotte bit her lip and arched her back, Isobel's eyes were drawn to her exposed neck and she suppressed a shudder of her own, it would be a moment's work to lean in and bite down on that soft flesh and feel the warm blood pulse into her mouth.

Charlotte glanced around, breaking eye contact for only a moment, wanting Isobel and wanting this, but not daring to hope that she could have what she now wanted.

12

"What about Nick?" she asked hesitantly.

"Oh he's coming with us," smiled Isobel.

"Who's coming where?" asked Nick as he placed the drinks on the table in front of him. His drink was already more than half gone, as was he. Isobel had watched him get through another pint at the bar. Nick was a man on a mission.

Isobel had a mission of her own. She poured the fresh Jameson's into her existing glass, but not before she fished the ice out of the new glass, why people did that when you ordered a straight drink, Isobel would never understand. She licked the liquid off her index finger and looked meaningfully at Nick.

"Looks like your luck is in, Nicky Boy. Charlotte here wants me to take you two home with me so we can all have a little fun…"

She sucked her finger and winked, rewarded with Nick's eyes glazing over lustfully. A heady cocktail of drink and lust overriding any coherent thought.

She raised her glass, "drink up then!"

Nick didn't need telling twice, he necked the remainder of his pint and smiled uncertainly as he watched Charlotte finish her large glass of white wine in three nervous swigs, he'd never seen her drink like that. It wasn't going to be the only thing he'd witness tonight that he had not previously seen Charlotte do.

"Shall we?" Isobel ushered the couple out from the booth, looking all the world like she was going to down her whiskey, they didn't see her surreptitiously place the glass back down, the drink largely untouched. They were too caught up with the prospect of what the evening held.

As they started out for the door, Isobel leant in towards Charlotte, "I'll see you outside. Nature calls."

She wanted to leave the bar separately to the couple, break any association anyone in the bar could possibly make. She smiled at the barman as she returned from her walk to the toilets, and as she left the bar and went outside, she walked right past the waiting Nick and Charlotte as though she were oblivious to them. As soon as she had cleared the bar window she called after them.

"What are you two waiting for?"

She kept up a fierce pace that she knew that Charlotte, in her heels could not keep up with. Nick stayed with his girlfriend which almost made Isobel like him. Almost.

The van seated three in the front and once she was in the driver's seat, she beckoned the couple to join her, "Charlotte first," she patted the centre seat proprietorially as she said this.

Nick watched his girlfriend clamber into the van, not an easy

12

feat in heels. The angle she entered the van in meant that she was leant forwards and she clumsily lunged over Isobel. Isobel took the opportunity provided to her, slipped her hand through Charlotte's hair, cupping the back of her head and she kissed her fiercely. She felt Charlotte exhale a breath into her mouth as she responded and kissed her back hard.

Charlotte almost fell to the seat as Isobel broke the kiss her head swimming from the kiss and also the wine she had downed only minutes before.

Nick stood in the doorway, slack jawed. All of his Christmases had come at once and he didn't know what to do. He was already out of his depth, but Isobel felt sure that he would rally his troops valiantly to the cause. This was not a chance that he would pass up. All the same she leant forward so he was fully in her eye line and he could see her face. She said nothing, but her expression conveyed two things, *yes, I just kissed your girlfriend* and *get in the van now!*

He almost leapt into the van now he had gotten over himself. As Isobel drove out of the car park she smiled to herself. He was rocking back and to in his seat, barely able to contain himself. He glanced her way several times, also taking the opportunity to look at Charlotte with eyes anew. He had seated himself next to his girlfriend, but Isobel noted that he was not touching her at all. He was avoiding contact as though to touch her now would break the spell and he'd wake up to his alarm to find that it had all been a dream and he'd been rudely awoken just as it was getting to the best bit.

Little do you know, Isobel thought to herself. For her part she was excited at the prospect of feeding. She had to keep a hold on herself so she did not break any of the rules of the road. It would not do to become over eager and therefore hasty. Every now and then, she mirrored Nick and took a look in the mirror at Charlotte. Charlotte was calm, but Isobel could feel the anticipation at the prospect of breaking a taboo. Charlotte hadn't been with another woman before and something had awakened in her. Something long dormant. She'd been with Nick for seven years and now that itch was making itself known. Nick wasn't the first boyfriend she had had, there had been others and she found that at some point in her relationships she was putting up with her lot. She wasn't unhappy and it was alright the life she had, but at the same time, she couldn't say that she was happy either. There probably was more to life, but she swallowed that thought back down and she just went with what she had, she thought she'd be unhappy if she started chasing unrealistic dreams. She'd almost forgotten the fun she'd had at school, the friends and the crushes. When it came time to date and mix it with the boys all of that just fell away and everything changed. Somehow she ended up with fewer and fewer friends and the friends she was left with weren't the fun bunch she'd started out with. She didn't know where they had gone.

Now this! She felt butterflies and she felt sensations coursing through her body that enlivened her. Her imagination was trying to go wild and she was pulling it back because she already thought she might explode at Isobel's touch. That kiss! Had she ever been kissed like that before? She didn't think so, or if she had, it was so long ago to have become a

12

memory cast in shadow.

She watched the ribbon of road and willed it to end at Isobel's house.

Nick's imagination was going wild. He'd not bothered keeping his on a leash. In his mind's eye, Charlotte and Isobel were writhing around and performing exactly to the script of his fantasy. The soundtrack of their moans was marred by his voice as he repeated over and over again: bloody hell!

Isobel may not have heard their thoughts, but she could read them all the same. People were obvious to her. She wondered how close to fulfilling Nick and Charlotte's expectations this evening would come. She knew they would fulfil hers.

13

The journey to the Big House in Brokmaster felt longer than it should have for all three of the occupants of the van, thanks to their wanting it to be over sooner it became belligerent and drew things out.

The silver lining for Isobel was the drawn out time added to that building anticipation. The more excited her meal got, the better. She knew her house mate would appreciate the meal she had brought back and that she had laid the groundwork already. She was not finished yet though and she already had an idea as to how the rest of the evening would go.

As she parked the van at the side of the house she frowned to herself. The Big House was sparsely furnished and this made tonight a little more difficult. Not by much, but Isobel would have to do something about making the Big House a little more... homely. Lived in. She would do some work as it was important to keep up appearances, no one should spot continuity errors and start unravelling her carefully crafted lie. That would not do.

13

These too were now far too excited and far gone to present a problem for her tonight. She had had them from the very start and they really hadn't stood a chance, poor lambs. Once anyone was the focus of her charms they couldn't help themselves. Actually they could and they did, she marvelled at how she merely had to flick that first domino and the rest fell down. Their dominoes. They had done nearly all the work for her and they slept walked exactly to where she wanted them to be.

That was what they were doing right now. She led them around the back of the house and through the back door. The house was in darkness and she did not bother switching the lights on.

"It's very dark," Charlotte's voice, trembling slightly with the excitement of what was about to occur.

Isobel shut the back door firmly and locked it. Taking her time, letting Charlotte's words hang there between them.

"Yes, I've only recently moved in and I haven't got used to the place yet. Found I prefer walking around in the dark instead of trying to find the light switches." She drew closer to Charlotte and kissed her gently on the lips, "besides, I think we should keep things like this, don't you? More intimate isn't it?"

Charlotte sighed a yes.

Isobel pulled away and stepped over to Nick, "you've been very patient haven't you?"

He grunted a reply as she slipped an arm around him and pressed her body against his. Yes, he was almost ready. No point in delaying the inevitable.

"I want to show you something," she said casually, and then she kissed him.

It was a passionate kiss that promised much and Nick was light headed when it ended. Some of that would be the rush of blood to his crotch, thought Isobel. She allowed her hand to brush his hard-on and was rewarded with Nick groaning. She supressed a smile.

Isobel took his hand and as she began to lead him from the back door, she turned to Charlotte, "be a sweetie and wait here for a minute will you? I will be right back, OK?"

She saw Charlotte nod uncertainly, she knew she'd wait, she had no other option and she had a secret hope that Isobel would return alone. She wanted Isobel all to herself, didn't want Nick to take over and get in the way.

Charlotte felt around her, her eyes had adjusted to the dim light that the night afforded and she could see that she was in a kitchen. There was a simple table with three chairs, she dragged one out and sat down. She would wait, it would be worth it.

Isobel lead an eager Nick along the hallway, their kiss had primed him and he was eager for more. The thought of having Isobel to himself, if only for a short while excited him, and it wasn't cheating, not if Charlotte was in on it as well.

Isobel opened the door to what he assumed was a living room, pulled him in and pushed him against the wall right by the door, laying a palm on his chest, she pushed the door closed behind them. This room was even darker and Nick struggled to see anything, including Isobel. He gasped as he felt her slip that hand that had been on his chest downwards and she drew closer as her hand went to his crotch and began stroking him through his jeans. He grunted as she moved against him, allowing her to lead at this point. Enjoying what she was doing and not wanting her to stop.

"Is this what you want?" her lips touched his ear as she spoke and he shivered with the pleasure of it.

"Yes," he growled, the word almost sticking in his throat.

"Good," she whispered, but then her voice rose as she added triumphantly, "it's always better that way!"

"What...?" he began, but she pressed more firmly against him, driving the breath out of him.

She clamped a hand over his mouth, digging her fingers into the flesh of his cheeks and as he tried to cry out he could feel her staring at him intently. She was still moving against him rhythmically and he felt conflicted. Then the hand she was stroking him with was undoing his jeans and freeing him, wrapping her fingers around him and stroking him expertly. He was responding to her even as he struggled against her.

Something was wrong. She was far too strong and the way she was looking at him was intense to be almost frightening, but the way she was moving against him and working his cock was sending him wild and he didn't want her to stop. His pleasure was building and that was all he wanted now. For her to keep going.

He felt something cold against his leg, then the same sensation on his other leg. His eyes went wide at the sensation, what the hell was that!? Whatever it was, it was now pulling his jeans further down, only that wasn't quite right, his jeans seemed to be sloughing away from him. He felt pulling and heard tearing and as more and more of his flesh was laid bare that cold sensation crept ever so slowly upwards. And still he was responding to Isobel's touch, his body betraying him and wanting her whatever the cost.

He tried to scream, but that hand of Isobel's held against his mouth firmly and little of the sound escaped. He struggled to breath as she continued to press against him, impossibly strong. And all the while she moved against him in a way that had his body betraying him. Her skirt had ridden up and she was stroking him against her. She was moaning softly and looking at him with an expression of naked lust. Fuck he wanted her. He could feel his pleasure building even as the cold sensation slipped higher, going above his knees and up along his thighs. What the hell was happening to him?

Higher it went, and it seemed to be teasing and playing as it approached that most sensitive of spots. He wanted it to stop, didn't want it to go there and yet he felt this need for release, he was reaching a point of no return and even as he tried to push against Isobel he knew it was too late. Then it was pushing up inside him, the shock of it taking him past the point of no return, and that was when Isobel's house mate fed.

The feeding would go on for a long time and now that this first part was over, it would not be entirely unpleasant for Nick.

* * *

Isobel released Nick, he stood there teetering on legs that were no longer his own, his body trembling, and then he was slowly and almost tenderly dragged to the floor. Once he was prone, she took a final look before leaving. He looked as though he were laying half covered by a silken black bed sheet, the naked upper half of his body gently twitched and lazily thrashed as though he were having a bad dream. She knew that as the night progressed that dark sheet would make its way up and over him until nothing could be seen of him, and yet later, when she came to take him away, no mark or evidence of what had occurred would be visible upon his body.

As she left the room, she turned and blew a kiss, "bon appetit!".

There was a skip in her step as she returned to the kitchen and the waiting Charlotte. Even in the dim light, she could see Charlotte smile as she returned.

"Come on," Isobel said as she extended a hand.

Charlotte took it and was happy to be led from the kitchen, up the stairs and to the bedroom. She didn't ask about Nick. Isobel never ceased to be amazed at how a person could square things for themselves. Mostly they didn't ask questions and closed everything down as far as was possible. In this case, no news was good news, and Charlotte was getting what she wanted, so everything was OK in her world right now.

The bedroom had a sturdy, antique wood framed bed, a bedside table, a modestly sized wardrobe and other than curtains that were currently open and allowing the light of the moon in, that was the extent of the furnishings. The room itself was large and this made the sparse furnishings look all the more inadequate and yet it all worked. The bed was the centrepiece of the room and Isobel and Charlotte naturally gravitated towards it. Isobel pulled on Charlotte's hand and drew her in for a slow and gentle kiss, feeling Charlotte readily respond and press her lips harder and more urgently, encouraging Isobel.

This was not to be. Not yet. Instead, Isobel pushed Charlotte backwards, the backs of her legs hitting the edge of the bed, she found herself seated. Isobel stepped forward, closing the gap between them. She looked down upon Charlotte and smiled wickedly.

Charlotte blushed, "this is my first time..."

Isobel chuckled, "no it isn't... this is just... better."

13

She crouched down and placed her hands on Charlotte's thighs, "and we can take our time."

"What about…" began Charlotte, but Isobel was already moving forward and silenced the question with a gentle but firm kiss.

They kissed tentatively and gently at first, Isobel pushing Charlotte backwards and down as they did. She joined her on the bed, raised up on one elbow, she kissed her on the mouth again and slipped a hand along her body, stroking and caressing. Charlotte moaned into Isobel's mouth as her fingers became more insistent.

True to her word, Isobel took her time. Stroking Charlotte's hip, then tracing a line down along her thigh, then going higher and teasing and playing up from her midriff and promising to centre in on her breast, but not quite delivering on that promise, her fingers stroking her neck and playing with her hair before moving on to explore more of Charlotte's still clothed body.

By the time Isobel unbuttoned Charlotte's blouse, Charlotte was flushed and wide-eyed. She watched Isobel expectantly and Isobel paused to smile down at her, building yet more of that anticipation, Charlotte quivering and yearning for her touch, to feel her mouth and tongue.

"Please…" she gasped, arching her back and raising her arms to pull Isobel in.

Isobel grabbed both arms and pinned them down, moving on top of Charlotte, "Oh no you don't!" she breathed these words against Charlotte as she leaned in, her lips only a hair's breadth away from her neck.

Charlotte groaned in response.

Isobel could barely contain herself now, but she wanted to prolong the moment, didn't want to rush it, the longer the build-up, the better it would be for both of them. She lowered her head and her lips found Charlotte's collar bone, from there she kissed and lapped and nibbled downwards. She released Charlotte's arms and they stayed where they were, she was caught up in the moment and didn't want to change anything right now. She had closed her eyes and her breathing was shallow. Isobel looked up at her as she slipped the strap of her bra downwards and exposed her breast. Charlotte sighed and bit her lip. Isobel lowered her head again and trailed kisses around and around in ever decreasing circles. Charlotte's back arched further, offering herself up.

Isobel suddenly lifted her head and switched her attention to Charlotte's other breast, repeating that slow and pleasurable path towards her nipple. Now though, she slipped sideways from over Charlotte and her hand found Charlotte's inner thigh and stroked upwards.

"Oh!" gasped Charlotte as Isobel's mouth and hand worked in unison, teasing and kissing and caressing. Building, always building.

13

Charlotte was now lost entirely to Isobel's attentions and she barely registered the final scrap of material falling away, her focus was entirely on Isobel's fingers and the way they traced their way up and down, edging ever closer and closer, sending sparks through her as they almost connected with the very centre of her. The anticipation of that touch was exquisitely agonising and she writhed under Isobel wanting nothing else in the world right now.

When it came, she barely registered a flash of exquisite pain at her breast, the wave of pleasure directly on its heels was all that mattered. Isobel sucked at her breast greedily as Charlotte had the most intense orgasm of her life. The waves of pleasure crashed through her again and again, threatening never to end. Her arms lifted and traced patterns in the air, then they fell, one finding the back of Isobel's head and pushing her more firmly against her breast.

Isobel responded and sucked down harder on Charlotte's breast. The rhythm of her sucking perfectly matching the pulses of pleasure that continued to wrack Charlotte's body. Isobel slipped her fingers inside Charlotte and matched that same rhythm and as Charlotte responded, she lifted her head away from her breast and kissed and licked upwards.

Charlotte moaned as Isobel's insistent mouth found her neck, her hand still at the back of Isobel's head, stroking and encouraging, her body moving under Isobel's, working against her fingers.

"Harder!" she gasped, feeling another wave of pleasure

making its way towards her.

Isobel obliged. Taking her time and increasing her movements just a little more each and every time. Her mouth was working harder and harder on Charlotte's neck, teeth grazing the skin. Her own pleasure was building and it was all she could do to remain focused on Charlotte and that building wave that was going to break at any moment and just before it did, Isobel bit down on Charlotte's neck.

"No!" Charlotte gasped and her free arm came up to push Isobel away. That her other arm remained where it was and if anything pulled Isobel closer did not register with her.

In the very next second, Charlotte's resistance was over before it had really begun. Her second orgasm was released as Isobel's teeth pierced her. This was even bigger than the first and Isobel moaned against her as she felt Charlotte's hot, sweet blood pulse into her mouth with wave after wave of Charlotte's orgasm.

Isobel fed upon Charlotte, sucking hard at first, but settling to a more gentle rhythm as Charlotte calmed. In the afterglow of her orgasm, Charlotte stroked Isobel's back and encouraged her, a gentle pleasure continuing to flow through her. At one point, Isobel started to pull away, but Charlotte wrapped her arms around her and pulled her closer, wanting her to carry on.

"No, don't stop," and she sighed as she was rewarded with Isobel pressing down against her neck once more.

13

Charlotte's caresses worked gradually lower and lower down Isobel's body and Isobel moaned and mewled against her neck as she probed with initially clumsy fingers, but then finding the right spot and moving with Isobel until she had her own orgasm.

As Isobel lost control, she bit down harder and that was when Charlotte lost consciousness, she bucked under Isobel twice and then lay still. Moments after this, Isobel rolled over onto her back, sated and fulfilled. She lay there staring at the ceiling. Motionless and unblinking.

14

Isobel lay stock still in the darkness of the bedroom. Usually, having fed and being satisfied, she would have this feeling of emptying. An involuntary meditative state, it were as though she was full of all that energy, a life force that filled her almost totally leaving room for nothing else.

Tonight there was some room for thought. She had enjoyed herself in a way that she had not in such a long time, if she ever had. Her body had responded and she gone with that feeling. She had genuinely wanted to give pleasure and not just as a means to an end. She had enjoyed *being* with Charlotte.

This thought made her turn her head. She gazed upon the slumbering woman and she found she was thinking about sparing her, allowing herself that possibility and instantly going further. She wanted to do this again and she wanted to do it with Charlotte.

A spasm of pain caught her unawares and a single blood tear oozed from her right eye as she squeezed her eyes shut and clenched her fists. She could not. Charlotte had been dead

14

from the moment Isobel had met her and there was certainly no turning back now, Nick lay dead in the room below, she had heard his heart cease beating soon after she had begun her seduction of Charlotte in this bedroom.

Why was she thinking this way? This was dangerous and unnatural somehow. She wasn't what she seemed and could not allow herself these sentimentalities. It was one thing to play the game she had always played it and allow her prey a good death, but now she was overstepping lines she should never go near, let alone cross.

Was it this form she had taken? Was she changing because she could feel like them? Was this a form of regression to something she might once have been? Or a romantic ideal of what she could have been?

Isobel could not remember her earliest years. She had always *been*. She knew that the stories of vampires were just that. Stories. Somewhere in the collective human psyche there was an awareness of the supernatural and things that were out there, waiting, biding their time until they pounced and dragged a person off into the darkness. The true nature of those creatures had never been captured adequately in a book or film. People wanted to be gods and like gods, they could not help but cast their creations in their own image.

The problem Isobel had was she was alone in this world of humans. She had never met another vampire that she liked, and so all she had was what she knew of herself, these stories and what she saw when she interacted with people. Her very nature was a problem because she herself was malleable. She changed and adapted so that people saw what they wanted to and some of that couldn't help but stick with Isobel.

Acquiring an unchangeable body had seemed to be a solution to this lack of constancy. Isobel could lock herself in, settle and be herself. But now this response and feeling was happening. She felt something towards Charlotte. How insane was that? That was like a dog having a relationship with a bone. She sighed, she needed a better analogy than that one, she could imagine a dog having a relationship with a bone, they bloody loved bones. Maybe that was what she was doing here. Masking a need within herself by fixating on something that was ultimately impossible.

Was she lonely? Was that what this was? Did she need to find someone. Had she come to the Big House to create a nest? She realised that she didn't have a clue. No referent points and centuries of just existing. A simple cycle of hunger and feeding. There was little else.

Who was she kidding, there was nothing else, and it had been centuries filled with nothing but the hunger and feeding that hunger. She was impossibly old and each passing year weighed down upon her, that and the lives she had taken.

She sat up suddenly, a horrible sensation assailing her.

What had she done?

Nick, he wasn't a pleasant man, but then there was a lot of that

14

about. A lot of men had this hereditary or learned entitlement when it came to their significant relationship. They took that woman for granted and behaved in a churlish and childish manner. Isobel saw exploitation in some relationships, but she'd been around long enough to see the way it worked the other way too. People were in things for what they could get and nothing was ever a one way street. Not usually.

She hissed and ground her teeth, Nick hadn't deserved to die. She couldn't bring herself to look at Charlotte. What had she been thinking? She'd existed on a diet of elderly people for such a long time, taking those with a matter of months to live, seeing this as the lesser evil. A theft of months as opposed to years. Doing Deaths work for her.

Prior to those years and the dry and flavourless diet of the elderly, she had selected her meals based on the worthiness of the person. She had found a sport in this. The most successful and therefore the worst of murderers did not get caught, until she came along and removed them from the equation. She hadn't just killed those who killed, she had found others with black hearts and she had ended them and made the world a better place, black heart by black heart. She was an angel and this was a righteous retribution.

There had been a reason why she had ceased that pursuit and switched her diet, just as there was a reason now, for her being here and trying something different. She could not recollect the why of it now, only that there was a poison of a sort when she took that evil upon and into herself, so she had had to change before something very bad had happened. Whether that was death or another kind of loss, she could no longer remember.

Tonight, she had not thought things through properly. She had been attracted to Charlotte and it had all just happened. She had made the decision not to feed near home. To take her hunt far enough away that it did not touch this place, but beyond that she had thought no further. Even Micky was a departure from her self-imposed code. Instead, she had released herself from those constraints and just gone with her base instincts.

She had enjoyed herself for the first time in an age, but at what cost? And what did this mean for her after today? What was she to do? She sighed, today had opened her eyes and reminded her of what she had been missing. Then she groaned as she realised that she was conveniently ignoring the woman on the main road, and before that the kills she had made in order to arrive in the state that she was now in. The rot had set in before today and she had let it ride. In fact, she'd been slipping for a while now. She'd slipped well before she had taken this form.

Isobel balled her fists and pressed the heels of her hand against her firmly shut eyes. Was she losing her mind? Was that even possible? To look at her companion downstairs she did not think so. How long before she ended up like that? For all of her talk of having never seen another vampire, there was the small matter of the companion that she had shared the years with, seemingly for forever. They had been together for so long that she didn't consider that thing to be separate to her, it was a part of her reality. Sometimes she thought it was the

14

only constant part of her reality.

"Hey."

Isobel winced at the unexpected touch. Charlotte was awake. Isobel felt arms encircle her.

"It's OK, Isobel. Men can be right bastards at times."

Charlotte had mistaken Isobel's agitated state for her grief and anger at her fictitious, feckless boyfriend. She really was a nice person. Isobel shuddered with something like regret. She had no choice though, the die was set.

She gently pushed Charlotte out from the hug and tried for a tortured smile, "let's not talk about him. I've got you now."

Charlotte's smile faltered a little as she saw the intensity of Isobel's look. Isobel pushed her back on the bed and straddled her. She kissed her lightly on the lips and then lifted off and stared down at her with that same intensity, then she brightened.

"You know, I could eat you all up. You're just so... delicious," she said mischievously, "in fact, I think I will!"

She leant down and showered Charlotte with light kisses and the occasional lick or nibble, starting at her shoulder and then working her way down. Taking her time, but once she left Charlotte's breast, there was no mistaking where she was heading. Charlotte arched her back and groaned even as Isobel's mouth got to her hip, then she snaked downwards and across, but just before she arrived where Charlotte was willing her to go she went lower, her mouth finding Charlotte's knee and then almost painfully slowly she went higher and higher, her hand stroking and playing along the inner thigh of her other leg. Charlotte was panting and moaning by the time Isobel reached the top of her thighs.

Isobel's breath on her was enough to send waves of pleasure through her, so when she felt her mouth she was almost delirious. Isobel knew exactly what to do and kept Charlotte on the brink with her mouth alone and it was only as she pushed her fingers inside Charlotte that she came.

Charlotte felt Isobel disengage her mouth as she was coming and her eyes flew open even as she lost control of her body. Isobel kept working her fingers in and out in time with Charlotte's orgasm somehow prolonging it. Charlotte looked down as waves of pleasure disoriented her and she locked eyes with Isobel something passing between them in that instant that added to the intensity of the orgasm bursting through her body. Isobel opened her mouth as she stared into Charlotte's eyes and she bared her teeth, two incisors unnaturally long and wickedly sharp, she felt Isobel's free hand squeezing down on her thigh, the nails digging into her flesh, she felt the pain from that grip. That pain intensified as Isobel's nails dug into her thigh and it seemed to pause time as the expression on Isobel's face changed to something nakedly lustful. Something hungry. A stream of ice slid down Charlotte's neck and down towards where Isobel's fingers were, inside of her, and she tensed, clamping around those fingers, her thighs trembling. Still Isobel worked those fingers in and out and Charlotte's body kept responding, betraying her even as she saw the danger that she was in.

The next seemed to happen in slow motion, Charlotte watched in terrified fascination as Isobel lowered her head down towards her pubis. An act that should have conveyed so much pleasure but now Charlotte knew her for what she was and knew the danger that she was in, but she was frozen in the moment and couldn't respond other than to mouth a *no* and gasp as she felt Isobel's lips brush against her sensitive flesh, and then she felt those teeth entering her thigh and as they did Isobel pushed her fingers deeper and deeper inside her, and Charlotte couldn't believe it as she came again, violently this orgasm crashed through her and threw her body against the bed. She almost lost consciousness as she came and as the orgasm subsided she fell breathlessly to the bed. All she could feel in the aftermath of her orgasm was the ebb and flow of Isobel sucking and lapping against her thigh and her now gentle caressing. She lay motionless but felt like she was being rocked to and fro. With each ebb and flow she felt a little calmer and serene and Isobel kept going and going until Charlotte's head swam and there was a moment of panic, she was aware that she had lifted her arm, but it felt like it wasn't her own. She pressed her palm against Isobel's head and she knew that she had intended to push her away, but it didn't feel like she was there any more, she had no more substance and her hand merely rested upon Isobel's head and moved against her in that ebbing and flowing motion, until it fell away and onto the bed.

She thought that she might have asked Isobel to stop, that maybe she whispered the words a little too quietly for Isobel to hear. She should try again and tell her. Tell her what? This was nice. Like that massage they'd had on holiday a couple of years back. Nick was nicer then. Nick was dead wasn't he? She'd known that even as Isobel came back for her and led her to this room. Had she cared? It didn't matter now did it? Peaceful. So peaceful. I might have a little sleep, was the last thing Charlotte thought.

Isobel kept feeding until it was done and she bestowed upon Charlotte a sleep that she would never awaken from.

It was for the best.

15

It was getting light when Isobel returned to the Big House. This was not ideal as a village like Brokmaster woke with the cock crow, so she knew she was likely to be seen and her worry on this front turned out to be entirely valid. As it was, it was deemed to be perfectly acceptable behaviour. There were comings and goings at this hour, it was the equivalent of rush hour, so had she rushed things and tried to get back in full dark it may have looked suspicious, whereas her arrival now was commonplace. Once again, her luck held.

The work of her morning had entailed taking Nick and Charlotte back home. There was a side road that she was able to park on and no one had seen her walk the two bodies into the house. Safely tucked up in bed, they looked like they had been there all night and would get up when the alarm went off in a couple of hours.

Looks can so often be deceptive and today the alarm would go unnoticed and unheard. Isobel looked down upon them one last time, her gaze lingering on Charlotte's pale and lifeless face. In this state, she was not the same. She was no longer

Charlotte and any regrets Isobel had were not here in this room, they had occurred in another place and they were already ghosts of their former selves.

Fire cleansed and fire removed any sign of Isobel and her companion, not that there were ever many signs to find and if ever an eagle eye saw something unusual, it would never point to a creature such as she. Not existing as far as humans were concerned did have some advantages.

Tomorrow, there would be news across the various medias about a fire and suspicious circumstances. Given a little time, there would be further news about a suspected suicide pact. Then almost everyone would move on to the next news article.

Of Micky, there would never be any sign. People went missing every day and he merely added to that statistic.

Isobel slammed the van door and walked briskly to the back door of the Big House and again slammed the door to the kitchen. Once inside she sat down heavily on one of the three wooden chairs at the kitchen table. As she sat there feeling utterly drained and despondent, she realised she was sitting in the same chair Charlotte had sat in only hours previously. She shot back up as though she was consecrating the spot and found herself propelled to the front room. She was in the room and speaking before she had time to think.

"How was it for you, eh?" she barked into the room.

"You should not speak to me like that," said the dry, dark and

15

ominous voice.

"I'll speak to you..." she began, but then she was clutching her temples and sliding down the wall to her knees.

"You forget yourself," said the dark voice.

Isobel barely heard the words, her head was still ringing. She glared at her companion. This was too much and after she had brought her a meal. The pain in her head intensified.

"And still you defy me," said her companion darkly, "worse still, you risk us both."

The pain stopped immediately that the last word was spoken.

"What do you mean?" Isobel pushed herself up to a seated position and attempted to compose herself.

"Playing with your meal like that. You seemed to enjoy yourself just a little too much," there was reproach and disdain in that voice and Isobel resented it.

"It's what I do," answered Isobel simply.

"Well you shouldn't," stated her companion.

"That's easy for you to say, but without that, what do I have left? Besides, they taste all the sweeter when their blood is up."

"Once they are near us, their blood is already up. You know this."

"It's not the same."

"You are not being truthful, you're hiding something. Perhaps you're hiding it so well you've hidden it from yourself. I question your motives because you do not seem to. If you are not in control of yourself then you will become reckless and that is when the trouble starts."

Isobel's hackles were up, she did not like being challenged, nor did she like being told. There was condescension here, but the worst of it was that her companion was right. She wanted to refute it and deny that there was any problem at all. There was though and it was all the worse for Isobel not really knowing what the problem was, she did not have the words and she feared that she was nowhere near understanding what was happening, that she did not understand herself sufficiently. In which case, how could she be in control?

She had wanted to say something for a while now. She had wanted to say many things. To ask her companion what they were to each other. They had been together for so long now that their meeting and origins had been lost in the mists of time. Her unanswered questions led to flimsy assumptions and laying between those assumptions were fears. Was her companion an older version of herself? Did she have this to look forward to? Why had they cleaved to each other in a way that felt like they could never part, that to part would be an ending to one or both of them?

15

She had fallen out of the habit of talking and exchanges with her companion were all too rare. She wondered if this had always been the way of it, or had they lapsed into this as the days rolled out before them and the capacity to talk dwindled. Their secret existence restricted their capacity to do anything. Yes, Isobel found some solace in watching the world of men and women and observing their perverse nature, but that emphasised the nature of her predicament and she never felt so alone as when she watched the living world around her. It were as though she was separated from the world where she should belong by an impossibly thin and invisible pane of glass. A small child staring into a fish tank, but in this case, the child was a fish and she was drowning in the stale air she shared with her companion. Her companion held her back, and yet she knew that was not really the truth of it. Her companion was a lazy focus for her, she casually ladened her companion with the blame and the responsibility for a life she didn't think she wanted anymore.

And now, here she was in a new state. She had a body and she could *be* in the world, but it was already going wrong. She knew that. Her companion knew that. There was a sense that this was doomed to failure, that anything she tried to do to break out of the monotony of her existence would only make matters worse. A bad seed had been sewn at the very outset and no good would come from this life of hers, however she tried to live it.

A spout of rage erupted from her frustration. She trembled with her barely contained anger. If she could not have this one thing then she would take the precious lives from others.

She would take that which she envied and she would show just what she was capable of, she would display her true nature and damn the consequences.

She felt the wave of anger and it frightened her. She really would lose control if she gave into her anger. She looked across the room into the dark where her companion was and she wanted to hate, but found that she could not. Knew that it would be unwise to take her anger out on her companion, now and here were neither the time nor the place. This was not about her companion, perhaps it would be so much easier if it was, at least then she would have a target for her rage and frustration.

Getting to her feet she looked poised to leap, then she made a decision.

"I'm going out…"

She didn't say where or for what reason, and she didn't have answers to those questions if her companion had asked. She just needed to get out of here and away from this place for a while. To be out in the world and maybe to feel like she was a part of it.

"Be careful, Angyal."

Isobel paused in the doorway. Angel. If she were an angel, then she had fallen from grace and she was living in purgatory. This wasn't hell, but it was a form of limbo. She was a hunter, a taker of souls. Maybe that was what angels were. If she were living out a penance then this was all a cruel joke for she had little choice, she either fed or she died. Not that she thought she could die. Not even if she stopped feeding. The state she would arrive at, were she not to feed, didn't bare thinking about. Barely alive, but still aware and in a well of never ending pain. Helpless and unable to put an end to her tortured state. Not that she could ever get there. Her hunger was elemental and to deny it was to inflame it and then, any semblance of control was lost.

Just like the deluded sheep that she fed on, she had few choices in this life of hers. Where she differed from those sheep was that she *knew,* and the pain of that knowing haunted her.

16

Somehow, a part of the morning had escaped her and this made her feel cheated and her mood would not lift. She walked with purpose through the village and carried with her an aura that made anyone that encountered her keep their distance.

As it was, she passed several villagers and all of them acknowledged her. By the third she had parked her stand offishness and allowed herself to nod acknowledgement, not quite able to return a cheery hello or hi.

In a short while, she found herself in the local shop. She was not completely set apart from the world and had in her possession items that people had become accustomed to to such an extent that they considered them essentials. These items included a laptop and later, she would order a few more things for the house to make it seem like it was actually being lived in. As she had walked, she had formulated a list that she would search for and buy. Furniture was a must, more bed linen and towels and a few bits and bobs in the kitchen that someone would likely find in the house of someone who was too busy to properly take care of themselves and went through phases of cooking nothing more than a microwave meal or a pot noodle. A few bottles of alcohol should also be present, half a bottle of red on the kitchen work surface. She would have to remember to leave a few dirty dishes by the sink too.

Isobel was well versed in how a house should look, so dressing her own was not all that much of a challenge. Nothing really presented her a challenge. She did not want for anything, she had an immense span of time ahead of her, in fact everything would be rosy if she could either find something to occupy her days or zone out from her life to such a degree that she could go through the motions as painlessly as possible. Loads of these people managed it, so it shouldn't be all that difficult. She suspected that it was something one could not do on purpose, that it had to creep up on them entirely by accident so that the transition went largely unnoticed. She also suspected that there was a necessary component of *nature* to these particular proceedings, that a person had to be predisposed to lapsing into a rut.

Then it hit her. She had already tried that, and it was her rut that she had climbed out of so recently. That was part of the problem, she didn't want to go back there and she couldn't find a new direction to go in. She wanted someone to come along and give her directions when she hadn't actually asked for any. That would work. Only it wasn't going to happen and if anyone approached her right now, she may very well tip their head back like a Pez dispenser and bathe in their blood.

Blood.

Always a happy thought that. She could sense blood from a hundred yards, hear the heart pumping it around a body and see the pulsing vein on a neck. She had only recently fed and already she was thinking about blood. That was just the start. The thoughts of blood and feeding and the euphoria she would feel as she fed, not to mention the pre-feed anticipation and excitement, well they started in as the odd drip here and there, then grew in frequency until she was swimming in them, then the storm came and she was thrown forward with no choice but to go with it.

Right now, she was surreptitiously watching the pulse, pulse of the vein in the neck of the female shop assistant. The owner would be out back somewhere, but right now it was just the two of them. The girl had nodded a welcome and then left Isobel to it, which was just how Isobel liked it, and it was certainly what she wanted right now.

She licked her lips and an involuntary moan escaped from deep in her throat. What was wrong with her? She couldn't tear her eyes away from that girl's neck and she found that she was breathing deeply of her scent. There was something about that aroma that was inflaming her. Making a point of moving further away from the shop assistant and trying to actually browse the items in the shop, intending to purchase at least a tin or two and perhaps tea bags and biscuits, she could not break the spell that was upon her. Try as she may, her eyes kept returning to the girl and for a second time she let forth with a moan. This was even more audible and the girl looked up and across at Isobel at the sound of it.

16

Isobel made a point of returning the girl's gaze with a neutral look of her own. The girl quickly looked away, flushing with embarrassment. The sight of this did not help Isobel one bit. She put down the tin that she had been intending to purchase and she decided to leave the shop as quickly as she could.

This was when Neil, the shop's owner emerged from the back room and spotted the newcomer.

"Hello there! We haven't seen you before, have we, Jess?"

The shop assistant looked up and smiled, "no, I don't think we have."

Isobel was inexplicably flustered and suddenly felt trapped. The shop was beginning to feel smaller to her and the walls were closing in. She felt an unusual feeling, one well known to most but alien to her: panic.

"I'm..." began Isobel, intending to respond properly to Neil's hello, but something was lost in translation from thought to the spoken word, "...just leaving," she said instead, and with that she brushed past Neil. The contact sending a shock of electricity through her, she gave the girl as wide a berth as possible, which was not very much at all because she was stationed at a till right next to the shop door.

The girl's scent intensified as Isobel went for the exit and she had to dig her nails into her palms to keep her focus and resolve. Opening the door was a blessed relief, the fresh country air washing over her and diluting the intensity of the scent that was threatening to overwhelm her.

As she walked briskly back home she understood two things. One was that she was still getting to grips with her new body and today she had discovered that her sense of smell had not only been heightened but affected her more directly and deeply than it ever had. The other was that the girl was on her period.

Isobel would have to put some work in so that she did not react so violently to those around her. Somehow, she would have to desensitise herself to the presence of blood.

"Yeah right," she muttered to herself.

She, a vampire, had identified a problem that she had and it was blood. Doing something about that was a big ask and then some. She had to do something though. She couldn't have a strange sort of panic attack every time she encountered someone on their period or whenever someone cut themselves.

And she'd just fed! Imagine the carnage if she was on the cusp of losing her battle with her hunger and the irresistible need to feed. Her mind raced and two thoughts leapt out from nowhere at her. Ditch the body and revert to her former self. She instantly dismissed that. Cauterise the inside of her nose. Get rid of at least some of this cursed sense of smell, because if she couldn't smell it then she couldn't react to it. It took longer to dismiss this latter notion because it had some merit. She soon came up with a couple of concerns though, she needed her sense of smell, it helped her stay sharp and out of trouble and she also thought that somehow burning her nose off wouldn't

16

stop her sense of smell anyway. Life had a habit of thwarting plans such as these. If she were a fictional character, her nose would of course regenerate. It would most likely sparkle too, whilst being a nose so perfect it must have come via several trips to a Hollywood plastic surgeon.

No, she just had to deal with it.

As she approached the Big House, her best efforts in dealing with this unfortunate set back to her walking abroad and sharing the world of men and women had her picturing a particularly delightful mealtime fantasy. It was so vivid, she was almost there, behind the counter. The counter that the twenty something girl was leaning against as Isobel licked and lapped higher and higher up her leg. She was pleased to note that she was possessed of some degree of self-possession and she had started right down at the bare ankle and taken some time to make her way up along the inside of the leg. She hadn't yet botched it, either by biting down there and then, or making a sprint for her intended goal. No she was slow and steady and getting closer and closer to the top of the girl's inner thigh and she was sliding both her hands up the back of the girl's legs to her firm buttocks and gripping them firmly so that when she buried her face in the…

"Hello!"

Isobel almost walked into John as she turned into her drive from the pavement. She reeled backwards as though he had landed a hefty punch to her chin and her eyes went wide to discover him right there in front of her. If the truth be told, the shock went further than that, his greeting had rudely teleported her from an almost real and very gratifying moment. Hell, she had it bad. And she didn't even know what it was that she had.

"You gave me a fright," she smiled uncertainly at John.

She had caught up with current events and her mind was here in this moment, but it didn't hurt to display some confusion and consternation. She had already squared her behaviour in the village shop, the real behaviour and not the fantasy she had just been entertaining. She was a busy woman and it was expected that she would be aloof and appear rude. If she kept things going in that vein then there would be those in the village who would describe her as 'nice enough, but on the spectrum, if you know what I mean?"

John raised a bundle by way of explanation, "thought I'd return this to you."

Isobel looked at it for a moment and having not instantly placed it, she thought back to the last time she had seen John, unconscious on the pavement outside this house. She'd grabbed the blanket from the house. For some odd reason, it had been hanging on the back of one of the kitchen chairs. The former occupant of the house had not had much by the way of furniture or possessions, but she had had this blanket.

"Very kind of you," said Isobel, "you didn't have to you know."

"Well I sort of did, and it's the least I could do. Besides, it's given me the excuse I needed to come and see you and thank you for helping me the other day and also to say hello."

"People say hello quite a lot around here," said Isobel voicing a thought she probably should have kept firmly inside her head, but it was out there now and would add to her legend.

John pulled a puzzled face and then recovered, "people are friendly around here, yes. I run the…"

"Broken Dragon," Isobel cut in.

The puzzled expression returned, how did she know that? "Yes, yes I do. Anyway, there's a drink waiting for you there by way of a both a thank you and a hello." He rubbed his chin thoughtfully, "actually, there's two drinks waiting for you, one as an introductory, special offer and the other is a thank you."

Isobel smiled a winning smile, "thank you. That's rather lovely of you. Now if you'll excuse me…"

She took the blanket from John and walked past him to the back of the house.

He found himself saying "yes of course," to thin air, and when he turned around, he was just in time to see the back of her disappearing around the side of the house.

He shook his head and smiled muttering, "nowt so queer as folk," as he started his walk back to the Dragon.

17

"I'm telling you, she's not right and there's something going on at the Bad House," said Don.

He was several pints in and in the mood to wax lyrical. He was also in danger of contravening several of the Broken Dragon's mores and norms.

"You mean the Big House?" said Janet, taking a big swig of her G&T.

"Starting to look like the Bad House to me," retorted Don.

"Careful Don," said John from behind the bar, "you'd best have some good reasoning behind this, you know we don't like rumour mongering and mud throwing here."

"I'm not like that," said Don, "you know I'm not."

John stared at Don, his face unreadable. Dangerous people who really were *like that* would say exactly what Don had just said. Also, just because you didn't have form didn't mean you weren't capable of bad things. There was a part of John that wanted to wholeheartedly agree with Don, there was something off at the Big House, but mostly he wanted to get over himself, move on and think the best of that place and by inference this village and his home.

Don shook his head, but he wasn't going to stop there, "there's the undertaker's van for a kick off…"

"That's not an undertaker's van," John guffawed at this, "the windows are tinted is all. They're good vans those. Wouldn't mind one myself."

John liked his cars and had a few out back. Like most car lovers, his desire for cars far outstripped any budget he could muster. It was a good van, up there with the few that he coveted. Ford and VW had upped their van game in recent years and some owners had taken that game a little further. Those vans had the potential to be wolves in sheep's clothing.

"OK, you tell me this," Don said indignantly, "why's a lady like that, driving a van with tinted windows."

"You're not being sexist are you?" Janet gave Don a warning look.

"No, I'm just saying someone like that…"

"Like what?" Janet held that warning look of hers.

Don looked uncomfortable now and John hoped he wouldn't

dig a hole for himself. Sometimes it was best to back down and leave a thing unsaid.

Don took the risk, and he'd thought this through. To a point. "How many people have you seen in the upper middle classes driving a van as their main mode of transport?"

John nodded his appreciation of the wording of Don's most recent question and he sympathised with the sentiment. There *was* something out of kilter with the Big House and that van added something to John's unease and curiosity. He kept trying to dismiss it and move on, but he had an itch there. He didn't like to think that that itch was just plain old curiosity, that he was that awful, nuisance, nosey neighbour twitching the curtain and watching the people around him as a form of inappropriate entertainment. He would have to get a life if he had fallen into those sad little ways. He was supposed to rise above this sort of thing and be the arbiter in the pub, the voice of reason. Instead, he was letting this play out after some token resistance.

It dawned on him that this was now the preserve of schoolkids. He pictured them in a tree house speculating about the goings on in the spooky house.

Did people ever really grow up?

"Plenty," replied Janet, "even people in the upper middle classes work. Some of them are even in the upper middle classes by virtue of the work they put in."

17

Janet's remarks sounded quite casual, but John knew they were pointed. He imagined that she had had her fair share of judgemental remarks and behaviour, especially as she hadn't even attempted to elevate her broad accent, she'd believed in hard graft and the substance that contained, everything else was just fluff and nonsense. She was another member of the middle classes thanks to the successes she had had, but maybe Don wouldn't blink at Janet driving a van.

John hoped a battle wouldn't be fought over that simple point when there was a lot more to it than that. People suited certain cars just the same as they suited particular dogs or gravitated towards a partner who kinda looked similar to them. It didn't always work that way, but often enough it did and when things didn't match up, they stood out. That was when people asked questions.

This was grey territory, John knew, because somewhere in that territory had been where he had operated as a police officer and he still had that nous, even now. He had to. He had to sniff out the potential trouble makers as early as he possibly could and manage the dynamic in the pub so that it didn't get to the point where the fuel of trouble ignited and a good night turned into a bad one. A bad one that would cast a shadow over the following days, weeks, months and even years. There was a skill to subtly steering things back on course and it took seeing things for what they were and what they possibly could be.

"Those vans have livery on them, don't they?" Don said.

Janet partially nodded, acknowledging the point, "there are at least as many vans without livery as there are with. I've never understood why people don't advertise their work or brand, but it happens a lot."

"Most of those people driving those vans are trades people aren't they?" said Don.

"Or deliveries," added John.

Don nodded to that one, "I just have this question mark over it is all. Not being a class warrior or anything like that, most of my deliveries are made by women driving similar sized vans, so it's not about her being a woman. There's just something not right, but it's more than about that van anyway. There's the way she acts."

"How so?" asked Janet. She was guarded and this was still dangerous territory for Don.

John watched with interest and wanted to know what Don was going to say, hoping he'd resolve John's own reservations one way or the other, give him a golden nugget that helped substantiate his gut feel or better still show him that he was being irrational. The latter may entail Don receiving a tongue lashing from Janet, and John would have to intervene there, he was aware that he was being a bit of a coward in sitting back and allowing Don to do the heavy lifting in this conversation.

"Have you not noticed?" Don asked, turning from Janet to John in the hope that either one of them would at least cite one moment of strange behaviour.

17

It didn't happen.

Don rolled his eyes, "surely you heard about her visit to the local shop?"

"I heard someone mention it the other day," said John, "that was something and nothing though wasn't it? People walk into shops and walk back out without buying anything all the time. I walk into rooms and haven't a clue how I got there, let alone why I went in there."

Janet made a murmur of agreement on that one, certain behaviours crept up on you and once you noticed them you realised you were another decade older and there was no turning the clock back.

"Well, I heard the story from Jess," said Don, "she was shaken by it. Said that woman was staring at her and behaving all wrong. Making growling noises. Then Neil comes out from the back and she gets all awkward and storms out of the shop."

John drew in a deep breath, "I think we have to be careful here," he said, "she's new to the village and we don't get that many new people come in do we?" he paused, but not for an answer, "she stands out because she's a she. I've already heard a couple of vicious rumours about her being a lady of easy virtue. Lock up your husbands and the such. No substance to it, just people with nothing better to do making things up. In this case, a single woman with a bit of cash. That's threatening to some. That she lives in the Big House makes her stand out that bit more and adds to the whole shebang. People see what they want to see and that's not necessarily the truth of it, is it?"

Janet nodded and gave a wry smile, she thought John had done rather well at putting this in its box. Don grizzled, unlikely to say anything further now, but he wasn't letting it go, that much was obvious.

For his part, having played Devil's advocate, John wasn't convinced. If anything, having presented his case and standing by every word of it, the Big House and the woman who now lived there really didn't sit right with him.

"Anyway," he added with a shrug, "we don't even know her name yet do we?"

And no one did.

Give it time, he thought to himself. Things usually fall into place given time.

Don obviously wasn't a proponent of giving things such as this time and his philosophy differed to Johns. He shook his head, "it's just not right. She's just not right. There's evil in that house. I've felt it."

John suppressed a shiver at Don's last words and did his best to act relaxed and natural, very aware that people who had to work on those things looked far from relaxed or natural. He'd pulled over his fair share of people attempting to convince him they had had nothing to drink, the acting of a pissed driver trying to be sober was farcical.

17

"Bloody hell!" groaned Janet, "next you'll be saying she was responsible for that car accident up on the main road!"

Don raised an eyebrow, "well…"

"Now you're just being ridiculous," Janet turned away from Don having said this and drank some more of her G&T, looked at the glass and decided to finish it off, raising the empty glass to John.

"Another?" this was a redundant word, more a pleasantry than anything else.

Janet smiled by way of a response and John poured her a fresh drink.

As he did, Don spoke to their respective backs, "She just turned up out of the blue. Don't you find any of this in the least bit strange?"

"What? Bought a house and turned up soon after the purchase? What's strange about that, Don?" Janet said this in a mocking tone and she also managed to sound weary.

"Did she though?"

John handed the drink to Janet and gave Don a quizzical look. Where was he going with this? He seemed to be heading into the nonsensical *Ah! But!* territory which singled people out as being just a bit irrational, if not heading off and out into the world of complete and utter irrationality. Don didn't strike

John as one of those types and he wasn't in his cups either. Not quite, anyway.

"Did she what?" John asked the question that would keep Don's thread going, mildly regretting it as he did.

"Buy the house? I mean, we always hear about houses that are available, even before they go on the market. They pretty much get snapped up before they go on the market here don't they?"

Good point, thought John.

"Did anyone know the old lady that used to live there?" Janet said this in a monotone, obviously getting bored of the conversation.

"Yes," said another voice that made all three of the locals look up and turn towards the source of the new arrival, "she was my aunt."

18

Isobel had heard enough of the conversation to understand what was being said and what was going on. Most of it was of no concern to her. Pubs were places of scurrilous gossip and hardly any of it went anywhere, it stayed right there in the pub once it had been vented.

That said, she also knew of the maxim, *there is no smoke without fire*, and her appearance in the pub as she was being talked about was fortuitous to say the least, she could move things along and maybe provide some distraction from that smoke, ingratiating herself with some of the locals would make life easier for everyone. And she was very good at making life easier for everyone.

"Why hello!" exclaimed John, the consummate host, "come in for those drinks have you?"

"Let's start with the one," said Isobel, "would anyone else like one?"

Both Janet and Don consulted with their mostly full glasses

and declined the offer of a drink.

"What will you be having?" asked John.

"Glenfiddich," Isobel said, glancing at the shelves of interesting bottles, "as it comes," she added.

John nodded and hand poured a generous measure, passing it over the bar to her with a nod and a smile.

"Thanks," she said, leaving the glass where it was on the bar. She would make a show of drinking it soon enough, "I'm Isobel," she said this as she held out a hand to Janet to shake.

Janet eyed the hand for a moment, the shaking of hands was a little formal for this pub, but an effort was being made and Isobel had singled her out as the first person she wanted to greet. Janet was not averse to a little solidarity and she took the proffered hand and shook it, "Janet," she said.

Isobel smiled warmly, then turned her attention to Don. Of course she knew who these people were, she had done her homework, but it wouldn't do to show off her knowledge of the village and the people who dwelt therein. More care to be taken there, Isobel could easily say the wrong thing and have them wondering even more about her. Always play it carefully, she thought to herself. A part of her resented this and wanted to be spontaneous. The only time she ever seemed to near a state of spontaneity was when she fed, but even then, she was looking over her shoulder and feared the prospect of discovery. For her, the angry villagers brandishing flaming torches and pitchforks were never far away and yet here she was, courting those self-same villagers, having left her castle to walk amongst them.

Don took her hand, he looked a little flustered and so he should, but he did his best to welcome Isobel, "welcome to the Dragon," he said as he shook her hand.

"Oy! Less of that!" smiled Janet.

"Never gets old that one!" chuckled John, "I'm John," he said to Isobel, "it's good to see you in here."

"Yeah," agreed Don, "I've never understood the people who live in a village and don't frequent their local pub."

"Takes all sorts," said John by way of a reply.

"Use it or lose it," replied Don.

"He's right, John. If you ever had to shut the pub, they'd be the first people to say what a shame it was," said Janet.

"That might be true, but can we change the subject to something a little less close to home, please. I dunno, you people can be so maudlin at times!" John grinned as he said this, but he was a superstitious soul and didn't want people speculating about his pub failing.

"How are you settling in?" asked Janet.

"Oh you know, I've barely had time to think about that. One minute I'm up in Town, the next I hear Aunt Maud has passed and here I am. It's been… busy." Isobel sipped at her drink, felt the burning sensation of the whisky entering her mouth and let it travel along her tongue and down her throat. She'd practiced this and found that as long as she took her time, she suffered no adverse effects by taking a little drink.

"So, are you staying?" asked Don.

Isobel looked puzzled, thinking the question through, "I hadn't really thought that far, but do you know what? I like it here and I could stay. Hadn't thought about going at all, so I suppose that counts for something doesn't it?"

"What is it that you do?" asked Janet.

"A bit of this and a bit of that really. Property investment mostly, I suppose."

Janet gave Don a meaningful look.

"What is it?" asked Isobel innocently.

"Oh nothing," said Don far too quickly.

"He wanted to know why you drove a van," winked Janet, "and said it wasn't as though you were in a trade."

"Weeeell," said Isobel, grinning, "I'd say being in a trade was a bit of a stretch. Let's not mention the tax efficiency

18

of commercial vehicles though, eh? It was either the van or a pick up, and the van won. I might convert it to a camper at some point in the future. If I ever get around to it."

"A camper, eh?" said John from behind the bar, he was pouring himself another lager.

"Yes, I quite like the thought of travelling around the country and stopping wherever takes my fancy, take a look around. Partake of the local delicacies and then move on."

"The life of a nomad, eh?" quipped Janet.

"Something like that, yes."

"All sounds very romantic," said Don, "until you get to the practicalities. Cramped living space that you'd quickly get sick of. Finding places you can actually stop. Half of those places turning out to be a bit crap…"

"You'll have to forgive Don," said Janet, "he's a right old ray of sunshine at times!"

"He's right though," said Isobel, "life on the open road isn't all it's cracked up to be, I'm sure."

"Depends how you do it and what mindset you bring to it," said Janet, "of course it helps if you've got a good budget and can treat yourself to a hotel from time to time!"

"Sounds like you've sampled life on the open road," said

Isobel.

"Nowt so grand," said Janet, "I've done a bit of travelling, mostly with work, but I've done camping holidays too. Always good to know you can abandon a leaking tent and get warm and dry somewhere, I can tell you!"

"We drove a Winnebago across the States when the kids were young," John had come around to the front of the bar.

John sometimes surprised even his most regular of regulars with his stories, just when they thought they'd heard it all, he would tell them about something else he had done before he came to be the landlord at the Dragon. It was easy to forget that John was one of the few incomers, he'd fit right in from the start and quickly became a part of the pub's furniture.

"That must've been hard, what with the young kids," Don stated this as though there were no other possible outcome than difficulty, mayhem and despondency when it came to children. He certainly wouldn't have risked a holiday carting his girls across a continent.

"We had our moments, but it was mostly good. Got to see a lot of America that way."

Isobel had another sip of her whisky, enjoying the warming quality of the spirit. She listened as the conversation wended and meandered and she contributed whenever she felt it necessary. Mostly she wanted to fade into the background so she didn't have to say much. She had come to show her

18

face and now she had done that. If talk of her visit to the pub turned out to be a damp squib with very little to say about her other than *she seemed alright,* then this was a good night's work, more so because this would help override speculation and talk of dark goings on at the Big House. Then it was a case of maintaining this and perhaps generating a little good will. That was a longer term prospect and she first had to complete this phase of gently ingratiating herself into the village, it's patterns and the gentle movements of its life.

"Another?" asked John.

Isobel glanced at her glass and realised that it was empty.

"I really shouldn't," she said, thinking that she should quit while she was ahead. She noticed that Janet and Don's glasses were nearing empty too, "but I will. One more Glenfiddich and whatever these two are having."

There were murmurs of appreciation and Isobel thought maybe she had earnt herself a small measure of goodwill right there.

They were part way into this next drink when the conversation seemed to jump randomly, "no bloke in tow then?" asked Don.

"Who says it's a bloke?" chuckled Janet.

Isobel raised an eyebrow and smiled and was rewarded with a grin from Janet and blushing from Don as he realised he may have missed the mark.

John intervened, sparing Don any further blushes, "do you think we're over the worst of this pandemic business then?"

This was relatively safe ground, although it risked comments on the shower of politicians that had added to the uncertainty of this era, appearing to feather their nests and certainly not adhering to the very rules they had imposed upon the rest of the population. But then it had always been the same, it was only that the spotlight moved around and away and then back again, shocking the population each and every time they saw what a rotten bunch politicians really were. They never did anything about it though, nor were they likely to.

"I hope so," sighed Don, "it's been absolute madness hasn't it?"

"You've got that right," agreed Janet.

"There could be another variant come along and stuff everything up couldn't there?" suggested John.

"Variants generally become less fatal though, don't they?" said Don.

"They're supposed to, but I wouldn't bank on it," countered John.

"I think we'll have bigger flu seasons," theorised Janet.

"How do you mean?" asked Don.

"Well, we'll have a flu jab and another jab. Maybe even a combined jab. Then it's a case of hoping there's not a nasty strain comes along and kills a whole bunch of people. It's been the same every year, we've just been unlucky recently."

"I hope you're right," said Don.

"Yeah, let's hope the worst of this is over and we have another hundred years of plain sailing," agreed John.

"What do you reckon, Isobel?" Don asked Isobel.

She shrugged, "it's all part of nature, isn't it?"

"It's a bit more than that, isn't it?" said Don.

"Not really. Everything dies. Nature has a multitude of ways of hastening that end. I doubt it'll be a hundred years next time, the population is growing and it's very mobile, so the scope for transmission and mutation of viruses and diseases increases. Then there are natural disasters that are increasing in frequency and size as the planet warms. I think the next decade or so are going to be really interesting."

"That's a bit grim isn't it?" said Don.

"That's rich coming from you, Don!" guffawed Janet.

"Grim?" said Isobel, "isn't the sentimentality attached to

nature and death fascinating. These are facts of our existence, but so often there's a value judgement made that bears little relation to the reality of the matter. Is it sad that salmon die as they spawn? They are eaten or they return back to the river, nourishing it. Species experience adjustments to their numbers and to their very nature. They adapt and change. People seem to be getting more and more squeamish about death and their relationship to death is getting worse. I see it all the time."

There fell upon the bar a silence that Isobel was at first oblivious to, as it dawned on her that her words had had this effect she slowly raised her now almost empty glass and eyed it curiously. She had not noticed its consumption and that in itself was of concern. She felt eyes upon her and decided now was the time to take her leave of the pub.

"Sorry," she waved her glass in front of her, "I get a little dark and introspective when I drink on an empty stomach. I'd best go before I climb onto my soapbox and really give it both barrels."

"Aw!" said Janet, "just as it was getting interesting!"

She took Isobel's hand just as she released the glass she'd now placed on the bar, "you will come again soon, won't you?"

Isobel was taken aback, Janet meant this and she felt the affirmation from both Don and John. She couldn't help looking from one to the other as they awaited her answer.

18

"Of course," she said, "I've…"

What was it that she had done and what was she going to say?

"…really enjoyed tonight."

And she had, she realised it there and then.

Isobel had enjoyed herself in the company of people, and it had not been a means to an end. No one had died.

As she walked back to the Big House, she smiled to herself. Yes, she had enjoyed herself and she felt… good.

She also felt hungry. Being around those people and enjoying herself had created an appetite within her and she was hungry earlier than she had anticipated.

19

"I need to feed."

Isobel was in the front room talking to her companion as the last light of the day waned and shadows lengthened across the land.

"So do I," came the reply from the darkness.

"So soon?" blurted Isobel.

"I could say the same of you," came the retort.

Isobel sighed. The logistics of providing a meal for two were more onerous, but there was no point in bemoaning the practicalities of the situation. Moaning would change nothing, it would only make matters worse.

"I'll bring something back," said Isobel absently.

"Something? I hope by that, you mean someone?" the voice was sharp and challenging.

19

"Yes, that is what I meant."

"Then why not say what you mean? You are going... soft."

Isobel sighed a sigh of frustration, but swallowed down any possible reply, instead she shook her head, turned on her heels and left the room.

She'd dressed up for this evening's hunt. She had started the way she had meant to go on and her wardrobe consisted of outfits that suited her and told a story that she wanted to tell. When she had shopped to dress the house, she had also added to her wardrobe. Boots and heels caught her eye and she pored over many pairs, buying a few as she went along. Shoes seemed to fascinate her and she enjoyed acquiring and wearing them. Underwear was not far behind in that respect either.

Being Isobel had given her a new lease of life, but as she left the house she pondered her companion's words. There was no doubt that she was different now. Her form had affected that, but now she had a question and it was a chicken or egg sort of question. What about her diet? Had this body driven her to change her diet? Or had she craved that change, the new body being only one symptom of that change?

She was hungrier and feeding on younger and more vibrant prey was making her feel brighter and more alive. She had felt pangs of guilt and remorse as she realised that she had shifted from those with little to lose and not even considered the rights or wrongs of this switch, having formerly prayed on bad and evil people and therefore performing a sort of justice.

Now she wasn't just being indiscriminate in her kills, she was actively targeting people in their prime and robbing them of a large part of their lives. Even as she slipped into the van and smoothed her skirt prior to starting the van's engine, she felt a thrill of excitement at the prospect of the fun she was going to have this evening and that trumped any qualms she had about those she was now targeting.

She wasn't out of control, she knew that, she had had too much time and experience of control to relinquish that, but this, for her, was a massive step change. The changes in her added to her levels of excitement, but they scared her too. What if she kept going? Where did all of this lead?

Then she was backing the van out of the drive and found her mind wandering to the girl in the local shop and how exquisite it would be to pay her a visit and spend the night with her. She barely registered the hour long drive to the hotel as she visualised how that encounter would unfurl and she was excited as she found a quiet spot in the car park with a path that went along the side of the main building.

The hotel was an imposing building set in its own grounds, with it being mid-week, there was a mix of residents. As Isobel walked in through the main entrance, she noted the signs guiding business people to the three separate conferences that were taking place today. Isobel knew that even if all three were day conferences, there would be delegates staying overnight. They would cite the long drive back after a tiring day, and some of them may mean it. Others would welcome a night off from home, there was a bar they could relax at and if they were lucky

19

they might not spend the night alone.

With the course delegates, travelling business people and various other guests, Isobel was sure she could find a suitable candidate for herself and then another for her companion. She supressed a moan as she thought about the evening ahead of her. This response surprised her and she steered herself away from the bar and towards the ladies conveniences instead. She felt the need to take a moment and compose herself. She could sense likely candidates from the reception area. Although it was early evening, it was already dark and there were plenty of people in the bar, some having started early. She could hear the laughter and flirting as she went past the open bar area and towards the toilets, she also noticed a few couples.

As she opened the door to the ladies she was thinking about Charlotte and Nick. Mostly, she was thinking about Charlotte. She was already considering the merits of retiring to the ladies as she went in and made her way to the sinks. Already there, adjusting her make-up was a brunette, she was carefully applying fresh lipstick. There was something sensuous about the way she slowly applied the stick and examined herself in the mirror.

The woman spotted Isobel watching her in the reflection of the mirror.

"You OK?" she asked into the mirror.

Mirrors were another strange trope to the whole vampire mythology, but not so far off the mark when it came to the dynamic between a human and a vampire. When a human saw a vampire, they thought they saw another version of themselves, but they only saw what they wanted to see and that was fine by the vampire, more than fine as the vampire was aiding and abetting them in this. Behind that false image wasn't exactly nothing, but the nothingness was symbolic of the awaiting oblivion.

"Yes, sorry, I was just admiring that lipstick of yours. What shade is it?" Isobel smiled a winning smile and leaned in towards the mirror.

The woman turned towards her and offered the lipstick, "You can try it if you like?"

Isobel took the stick from her, looking into her eyes as she lifted it from the woman's fingers, allowing her fingers to linger for a moment as they touched, "thank you." She almost mouthed these words.

She turned on her heel and leant forward to apply the lipstick. She could feel the woman's eyes on her. Oh-oh, she thought to herself, that's bad, I might get the wrong idea. It was a little too late for that though and Isobel was getting carried away with her thoughts already. She finished applying the lipstick and then turned to hand the stick back.

She was about to make a resolution to be good and at least check the bar out when the woman took her a little by surprise. The woman was stepping back towards the cubicles and opening a door, her eyebrow raised by way of an unspoken

19

invitation.

Isobel couldn't help but step forward to close the distance between them, but as she did, the woman slipped into the cubicle, never taking her eyes from Isobel. As Isobel followed the woman into the cubicle and closed the door behind her, the woman closed the toilet seat behind her and sat down, pulling her skirt upwards as she did so.

Isobel stood there looking down at this woman. How had she taken charge of the situation? Isobel smiled wickedly, a smile that was intended for herself as much as anything else. This was not all the woman's doing, it was mostly Isobel's. Her excitement was contagious and the woman had been willing and impressionable. Isobel was manipulating her surroundings without even being aware of it. This was powerful stuff, she thought to herself. She took a deep breath and restored some calm, readying herself for her next move, but in that pause the woman took the lead, parted her legs and brought a hand down between her legs, pulling her skirt even higher and then slipping fingers downwards.

Resting her back against the cubicle door, Isobel watched as the woman pleasured herself. They kept eye contact as the woman stroked her fingers to and fro and now the woman's eyes were glazing over with lust. Just as it was about to get interesting, and vocal, someone walked into the ladies and broke the spell.

Isobel and the woman exchanged a smile and Isobel leant forward and kissed the woman, lips brushing against each other and a tongue gently probing. She broke away from the kiss and leant further forward so she was speaking in the woman's ear.

"Do you have a room here?" she asked.

"Yes, but…" she began.

"You're sharing it with your lover?" guessed Isobel.

"Yes."

"Is he in the bar right now?" asked Isobel.

She nodded, "we're both at the conference here."

"And you didn't take separate rooms?"

"He's the boss," said the woman.

Isobel shrugged, "well he's going to be busy for a while yet, isn't he?"

The woman shrugged, "I guess he is."

"So why don't we take this to your room?"

"What if he comes back?"

"Then I'm sure we can accommodate him, one way or another."

19

The woman smiled, "he'd think all his Christmases had come at once."

"I'm sure he would."

Isobel opened the cubicle door and they left before the occupant of the other cubicle saw them. The route to the woman's hotel room was quiet. Everyone was either in the bar, eating, or safely ensconced in their room. Isobel had ushered the woman in front of her and allowed her to lead the way. She watched her as she walked. The heels she was wearing accentuated her firm, shapely legs. Isobel enjoyed watching the movement of her buttocks as she walked down the corridor. It was all she could do to leave her alone as they had shared the lift up to the room, but she knew waiting until they hit the room was the right thing to do, especially as the woman had half expected her to make a move in the lift and it would have been so easy to do so. No, leaving her to stew was the best thing and Isobel could sense her anticipation. It excited her all the more.

Pulling the key card from her handbag, the woman swiped it through. She opened the room to the door and waved Isobel in. As soon as Isobel had stepped into the room, she turned and pulled the women inwards. The woman was already stepping forward, so her momentum carried her into the room and Isobel took her by the waist and turned her so those buttocks of hers were against the side table. Isobel stepped forward and found her lips, kissing her hard. Hands slipping along her back, eliciting moans that she felt more than heard as the woman responded to her kisses and kissed her back just as hard.

Isobel felt the woman's warmth and the beating of her heart provided a soundtrack to their protracted kissing. It would be a moments work to feed on her right here and now, but there was no need to rush. Despite that, she considered wasting little time in this room and finding a second, willing victim. She would that this were an idle fantasy flitting through her mind as her lust threatened to unhinge her, but she could feel the hunger and it was growing into something almost unstoppable. There was always a huge compulsion and it did not do to ignore the signs as the hunger began to make itself known, but the power of this was unprecedented.

As they kissed and the sensation of the woman's moans into Isobel's mouth inflamed her, she was almost taken by surprise when the woman slipped a hand between them and pushed a finger along the very edge of her panties. It was Isobel's turn to moan and she parted her legs further to encourage the woman. There was no need for a second invitation, the woman knew what she was doing and Isobel straightened so she had better access. They stopped kissing and a look was exchanged between them as Isobel stood before the woman allowing her to continue. She undid her shirt as the woman's fingers became more insistent. The shirt fell to the floor and the woman leant forward, pulling the straps of Isobel's bra down off her shoulders, her mouth exploring her breast hungrily. As her lips and tongue found the bud of her nipple, two fingers pushed inside her. The index finger of her other hand stroking expertly. Isobel's hand found the back of the woman's head and encouraged her to kiss and suck harder. As the woman's fingers probed and stroked, she gyrated in time with her ministrations and in no time at all she felt the

19

familiar build up. The pleasure swept over her and her legs trembled as she came. The speed and the power of her orgasm surprised her and as she came she pushed the woman harder against her almost suffocating her against her breast, feeling her teeth against her skin sent shocks of electricity through her and she growled deep in her throat as her legs continued to tremble violently.

Barely before the waves of pleasure subsided, she turned and span the woman onto the bed, the woman's legs pitching up as she landed on the mattress. Isobel deftly caught her by the ankles and held her legs there. Now it was her turn.

She brushed her lips and tongue against the woman's ankle and then she worked down the inside of her leg almost to her inner thigh, then she turned her head to consider the other leg. The woman groaned as Isobel returned to the neglected ankle and took her time, licking, kissing and nipping upwards along the stocking clad leg. She slipped her hands along those shapely legs as she kissed until she was tracing a line with her fingers, ever closer to her objective.

The woman sighed with pleasure, closing her eyes, throwing her head back and arching her back. Hands grabbing handfuls of the duvet as she anticipated Isobel's mouth on her. She could feel her breath on the thin material of her knickers and the shock of feeling that material slipped to one side made her gasp. She could almost feel Isobel's lips and tongue. Almost, but not quite. Then Isobel's tongue snaked out and the feeling was pure bliss. She almost growled with the pleasure of it.

Isobel lapped against the woman whilst probing with her fingers. Teasing and playing, but not quite penetrating. Not yet. Just as it was getting too much, her hands slipped under the woman's buttocks and squeezed and instead of fingers, it was Isobel's tongue that penetrated the woman.

She teased and played and kept the woman near to orgasm for an age until she could bare it no longer. When she was at that tipping point and her body was quivering with excitement, Isobel moved up the bed, stroking the woman's pubis gently, so very near her sex and so close to releasing her with all but a few strokes.

"Will you come for me?" she asked the woman.

"Yes!" she gasped, "please! Don't stop!"

"You're all mine," Isobel whispered, kissing the woman's neck gently.

"Yes! Just do it! I want it so much!" she groaned.

"You want me to?" Isobel punctuated each and every word with a deliberate kiss and nibble with her teeth.

"Please," keened the woman, drawing the word out as she quivered under Isobel.

Then she almost cried out, but the noise cracked, trapped in her throat as Isobel slipped her index finger down over the woman's sex and at the same time her teeth penetrated the woman's neck. The woman's eyes went wide and with her free arm, she pushed and pushed ineffectually against Isobel's shoulder. Her feet beat a tattoo on the mattress as a dual wave of panic and pleasure hit her and as the waves of orgasm swept over her, that initial pain was forgotten and all that was left was the pleasure and the insistent sucking and lapping at her neck.

Isobel slipped a finger inside the woman and gently moved it back and forth giving her a stream of constant pleasure. The woman sighed and began stroking Isobel even as she muttered into the room.

"Oh hell! What are you doing!? What is this? Oh shit, am I still coming? Did you bite me? You're... I think I'm... you're going to make me come again? Please... I... Oh!"

And she came again, a slow, gentle orgasm that held her for a long time and by the time she came out of it and her head cleared sufficiently she was too far gone to do anything other than to submit to Isobel.

* * *

"Honey! I'm home!"

Isobel had heard the hotel room door open, but she was not about to allow that to disturb her. She carried on feeding.

As it was, the man needed to empty his bladder of all the drink he had consumed and he went straight into the en suite without approaching or even looking towards the bedroom.

"Alan..." whispered the woman.

Alan's arrival seemed to break the spell for the woman and she gave forth with a flurry of movement. A crazy rally. Her arms and legs scrabbled about the bed, but she could not budge Isobel. Isobel was too strong. Unnaturally strong. Her eyes were wide again and filled with panic, her mouth opened ready to call a warning to Alan, but Isobel was too quick. She clamped a hand firmly against the woman's mouth and she sank her teeth deeper into her neck, sucking harder at her and feeling the woman's blood fill her mouth.

The woman's eyes swam and then rolled. Her cries stifled against Isobel's hand. Isobel sucked harder and more insistently and the woman's resistance ebbed away with each passing heartbeat. Isobel's stifled mewling and moaning drowned out the woman's sigh as Isobel released her mouth and focused on her feeding.

She whispered "Alan," once again, too weak to do anything else.

The woman moaned with something like disappointment when Isobel ceased feeding at her neck and rolled over so she could find her feet as the man stumbled out of the bathroom and towards the bed. He was intoxicated and had returned to the room with only one intention.

19

"Bloody hell!" he exclaimed as, in the dim light of the room, he saw not one, but two women on the bed, "you could have told me, Zoe!" His face, already flushed with drink, became even redder.

Isobel smiled wickedly, "I was just getting her warmed up. Now I think it's your turn!"

He stood transfixed, his mind struggling to catch up as Isobel went to her knees and unzipped him. He'd been drinking a lot. Almost too much, but Isobel worked him expertly with her mouth and was rewarded by his groans and the swift stiffening of his member.

Once he was ready, and that took precious little time at all, Isobel got to her feet and pressed herself against him, taking him in hand.

"Why's…" he drawled, "Is Zoe asleep?"

"She drank too much," said Isobel as she stroked him up and down, "then I wore her out, poor lamb."

Alan grunted, "shame."

He didn't sound too disappointed thought and he slipped a hand between Isobel's legs, fingers fumbling and clumsy, but he found her and pushed upwards.

"There's a good boy," said Isobel huskily, "shall we see who comes first? That would be a good game to play wouldn't it?"

Her words sent shivers through him and those shivers were amplified by what she was doing with her hand. She moved closer so she was rubbing him against her, and with her free hand, she cupped the back of his neck. She moaned against him and began panting. Responding to him and egging him on. Her murmurs and moans encouraged him and she could feel him twitching against her as he got more and more turned on.

She knew before he said anything, could feel that tell-tale trembling and quaking coming up through his legs and into his body.

"Oh wow!" he groaned.

"Oh dear, you're not going to lose are you?" she said sexily against him, "hold back. Don't come yet…"

"I…" he gasped, but she could feel him tensing his body and fighting it. Holding back as best he could. Wanting to do this for her and knowing it could only make it better for him.

It didn't help his cause that she was playing with him with her fingers and he could feel the heat of her as she ground against him. Her mouth insistent against his neck. Her body gyrating and moving against him. However hard he tried, he was going to come all too soon. She knew that because she was going to make him come. All she had to do was open her mouth wider and graze her sharp teeth against the skin of his neck and then…

19

She moved closer to him and angled herself so that he slipped easily inside of her and she took all of him in.

"What the…!" he started to protest as he felt those sharp teeth against his neck, but then she bit down further and his stiffened and panicking body couldn't hold her back and neither could it stop his own orgasm.

"No!" he gasped.

But as she sucked greedily at his neck she also ground against him to the same rhythm, enfolding him and milking him, drawing him into her. And then it was happening. She could feel him pulsing inside her and into her mouth at the same time, and at that moment her own pleasure erupted. She could feel herself tightening around his engorged cock and despite himself he carried on moving with her and heightening her pleasure. The pulses of his cock matched the pulses of his blood as he filled her.

She kept him inside her and moved slowly up and down as she fed. Sucking and moving in one fluid motion that sent waves of pleasure through them both. One thing she found curious was that the usual change in men after the act, the flaccid cock and the typical need to roll over and sleep, did not happen when she fed. The act was highly sexually charged and men always, always stayed hard. He felt good inside of her and his pleasure remained as she guided him down to the floor. His back sliding against the wall and her firmly pressed against him, she allowed him to sit on the floor and she crouched over him, her mouth never leaving his neck and her body never ceasing its now languid and unhurried up and down movements.

"Oh fuck…" he moaned as she rode him expertly, encasing him and closing in around him, milking him yet again, his pleasure building once again, "oh that's so good."

He was stroking her gently now. All of the clumsiness gone. Urging her on and talking softly. She could feel him reaching his second climax and she didn't want him to get there too quickly and not like this, not like they were.

She stopped feeding and slowed her movements, coming to a stop and holding him there.

"Don't stop!" he quietly begged, his eyes brimming with disappointment.

She smiled at him then looked down between them. He followed the line of her gaze.

"Oh," was all he said.

She slipped off of him and leant down and kissed and licked the shaft of his cock. It twitched and throbbed and she could tell how close he was, he wasn't going to last very long at all. She parted his legs and moved between them, lowering her head until she was kissing his inner thigh, she enclosed his cock with her fingers, moving them up and down the shaft lightly and slowly. This close to his sex organ, she could feel the heat of him and hear the pulse of his blood. She trembled

19

with anticipation and let out a long, low growl which exposed her teeth. His pulse was quickening and she knew he could hold back no longer.

Neither could she.

"What?" was all he said before she bit down for a second time.

All of him stiffened, he went rigid and he tried to push her off, his hands against her shoulders, bracing himself against the wall, but she had surprise as well as strength on her side. In any case his heart wasn't in it, her hand had tightened its grip and she was firmly milking him. He groaned and his back arched and he came hard as she fed from his thigh. As he came, she sucked hard and felt him bucking under her and the rest was a blur. Somehow those resisting hands slipped from her shoulders and reached for her. Pulling her closer and between his moans he was urging her on. Talking to her and asking her to suck harder and not to stop. Her hand never left his cock and although he didn't come for a third time, he was never far from the pleasure of another orgasm, his second barely subsiding as she moved against him and continued to give him pleasure as he gave her his life blood in return. She came to herself as they both subsided from the moment. Him stroking her back as she continued to feed. Her hand still encompassing his member which was gently throbbing and sending waves of pleasure through him until she was finished and he slipped away forever.

* * *

"What have you done?"

The voice was quiet and tremulous.

Zoe.

Isobel could have sworn that Zoe had slipped away when they had so rudely been interrupted by Alan's drunken entrance. No matter, she was not far from that gossamer veil even now. Isobel wiped her mouth whilst she had her back to Zoe and the bed and took a moment to compose herself before getting to her feet and turning towards the prone woman.

"You must have passed out. When we were…" Isobel smiled down at Zoe, her meaning was clear.

Zoe's hand went to her neck, but it was Alan she was looking at, "you… *bit* us!"

Isobel leaned down towards the woman, stroking a strand of hair from her face, "It's OK, Zoe. It's OK."

"No! I…"

But Isobel carried on repeating those words, *it's OK*, and there was a manner of spell in them as she drew closer and closer to Zoe's neck.

"Please, I…"

Zoe tried to get up from the bed, but Isobel was already leaning over her. A hand slipping along Zoe's arm and holding her wrist even as her lips brushed her neck sending a jolt of electricity through Zoe. Zoe knew what that touch meant and although she said nothing and did not let out a cry, she struggled with her free hand and her legs. Pushing up from the bed and only achieving one thing.

She presented her neck to Isobel and Isobel was not going to refuse this gift. Her teeth slipped into Zoe and the woman let out a long and low grown. Her legs kicked outwards several times and then the muscles in her thighs trembled as Isobel sucked down on her neck and fed. Zoe moaned rhythmically in time with her body moving up and down and in time with Isobel's sucking at her neck, each suck elicited a similar upwards movement from Isobel's body.

Soon enough, Zoe gasped a single, final word, "Fuck," as an inexplicable orgasm carried her away from consciousness. This time, Zoe would not wake up, but Isobel lay quietly against her, sucking gently until she was certain that would be the case.

20

It didn't take long for her to tidy up afterwards.

What took up a little more time was the moment she snatched before leaving the room. Something came over her and she couldn't help but take a seat on the armchair in the room, part her legs, close her eyes and relive what had just occurred in the room. As her fingers wandered, so did her mind and it went far beyond the confines of the hotel room.

She came hard and stifled her cries by biting her lip. As her head cleared, she sighed. She had yet to find takeaway for her companion. Alan was supposed to be the takeaway, but she'd been horny and then she'd been hungry. She found the two difficult to separate and she was already getting excited at the prospect of number three of the night even though she was not supposed to be feeding and had always been sated after one sitting, never mind two.

Isobel needed to move quickly, time was ticking and her companion would not be best pleased if she were to delay any further.

20

As she reached the ground floor of the hotel and walked across the reception area, she felt lightheaded and a dull pain swam just behind her eyes. Her peripheral vision faded and she had to slow her walk. When that didn't help, she stopped and leaned against the back of an empty chair, her left hand reaching for the seat back to help brace her and keep her from stumbling and maybe even falling.

Had she overdone it? Was this the come down from the euphoria she had so recently experienced. She didn't think so, but this almost debilitating feeling had come on so quickly and as though from nowhere.

"You should sit," it was a woman's voice. There was a strength there and the words were nigh on a command.

A hand took her own, right hand, and guided her around the seat she had been leaning on. Isobel almost meekly took the seat. She made a concerted effort to push the fog from her mind and it was a push. When she concentrated and imagined it as an object, she was able to bring some much needed clarity back to her mind.

"It still gets me like that when I'm not prepared and expecting it," said the woman.

Isobel, now she was back in possession of her faculties, looked at the woman for the first time. She stifled a gasp. She could have been looking in a mirror.

The woman looked at her curiously, "you've never met one of

your own kind before?"

Isobel shook her head dumbly, unable to muster the words as the shock revelation of her meeting hit her full on. No wonder she had felt disoriented! This woman was powerful, seemingly more powerful than her, and even with the effort she had made to clear her mind, she could feel her influence. She looked around her at the now changed world. As she returned her gaze to the woman, the woman smiled.

"They are easily led aren't they?"

Isobel nodded and smiled. She felt herself relaxing and that sent a shrill of panic through her, she redoubled her guard. This encounter was new territory and she had no idea what this vampire wanted and what she was capable of.

The vampire leant forward and offered her hand. Isobel eyed it warily.

"You do well to be cautious," the vampire said, leaving her hand exactly where it was, "but there are few of us around and it has been an age since I met another of my kind, so I'm only being friendly. But I would say that, wouldn't I?" and she winked, her eyes sparkling mischievously, "I'm Camilla."

Isobel took the hand, there was a power to that contact, the hand itself like warm marble, "I'm Isobel," she told the vampire, "you're older than me, aren't you?"

Camilla withdrew her hand and smiled wryly, "a lady never

divulges that information in polite society." Again that curious look. She shook her head, "you're mistaking age with power. For us, age is an irrelevance and it certainly has no bearing on power."

Isobel had a flash of something in her mind, "you're thinking that I'm more powerful than you are..." her brow creased, "...and dangerous. You fear me?"

Camilla looked shocked, but she banished that look swiftly. Cocking her head to one side, she eyed Isobel, "you are an enigma. Yes, I will be honest with you, I feel fear in your presence, but I doubt I am danger." She leant forward, "am I in danger Isobel?"

"No," stated Isobel in a heartbeat, "no you're not. But am I?"

Camilla chuckled a dry chuckle, "not from me you're not. The only danger you should fear is the danger you present to yourself."

This was a pointed comment and Isobel felt another surge of what she could only describe as *knowing,* "why do you think I don't know what I am, and why is that such a terrible thing."

Camilla looked aghast, "you're in my head?"

Isobel shook her head, "no, it's more that you're broadcasting to me."

"Doesn't that... cause you problems?" asked Camilla.

Isobel wondered for a moment what she could possibly mean, "oh!" she leant forward to whisper, "with the *natives?*"

Camilla nodded.

"It's not the same with them. I can read them, but I suppose it's more like an owner knows their pet. They are... predictable."

Camilla smiled, "more so when you are influencing them."

Isobel shrugged, "giving them what they want."

Camilla's eyes widened, "interesting."

"Is that not what you do?"

Camilla thought about this, "no, I give them what I want."

Isobel smiled, "but if you go with their flow and they get what they want then you get what you want, only it's so much... sweeter."

"It seems that I underestimated you. You are not as... *green* as you first seemed."

Isobel saw behind that word *green* and even without her newly discovered ability in this arena, she would understand that it was a word loaded with meaning. She chose not to vocalise Camilla's initial impression of Isobel, it was obvious that she had seen the way Isobel had been wrong-footed by her presence and this had led her to believe that Isobel was weak

20

and naïve, but once in her presence she had known there was more to Isobel and as she became aware of this her natural defences had come to the fore. Even so, Isobel could read her and even in the face of Camilla's undoubted power, Isobel knew she was the more powerful of the two. She was the older. And she was *different*.

Of course, Camilla could have mislead her on this, whether she did so via a conscious deception or thanks to an erroneous belief. The latter, seeing Isobel as tremendously powerful, would be the next best thing to Isobel actually being more powerful, but Isobel wasn't relying on Camilla alone to substantiate this fact, she could feel the power within her as she reacted to the other vampire's presence and as she attended to this she for the first time fully noticed her surroundings and what was happening around them.

Isobel turned her head and watched the reception desk. The woman at that desk was staring intently at her screen, barely moving. Totally engrossed in whatever it was she was looking at, Isobel wondered what it was that could be so interesting. She carried on watching and it was only when the woman attended to an itch on the tip of her nose that she had an inkling as to what was going on. The movements behind that desk were impossibly slow. She rose from her seat silently and walked over to the entrance to the bar.

Somehow, she had zoned out from all of her surroundings, but now that she attended to them, she could hear the macabre sounding music in the background as it was drawn out to such a low speed it sounded like the devil himself singing.

Similarly the background hubbub of the bar added an eerie layer of sound: hell's choir chanting along to their master's dirge.

Intrigued, she walked further into the bar, conscious that she had left Camilla seated in the reception area. At the bar, there was a man in a business suit, top button of his shirt undone and tie pulled down. In his hand was a tumbler of whisky and it was pressed to his lips. She gently removed it from his grasp and took a sip before placing the tumbler on the bar. It was a good single malt. The hotel had taste.

She smiled to herself as she casually walked away. One moment he'd been drinking from his glass, the next the glass was no longer in his hand and at his lips, it was on the bar. Isobel wondered whether he would finish the drink, preferring to go to his room and try to sleep off whatever had just happened.

Walking around the bar, she took her time, looking over the inept players in a bizarre game of musical statues. At a table, she exchanged everyone's drinks, amusing herself with some low level chicanery and doing it, only because she could. Pausing for a moment, she wondered whether there was anything else she should do while she had the opportunity, made up her mind and walked behind the bar.

The barman was in his twenties and obviously worked out, but she'd chosen him because he was stood up and easily accessible. She stepped right up to him, looked him in the eyes, then leant in for a slow, sensuous kiss. She stroked his crotch

20

for good effect and smiled through her kiss as she felt him ever so slowly respond. Reluctantly, she stopped and with that, left the bar, knowing that she had had an effect on several of the people in that room and wondering how they would square those inexplicable, fleeting, subliminal moments.

Camilla was still seated as Isobel returned, "weren't you tempted to come over to the bar?" she asked Camilla innocently.

Camilla replied wordlessly, with a strange expression on her face.

"What is it?" asked Isobel suddenly concerned, but she knew the answer even as she asked the question. Camilla couldn't leave her seat. She could converse and interact with Isobel in something like her real time, but that was the limit, "this is all me?"

Camilla nodded gravely, "and I think you should stop it now."

Isobel took a final look around, "let's leave here before I do though."

Camilla grimaced, not wanting to show weakness. This wasn't peculiar to Isobel, Camilla just wasn't in the habit of being weak, let alone having to admit it. Isobel reached out a hand and Camilla took it, immediately understanding what Isobel was offering. As soon as their hands joined, Isobel's spell was over for her. They left the hotel by the front door and walked out into the grounds, taking a path out around the side of the hotel.

"So what now?" Camilla asked.

Isobel stopped, barely aware that she still had hold of Camilla's hand, "I suppose we go our own ways."

"You're not..." began Camilla.

Isobel stopped and turned to Camilla, stroked strands of hair from her face, "why would I do that?"

Camilla was visibly relieved. The episode in the hotel, just as she had thought that she was in no danger from Isobel had shaken her. Isobel was very dangerous indeed and her influence on her reality and the way she had seen the world was so powerful that she had, for the first time in her existence understood what it would be like to be prey. She *was* prey. Isobel was on a whole other level from her.

This was her cue to take her leave and she was not going to hesitate to do so, she wanted to put as much distance between them as she could. Camilla had heard tales and hushed recounting of legends, but that was all they were, myths and legends. Tonight, she had learned that there was something else that walked the Earth other than vampires and it was stronger than them, and having crossed paths with it, she wanted out.

"I'd like to meet again," Isobel called after her.

20

Camilla did not turn in order to respond, "that would be… nice."

Camilla walked briskly and purposefully to her car. Each step away from Isobel was a relief. Nearing her car, she found the fob in her handbag and pressed it, the indicators on her Mercedes lighting up the night briefly. Lighting up the night and lighting up Isobel.

They stood across from each other. Camilla coming no nearer to the creature that was leaning against her Mercedes in a proprietorial manner. Something had changed and Camilla now knew she was in trouble.

"Change of plan," said Isobel airily, "the night is still young and we've only just met, so I think we should spend a little more time together."

"I'm… sorry… I can't, I need to get back," Camilla moved towards her car, hoping against hope that Isobel would leave it at that.

Isobel remained where she was, looking like she didn't have a care in the world, "back to what, Camilla? It's not like there's a baby sitter at home is there?"

Camilla slowed, shaking her head. No, there wasn't.

"You've no intention of going *back* anyway. Not when you have Quentin and Uma to go and see."

Camilla gasped and looked poised to make a run for it, but she never got the chance. Isobel appeared from nowhere and had her in an iron grip. Camilla may have been made from marble, but she was no match for Isobel's strength.

"Please," she sighed the word as Isobel pulled her tighter.

"Please?" Isobel sneered at her, "that's what *they* say. Have some dignity!"

"We don't have to do this, Isobel."

"You didn't have to try to kill me either…"

"That's…" stammered Camilla, "I didn't…"

"You don't have to explain, Camilla. I already know. You told me everything, and that includes where I can find Quentin and Uma."

With that, Isobel walked Camilla to the van. To a casual observer, if a casual observer could override the effect Isobel would have on anyone in the vicinity, they would see two women casually walking to a vehicle. That Camilla was taken unwillingly was not at all obvious. She resisted, but she may as well have tried to move an entire mountain with her bare hands.

Once inside the van, Camilla felt a weight upon her, as though the very air held her in place in the passenger seat. She knew this was a fight she couldn't begin to fight, let alone win.

20

"Where are you taking me?" asked Camilla as Isobel fired the van up and drove it from the hotel car park.

"To see a friend," was all Isobel said.

Nothing more was said as they drove to Brokmaster, but Isobel was busy gleaning all she could from Camilla's mind, whilst she still had a mind left to probe. If only she had known the questions to ask and where exactly to look...

21

Once back at the Big House, Isobel was in no rush to hand Camilla over to her companion, her thoughts on that transaction were mixed, she wasn't sure how wise it would be to give Camilla over.

In the kitchen she compelled Camilla to sit.

They remained in silence for what felt like an age to Camilla, eventually Isobel spoke, "you ruined my plans for the rest of the evening," she told the vampire, "I was about to help myself to a little take out, and then you came along out of the blue. A pleasant surprise, or so I thought. I'd avoided my own kind for such a long time that I can't even remember meeting another vampire."

"You're not a vampire," Camilla's voice was strained and full of emotion.

Isobel smiled awkwardly, "why would you say that?"

"Look at me!" Camilla cried, "I'm a vampire! You're a…"

21

She stopped and glared at Isobel.

"Go on, you may as well say it..." Isobel tutted at Camilla as though she were a naughty school child, not a powerful, centuries old vampire.

"N..." Camilla was shaking with the effort of defying Isobel.

Isobel grinned, she was literally squeezing the word out of Camilla.

"...monster!" she blurted the word out, then choked. Specks of blood coated her lower lip and chin.

"I'll show you I'm a vampire," Isobel whispered darkly.

With that, she grabbed Camilla's wrist and dragged her to the front room of the Big House.

As they went through the door into the front room, Isobel threw Camilla into the middle of the impossible dark. Camilla slid across the bare wooden floor and lay there, disoriented by the darkness that now surrounded her, disoriented by Isobel and by her own fear. She tried to adjust her sight in the darkness of the room, something that came naturally to her and required no conscious thought, but this time it would not happen, as though something inside her had broken, but she knew that this was not the case, the problem lay outside her. In this room. The darkness seeping through her eyes and into her mind.

"What have you done?" she cried into the darkness of the room.

There was the sound of Isobel's heels walking across the wooden floor, then she appeared out of the folds of darkness and crouched down in front of Camilla, "done?"

"This isn't right!" Camilla almost rallied in her indignation, "it's unnatural. An abomination..."

But Isobel wasn't listening. She should have listened, but a switch had flipped inside of her and after that there was only the hunger. She fell upon Camilla in a frenzy of tooth and claw, she went at her like a beast. Somewhere in the chaos she was aware that her companion had joined her. Her companion had of course been there with her from the outset.

Camilla did not stand a chance.

The vampire's terror and anguish was like nothing that Isobel had ever tasted, it filled her with an energy that was almost overwhelming. If she had been formidable at the hotel, she was now unstoppable, she laughed as she gorged herself on the vampire's blood and she did not stop until there was nothing left. Dizzied with the fizzing energy that now filled her, she rolled onto her back and stared up into the nothingness of the dark that shrouded the room.

She could hear her companion feeding, even after she had finished. There should not have been anything left to feed upon, but her companion seemed to feed on something in

21

addition to the blood of her prey. After a while, the sound of feeding subsided and the room fell into an ominous silence.

"You should not have done that," said her companion from the deepest corner of the room.

Isobel lay silently for a while. She had emptied herself of everything other than the energy coursing through her and she resented the intrusion.

"Why not?" her voice was monotone and mocking of the authority of her companion.

"It is not done," said the companion.

"What isn't?"

"Vampire should not feed on vampire."

"Who says so?"

"It is written, and it is a heresy to do so."

Isobel rolled onto her front, propping herself up on an elbow, chin resting on her cupped hand, "and yet you fed."

"That is different..." there was a sadness in those words. A deep sadness. Isobel felt them and they struck a chord. Some people talked about the shame they felt after sexual acts. The shame was prevalent and even those who said they did not suffer this shame felt it all the same. Sex and shame had come as a package ever since a serpent offered a woman the knowledge of self-awareness. That awareness had awoken and known the woman's nakedness and what that bare flesh could mean both for her and for others.

The flesh was weak and corrupt. The hunger that Isobel and her companion suffered was debilitating and it ruled them. They were not themselves and Isobel had been hostage to it for so long she no longer knew who she was.

Her thoughts turned to Camilla's two vampire friends, Uma and Quentin. They may have more answers for her. Already, she knew that her encounter with those two would likely not end well and it saddened her further that she had already reached a terminal conclusion, a conclusion that was foregone and precluded any alternative. She would wait until she needed to feed again and then she would find them, one after the other.

A spark of excitement arose in her at the prospect of meeting them both in the space of one night. The potential of that meeting and the feeling she would achieve having fed on two vampires would be beyond imagining.

"Careful, Angyal."

The companion's dry voice was softer somehow, and her calling her an angel told her all she needed to know.

"She would have killed me," said Isobel sadly, "as would her two friends. She *knew* that."

21

"Why do you think you avoided others of your kind for so long?" came the voice from the shadows.

"I thought it was what we did."

"No, it was what you had to do."

"But why?"

"It was better that way. Easier."

"I really am alone in the world aren't I?"

Her companion remained silent, did not feel the need to validate her existence.

"I'm going to bed," Isobel was already on her feet.

She was about to say she would deal with Camilla's remains in the morning. There was no rush, she was a vampire. Had been a vampire. But when she looked down to where the stricken vampire had lain, of Camilla there was no sign.

Isobel paused, her mind whirring. She was a bundle of contradictions and the world she saw seemed to be built in a similar, contradictory way. She took herself off to bed, thoughts bombarding her. She resolved to rest and then to go out into the world as her alter ego. To sample a simpler life at least for a while. Take advantage of the calm of the next few days and leave the pending storm of her approaching hunger to one side, it would present itself in due course, as it always did, as the dark cloak of the moon followed the sunshine.

"Be careful, Angyal," said her companion as she shut the door of the front room.

22

Another day had dawned and Isobel had taken the presence of sunlight in her bedroom as a cue to go downstairs. With no thoughts on what to do with her day, she opened her laptop and listlessly flicked from one website to another. The news bored her today, and she felt like it always did as she conveniently ignored other days when she had been full of an inexplicable joy, enjoying the news articles that provided her insight into these strange creatures she shared a world with.

Each new tab she opened was approached with some degree of interest, but in a matter of seconds that interest dissipated like so much steam from a kettle. Once or twice she looked at the kettle on the kitchen work surface and considered making a cup of tea just for something to do. It presented itself as an opportunity to take a break. The redundant mug of tea she would be left with would most likely upset her, and it was for that reason she did not get up from the laptop and the table for a full hour. Then, as she looked at the kettle once again, she remembered the whisky she had drunk and that it had not caused her any unpleasant side effects.

Instantly, her mood lifted at the prospect of having tea in her life. Not just the brew itself and discovering after all this time that she could drink it, but to have the ritual of tea making in her life and potentially being able to share that with someone.

Yes, that would do nicely, thank you.

She got up and felt a nervousness as she went through each step of tea making. She was momentarily bothered by the lack of milk in the fridge, but that passed and she resolved to buy milk, should this initial tea adventure go well. The brew made and mug in hand, she rested her bum against the kitchen unit and breathed in the aroma of the tea. This was good, she thought to herself. And it was. She should have indulged in the tea making ritual before now, even if the drinking of the tea was not to be. She knew she had avoided it because all of that effort had to end in her consuming the tea. Without the satisfactory ending, the rest of it was pointless and saddening. A small reminder of her existence.

She took her mug back to the table and placed it there, waiting for it to cool sufficiently that she could drink it. She leant back and took in the scene on the table now. Everything looked better for there being a mug next to the laptop. More complete. More real. Isobel looked upon it, savoured the scene and found it to be good.

Looking forward from this moment, she could see a day where there were two mugs of tea on this table. That might have been why, via a myriad of websites and click throughs she found herself on a dating site.

22

Barely paying attention to the online sites that she was visiting, she wasn't aware of how she had got to this site, but now she was focused and her interest was piqued.

Where to begin?

Thankfully, there was a section on this site welcoming newcomers and giving them some background, information on how things worked here and the dos and don'ts of the dating game.

Game, thought Isobel, and she supposed that it was. It was all a game and she was a game changer. The site and the very concept of online dating intrigued her. She clicked on a couple of articles and read them. True romance could be found online, it was all a case of approaching it in the right manner.

The slant of the articles seemed strange to Isobel, they depicted men as another species and she was in no doubt that if this was how it was from the female perspective then it would be the same on the other side of the fence, not to mention the various combinations of relationships that people could partake in. It really was all a game. A game with strange, almost nonsensical rules.

Isobel relished the thought of playing.

Her mug of tea cooled and remained untouched as she moved on to the profiles of the available men, or supposedly available men. Supposedly men, for that matter. She had been warned of catfish in the opening guidance.

Apparently, the trick was to see beyond the profile picture and the profile itself and envisage the real person. If you couldn't, then it didn't ring true and you should walk away. In no time at all, Isobel wondered whether there were any profiles that she wouldn't walk away from if she were one of the usual players of this game. She was glad that her angle was somewhat different and the game she was going to play so much more enjoyable.

Isobel marvelled at the profile photos. Some men felt the need to show off a car or a boat. There was a subset holding aloft large fish. Isobel wondered whether this was a sexual thing, and she supposed to one extent or another, it was all sexual. Apart maybe from the men who felt the need to throw a large obstacle in the way, like their dog, their friends or a hobby they were obsessed with. The gist of those profiles was that if you couldn't accept those things in this man's life and play second fiddle to them, then jog on buster.

Isobel absently sipped at her now stone cold tea as she swapped over on the site so she could review the profiles of some of the women. As research went, this was fascinating. Similar patterns emerged, if anything, those women who were pet obsessed were even more fierce in this assertion and it was clear that there was no actual room for a man, unless he was willing to sleep in the doghouse. Playing second fiddle to a dog probably wasn't most people's bag.

Every now and then, Isobel paused at a profile and took a little more time and little more interest. There were several strong candidates on this site and this would be a welcome variation to her usual practices. Isobel conveniently ignored the recent

22

changes she had been making, she was keen to do more and go further, so she saw the ground she had already covered as an irrelevance. She had further to go and that was all that counted right now.

Yes, this was an interesting tool, and it should help guarantee her a certain quality of meal. That was, as long as the dish of the day had not been too economical with the truth. If they had, then it would go badly for them, thought Isobel, smiling darkly to herself. She'd looked through enough profiles to see the patterns and get a feel for the sorts of people available on this platform. She found herself attracted to the arrogant chancers and grifters. The people who set themselves apart and used others. It was all so easy if you looked at it the right way, and as a menu, this really worked well for Isobel.

She took the plunge and registered using a borrowed identity, the photo she used was not a photo of Isobel, but she was doing the opposite of catfishing as well as presenting herself in a light that would work for her targets. They would see what they wanted to see, and Isobel was always going to be an improvement in the flesh. Then she looked at the enhanced detail that she had access to now that she was a member. All this did was confirm the categorisations she had already made. The next step was to contact some of her favourite options and await their response. She sent out ten short messages.

Her hand paused over the lid of the laptop. She found that she did not want to wait for a response. Now that she had embarked upon this exciting venture, she wanted instant gratification. Entering into the online dating world had created a hole all of its own and that hole was already filling with sadness and frustration.

Closing the laptop she wondered whether this was a new development. Was this hole an additional hole in her life, or was it only representative of the lack of something that had always been there and continued to be a part of her existence. She sat with her hand atop the laptop and wondered at this existence of hers. Lonely and set apart and yet here she was, in a house, in a village, living the dream that many people had. A move to the country and all that that entailed. She'd even been to the pub and enjoyed herself, and she may go again this very evening.

That she was living two lives should not have concerned her, she knew that. She saw enough of that duality around her. People compartmentalised their lives in order to function. They could be absolute bastards at work, pious when they attended their church at the weekend and a sweetheart at home. Reconciling these incarnations of what should essentially be the same person was a fool's errand, so if other people could do it, then why couldn't she?

The encounter with Camilla was unfortunate and it had shaken her at the time, but she had come into this day calmer and focused on the days ahead. Besides, she had plenty to look forward to and now she had a meal plan and this would be supplemented by her visits to both Quentin and Uma.

The detachment she felt did not concern her. At times it did, but not now. She felt a cold antagonism towards the vampires

22

she had yet to meet. As far as she was concerned, they were in the same mould as Camilla and now that Camilla was missing they were a threat that would have to be neutralised. The yearning she had to do this was the hunger. That was all there was to it, the ever present hunger was responsible for much and as it took up such a large part of her it devolved her from having to take responsibility herself.

With no one to effectively challenge her, Isobel would continue like this. Her companion tried and she thought that maybe once she had taken her companion more seriously, feared her even, but those days had passed. That they had only recently passed did not matter to her at all. Neither did her resolve to eliminate two creatures that were similar to herself. She had taken Camilla's words to heart and she was using them for her own means. If she was a monster, then it was a monster they would see.

That suited Isobel fine and she failed to understand that she was hurt and acting from that hurt place. That what she sought above all else, she herself was making impossible to find. Her reality right now was that the world was monstrous and that she had to be even more monstrous in order to fight it.

And yet, somehow she managed to walk out of that house later that day and spend a pleasant couple of hours in the pub, this time taking a seat near a table of farm workers celebrating a birthday. Their happiness and laughter was infectious and Isobel could not help but get carried away by it. Only she could help it and she did, for it was her influence that led to such a memorable night for all that attended the pub that night.

Again, she marvelled at a night where she had been in the company of beings she saw as something *other* and also as food. She marvelled at the way she had joined them in simple celebration and actually enjoyed herself. This was no longer unique because she had managed to do this one time before this and she dared hope that she could do it many times again.

As she walked home, a decided roll to her walk, having imbibed more than a few large whiskies, she chuckled merrily. She had enjoyed herself thoroughly and yet she hadn't killed anyone. If someone had told her even a few weeks prior to this night, that this was not only a possibility, but that she would be indulging in a spot of socialising and having the life of Riley? Well... she would have most likely killed them for their impertinence. She laughed at her own joke as she walked home, and this was a part of what she liked. Home. Not just the sanctuary of the Big House, but all of it. The village. The people. The setting. Her life.

Life was good.

It was a shame the hunger was already stirring and that she would have to take life soon enough...

23

The imposing Big House seemed to rear up above the rest of the village, and yet it was no taller than its neighbours. The house was dark and brooding and spoke of something fearful, and yet it was anonymous and more often than not, unnoticed and unremarked.

In more recent times, the Big House seemed to go through regular cycles. It were as though the structure was alive and prone to extremes of mood, sometimes grim and borderline dangerous, at other times bright and breezy and full of the vim and vigour of life.

These moods were Isobel's moods and they accorded with the state of her hunger. Always the hunger. Her hunger was her engine room and also her reason for being, however much she sought to forget or deny that, the hunger would rise forth and it would always have its way.

Today, Isobel had a spring in her step and bowled into the kitchen as though she were performing for a nineteen fifties washing powder ad. She launched into the tea making as though this were the most natural thing in the world and she smiled benevolently at the closed laptop, congratulating herself on leaving it be on her way through the house the night before. She had shown resolve and patience and in making the tea before opening the laptop, she was continuing to remain in control.

Control was what it was all about. She was the master of her destiny and she would choose the course of her life. This did not mean that she was not excited at the prospect of replies to the messages that she had sent and this showed as she opened the laptop and tapped away in a frenzy until she was on the site and into her messages.

She had replies!

Ignoring several random messages from people other than her intended targets, she opened the replies that had come in from her original messages. There were four of them. The first upset her and nearly crushed her upbeat mood, a mood that was already heading downwards at seeing that she'd had replies from less than half of the messages that she had sent out, and mostly it was the women who had come back to her. One of the two from the men read:

Sorry, you're not my type.

At least they apologised, she thought to herself, trying to find the positive. That didn't really work. Bastard! She fumed to herself. Of course I'm your type you complete moron! I'm everyone's type! They don't have a bloody choice when it

23

comes to me!

She hadn't banked on not getting her way and she couldn't understand it.

Drinking tea helped. It provided a natural pause and the opportunity to partially reset.

Of course, her influence did not extend across the internet and she reminded herself of another, very important thing.

This was a game.

She smiled and replied to the rejection.

Two things.
 I am your type, you just don't know it yet.
 And, I have some very special friends who are certain to be your type...
 ...only, you don't get to play with them without meeting me first.

Another smile as she pressed send. The guy in question was in the category of *player* and although he undoubtedly had his pick, meaning his game was a numbers game – take the least effort, go for the best low hanging fruit and move on – this would open him up to another dimension. Two or more for the price of one?

People were simple and if you knew the rules to their games you could play them. Isobel was also a player and she always played to win.

The remainder of the replies were positive, if a little cagey. People cautiously feeling their way, their initial response not giving too much away and inviting Isobel to give a little more and provide some substance to the engagement. She had no doubt that they would quickly get into their stride and soon enough she would have dates booked in her diary. The thought excited her, but there were other feelings bubbling away there.

Another message coming through distracted her. It was a follow up message from one of the randoms. Curious, she opened it and instantly regretted it.

Bitch!

Always a great way to open an exchange, thought Isobel.

You're all the same.

Oh really?

I write to you and you ignore me! Where is the respect? You think you're better than everyone else don't you? Such a lack of manners you pig-bitch!

Darling, I *am* better than everyone else.

She scanned down this trail of messages. His opener was abrupt and inept. Some would say rude. Commanding her to message him may have seemed like a good idea and was supposed to work if you read certain genres of erotica, but in practice, just like comedy, it was all in the delivery.

23

Isobel pressed reply and messaged the man back. Not to apologise or to engage him on his battleground, instead she suggested meeting up so she could make it up to him. The man was an idiot and a menace and she would be doing the dating scene a favour. She also found him curiously funny. Hilarious even.

Pressing send, she went on to the other two random messages. One was asking her if she had found god. She replied and said she hadn't, but did they have a contact number and address should she find him in her garden shed. She didn't expect a reply and it would be just as well for the bible basher if they left it at that or they would be meeting their god sooner than they had expected.

The third and final message was a single photo and three words:

Fancy a ride?

The photo was of a quite impressive dick standing to attention.

Isobel wondered whether the dick belonged to the sender of the photo, after all, she had doubted half of the boats and cars belonged to the sad wannabes who felt the need to photo themselves with those status symbols.

"Only one way to find out," Isobel muttered to herself.

Spread your treats, she reminded herself as she replied:

Does this gambit work often for you?

The guy was online and a reply pinged back less than a minute later.

It's never failed.

She smiled.

It's an impressive tool, do you know how to use it?

Another swift reply:

I've had no complaints.

She rolled her eyes:

Which is what happens when you have a one night stand and then block people...

The next reply took a little longer:

I don't do that. More often than not it's the other way around. What's a guy to do?

Isobel thought for a moment, mostly she was calculating a date to hook up that was soon enough to keep this guy hooked, but far enough off that she was not eating too soon:

OK, why don't you take me for a ride on that thing on Friday?

23

This reply was almost instantaneous:

Not sooner?

Isobel replied with one word, no.

Friday it is then.

Isobel smiled and felt a strange delight at the prospect of their meeting on Friday. It wasn't quite love's young dream, but it was affecting her that way all the same. She didn't question it and she enjoyed it for what it was. Although what it was was dangerous and the sort of thing that would more often than not lead to trouble…

24

Thursday came along relatively quickly. Time can do that sometimes.

Isobel visited the pub again and although this visit was nowhere near as raucous there was something relaxing and calming about her visit there, it was like a home away from home, although if truth be told her home was not all that homely. The Dragon was far better, it had a vital ingredient that was missing in the Big House. People.

There was also a visit to the local shop and this time, there was no drama. Isobel included milk in her purchases and found that the addition of milk to tea was a winner as far as she was concerned. She didn't want to try sugar though, she had seen what sugar did to people and she could do without that, she figured she got enough of a fix elsewhere and the addition of caffeine and alcohol to her diet was pushing things far enough as it was.

The time betwixt Thursday and Friday promised to drag. Isobel could not remember a period such as this before in her life. It made no sense to her. She was filled with an irritable sort of excitement and did not know what to do with herself.

She went online a number of times as though that would fix the problem, provide a distraction that would get time moving along properly again. The rude man had responded saying he would meet her. He made it sound like he was not only doing her a favour by granting her an audience, he was also doing it under sufferance.

"Oh, you will suffer!" Isobel said under her breath as she firmed up the arrangements.

For some reason, he wanted a lunch time meeting, not to meet in the evening. Of course, he knew a place. Isobel was sure that he did. She suspected that his need to meet at lunchtime was driven by the existence of a wife or girlfriend and most likely children. Leaving children without a parent would usually at least give Isobel pause for thought, but with a father like that, they would do better with a clean slate. Let them find their own way in life, it would be better than the example he would set them.

She settled on Friday lunchtime, for no better reason than it would break up the day and give her something to do.

The hunger was not making itself known, but this did not cause her concern, the fluttering excitement was distracting her and she would not be surprised if, when the time came to feed, she would be ravenous. She doubted she'd be unable to feed. That was such a remote possibility, it may as well have been an impossibility.

Spending more time on the dating app, she found more profiles and sent more messages. She found that replies from the women she messaged generally took longer to come through, but that they were more likely to respond. Her pet theory here was that over a longer period, the women would continue to reply consistently and win most of the marathons. The men were sprinters, putting in a lot of effort in those early yards, after that, all bets were off. Isobel smiled to herself. Few of her love interests would make it to a second date. On past performance, none of them would.

Having cultivated a month or more of meals, there was very little else for her to do. So, having taken the laptop upstairs with her, she closed the lid and stared at the ceiling and allowed her mind to wander. In her current state, the waters of her mind lay stagnant and all she had to entertain her were emotions, the predominant of which was frustration.

After a while, she went downstairs and into the front room. She stormed into the room and then stood there in the pulsating darkness, wondering why the hell she had come here.

"You're listless," her companion observed.

"Can't sleep," said Isobel.

She was rewarded with a dry chuckle, "you have never been able to sleep. Your kind do not sleep."

24

Stating this simple fact was not why Isobel had come here. She wasn't clear on why she was here, but it certainly wasn't so her companion could poke her with facts.

"You know what I mean," said Isobel tetchily.

There was a pause pregnant with affirmation. Of course her companion knew what she meant, but that did not mean she was going to provide any comfort or reassurance. Her companion didn't hold with that and had not spent any time or energy cultivating a bedside manner.

"There is no rest for the wicked," said her companion eventually.

"So they say," said Isobel, "although, whoever the *they* who say this are, I'm sure they have no clue."

"I wouldn't be so sure," said her companion.

Isobel considered this for a moment, "Hmmm, pious, religious types who nurture zealous beliefs and consider themselves to be a step up from everyone else? You think that type of wicked person doesn't sleep?"

Another dry chuckle, the rustling of ancient, desiccated leaves, "yes, they most likely sleep like the dead."

For that was what they were. There was a certain type of person who embraced religion in an outwardly devout manner, but something was corrupted within them. They treated their fellow human beings as though they were not saved. They constantly judged and didn't even realise that somewhere along the way, they had taken it upon themselves to do their god's work for her. This of course was the ultimate of blasphemies. Human's may have been cast in the image of their gods, but they were deeply flawed. One of the worst of their flaws was that they were blinded so easily and were not quick to understand this, let alone to do anything about it.

Isobel had been around humans long enough to see this type of person conduct their lives in an unsatisfactory, cruel, wicked and evil manner and yet lie to themselves every day of the week barring the day they attended their place of worship. They reserved this day to lie to their god, mistakenly believing that she would forgive them everything. Not that there was much to forgive as far as they were concerned.

If asked what was needed to render them perfect beings, not one of them would be able to answer this question adequately. They already believed, with every fibre of their being that they were saved, but also that they had already arrived. All that was left was the door to be opened and for them to be waved in.

Against all evidence and against her own experience and beliefs, she hoped that there was a heaven and a hell. The best seats in the house would be at the entrance to hell. The entertainment provided by the shocked and confused righteous as they were ushered in would be priceless. Not even purgatory for these people. They were too far gone. They had done the devil's work every day of their life.

24

Yes, those wicked people would sleep a full and satisfying eight hours every night.

If anyone wanted proof that life was not fair, there was proof.

"Why are you here Angyal?" asked her companion.

Isobel drew in a deep breath. Why was she here? She could think of only one thing she could say, but this was not the reason for her being here. It would have to do though.

"I'm... going out later," she said, "would you like me to bring anything back?"

There was another pause and Isobel dreaded the potential response from her companion. That it was too soon. How could she be hungry. What was happening with her? The changes were too much. So many potential recriminations and all of them merely the voicing of her own thoughts.

When the reply came, it was an anti-climax, "Nothing for me. I am not hungry, Angyal."

Isobel left the room awkwardly, not wanting to stay, but feeling like her business here was not finished. She often felt like this in this room.

As she closed the door to the front room she paused, leaning back against it. She found she was staring at the stairs, but not wanting to approach them. She remained listless and unsettled and going upstairs would only make it worse.

She nodded her head as she made up her mind, launching herself from the door she went through the kitchen, retrieving the keys to the van as she went. She would go for a drive. That was what some people did when they had this feeling and did not know what to do with themselves.

* * *

Driving through the quiet night was a kind of therapy. The headlights lit up a ribbon of the road and Isobel watched as it was swallowed up by the van. She was in control right now and she was enjoying herself, but there was something missing.

She frowned as she considered this and then her eyes fell upon the radio. Music. That was what was called for. She turned the volume dial and the radio came on. There was no need to change the radio station, fortune shone down upon Isobel via the pale full moon in the sky and the van's cabin was filled with music that made her smile and move in her seat with the beat.

She had no intended destination, she just wanted to drive and to spend her time doing something engaging and enjoyable and that was what she did. She would never quite know how she arrived at the bridge as the woman walked onto it. It were as though they had both been drawn to this spot at this precise time and their meeting was predestined.

Isobel passed the woman, singing her heart out to a tune she

24

hadn't realised she knew the words to. She nearly missed her, but movement caught her eye and she wondered why someone would be out walking at such a late hour, let alone here, along this road where she had not encountered a single vehicle.

How had the woman arrived here? Now Isobel was attending to it, the woman was not dressed in clothes at all suitable for a stroll. She guessed that somewhere nearby there was a parked car, the engine ticking as it cooled in the night air. That just left the reason for the woman to be here and Isobel suddenly knew. This was no sightseer and the bridge was a means to an end.

She was out of the van before she had even realised she'd parked it off on the side of the verge beyond the bridge. This woman was not going to jump. Not yet, anyway. Suddenly, the prospect of a free meal was far too tempting for Isobel.

"It's late," Isobel said from just behind the woman.

The figure in front of Isobel had been slowing her pace and now she stopped entirely. The surprise of Isobel's presence should have made her body tense and perhaps caused an involuntary cry, or at the very least a loud exhalation, but the woman was so intent on her course of action that these things failed to happen. This woman, Isobel now knew, had already left the world and her intended jump was a mere formality, a dotting of an i and a crossing of a t.

The woman said nothing, just stood there with her shoulders slumped. Her body telegraphed despondency and bleakness.

There was the smell of tragic loss about her. For a fleeting moment, Isobel had this inexplicable desire to help her. Even in the face of absolute defeat, hope flared up. Surely she could make a difference in this woman's life, her of all people?

As quickly as it had arisen, she quelled it. That was not her. Even if it was within her power, she could not change the outcome for this woman. She felt a wave of sadness as she realised that she also would not lift a finger to help her, and she went on regardless. This was her nature and she could not go against her nature.

"Come with me," said Isobel.

"Why?" the woman said this, but it was obvious she was not interested in any answer.

"I'm hungry," there was something in that word. *Hungry.*

"You're...?"

The woman turned towards Isobel. She was dressed for work, an office job. The jacket of her skirt suit was undone and as she turned, Isobel spotted a small damp patch on her blouse. If Isobel had not already known, she would as she saw how the woman's breasts were leaking.

"I need you to feed me," Isobel allowed her hunger to come through those words. The hunger and the wanting and the need.

24

The woman responded by raising both her arms, welcoming Isobel. Instead of stepping into the embrace, Isobel first guided her back along the bridge and into the privacy of the van. Ushering her into the back of the van, the woman meekly stepped in and immediately sat on the bare metal floor behind the passenger seat. Again she raised her arms and this time, after closing the van door behind her, Isobel moved towards the woman and that embrace. She dropped to her knees beside the woman and waited for a moment as the woman undid her blouse and unhooked her bra and then she carefully and gently lay across her lap, facing her.

The woman gazed lovingly down at Isobel as Isobel brought her mouth to her breast and began to lap and suck gently at first and then with more hunger. The woman stroked the back of Isobel's head softly, encouraging her as she fed.

Suddenly, she cried out and gasped as Isobel bit down.

"No!" she cried, "Too hard! You're hurting me!"

But Isobel did not stop and her teeth went deep into the woman's breast and she was rewarded with the pulsing of hot blood into her mouth. She sucked upon it, drawing it into her mouth as the woman tensed and bucked under her and after a moment or too more the woman settled and the initial pain was gone. Isobel lay there moaning softly at the woman's breast and the woman silently watched her for a long while.

Towards the end, something changed and the gentle pleasure the woman was feeling began to build into something more insistent. At this change, Isobel's feeding became more urgent her mouth working against the woman's breast.

"Please, no more! I can't!" the woman groaned, her legs were scrabbling up and down on the floor of the van, a heel squealing against the metal. Her movements only serving to push Isobel against her breast more firmly as she sucked down harder.

Now the woman was pushing against her, trying to push her away, but Isobel slipped her arms around the woman and held her.

"No!" she gasped, and then her body began to tremble and Isobel moaned against her, feeling an exquisite pleasure as she took the woman, for her, this was the best bit and even though the woman had accepted death less than an hour ago, she now fought it and it was that fight that gave Isobel so much more.

The woman now bucked violently, her body convulsing, muscles tensing and releasing, tensing and releasing and then she was moaning too, an orgasm taking her by surprise and taking her beyond the point of no return.

It wasn't over yet, but now, in the aftermath of that orgasm, the woman slumped and accepted Isobel, echoes of her orgasm jolting her body every time Isobel sucked down.

25

Friday came along, despite Time's best efforts to keep it at bay. Isobel hadn't quite resorted to counting the remaining seconds to make them real, but she had been close. She was thankful that the lack of rest had few consequences for her, if any. The fallout from it was a kind of psychosomatic symptom and perhaps by virtue of the world of people and her diet on them. She was keyed up, frustrated and edgy.

She began her day with the ritual of tea. This brought with it a modicum of calm, but nowhere near enough to make a significant difference to her mood. So, she went back upstairs and changed. She had only dressed, fifteen minutes ago, but in the mood she was in, this change of clothes was much needed.

She rushed her clothing change, almost fighting to get re-clothed in the new outfit of choice. All of these garments were new and had a certain smell to them, especially the training shoes. She bounded down the stairs carrying the now empty shoe box and packaging from the clothes, dumping the rubbish in the two wheelie bins at the side of the house as she passed them. She broke into a run as the bin lids slapped back down into place. No need for her to stretch or warm up, these activities were superfluous and anyone who encountered as she left the driveway would assume she had done with that business indoors, or around the back of the house.

Neither was she running in order to keep fit. She didn't work like that and she really didn't need to. She was a simple creature, whose existence was all about the building hunger and sating it. The bit in between was hers to do with as she pleased.

The reason for her run was to get out and see a bit of the world around her and what better way to do it than to run? Running could be a solitary pursuit and she would make darn sure that it was as far as she was concerned, and not only because being in close proximity to a hot and sweaty human was not the best of ideas for her. She didn't want to lose control and then have to deal with an incident so close to home.

She set a leisurely pace through the village, quickly crossing it's breadth and reaching a kissing gate that she slowed to slalom through. Now she was on a foot path that rose upwards and out of the village. She increased her pace as she established that there was no one around to see her. Some of the paths around Brokmaster were not clearly marked as they were not used all that often thanks to them not being public rights of way and not appearing on any map. With her enhanced senses though, she knew exactly where the paths were and easily found the styles at the far ends of the next three fields. She was heading for the woods, there was something appealing about the soft ground there and the dappled light, the cover of branches and leaves would afford.

As she reached the boundary of the woods she slowed and then turned, looking back down at the village and taking the view in. It was a beautiful part of the world and so few people knew of its existence. Brokmaster was one of the most secluded postcodes in the United Kingdom and Isobel liked it that way. She was glad to be alone and enjoying this view, no need to fake being out of breath. She hadn't broken into a sweat and neither would she. Her body did not need to regulate its temperature in that manner and if it did, her perspiration would have stained her clothes red. As it was, tears were a problem, albeit a rare one, as she seldom cried.

Turning to run the path into the woods, her thoughts turned to her tears. Since she had moved to this small village to live a new life, her emotions had surprised her. She had been on such an even keel prior to this. Nothing had phased her and she felt very little. No wonder, she thought to herself, she had slipped into such a drab existence, there were no variations to it whatsoever. She had come as close to being dead as she could be without actually going through the process of dying. She'd been going through the motions and was gradually drowning in a sea of grey.

No wonder this new life of hers was evoking emotional responses. She had been so long in the semi-darkness that this gentle existence of her was over stimulating her. She hadn't gone crazy and she was taking her time and spreading her treats, but it was still a wonder that she had not been overwhelmed by the vibrancy and light of this world of hers.

Then she was distracted by a flash of white. The tail end of a solitary deer spooked by her appearance. She felt elation at the movement and what it promised. She picked up her step, but kept to the path. Turning her head this way and that, sniffing the air around her and listening intently as she sprinted in a parallel direction to the deer. Faster and faster she ran, closing the distance between them.

Once she was flanking the deer, she could see its eyes wide with fear. The deer could see her for what she was and it knew it was running for its very life. Isobel was the apex predator on this patch and it was entirely her decision as to whether this buck lived or died. The thrill of the chase. There was nothing like it. She felt her power in this moment and there was a beauty here. Hunter and prey moving in unison, performing a dance that could end at any moment.

Or not.

She slowed her pace, dropping down one cog and allowing the buck half a yard. She watched as the body of the deer changed subtly, it's speed increasing and a message of hope thrumming in every muscle and fibre of the animal. It was getting away. It would live another day.

Isobel's mood lifted even further and the level of her excitement surged forth. She bared her teeth in something like a triumphant grin and in that moment, it looked like it was all over. She had spared the deer and the dance had ended for her.

25

And then she leapt…

* * *

"Are you alright dear?" asked an elderly lady as they approached each other on the pavement.

Isobel raised a quizzical eyebrow, wondering for a moment what the old woman meant, "oh! Yes! I fell in the woods when I was running."

"Are you hurt?"

"No, only my pride! I'm muddy though!" superfluously, she waved her hand along her muddy clothes.

The old lady smiled as they passed each other, "straight in the washing machine with that little lot!"

Isobel gave forth a brief laugh by way of answer. She would be putting all of this outfit in the wash and she was going to have a soak in the bath. There was something calming about water and a bath would take her right up to the allotted hour of her first date. It would also cleanse her of the mud she was caked in and the blood that the mud had been used to conceal.

Friday was now going along at a pleasant and enjoyable rate and the best was yet to come.

26

It was no surprise at all to Isobel that the rude man who she had arranged to meet at lunch time was no better in person than he had been behind a keyboard. The years since his profile photo had been taken had not been kind to him. He had ripened and then gone to seed. He was obviously attempting to hang on to those marginally better days, refusing to accept that he needed a larger size shirt, the buttons of which were threatening to part company with the burgeoning material and shoot across the room. He had carefully placed long strands of hair across his bald pate. He had yet to accept his baldness, and this was something he could do little about, but still he tried, making him look ridiculous but somehow staying true to his form.

The venue for their rendezvous was a cheap hotel bar. The intent of this odious man was obvious and that he was on the clock added a further awful dimension. He even resented buying her a drink at the bar and his impatience meant that their small talk was stilted and awkward. He threw his rum and coke down his throat and didn't bother looking at Isobel's glass, which was still very much full.

26

"Shall we?"

Isobel feigned innocence as he looked up at the ceiling as though the room he had booked was directly over the bar, "shall we, what?"

"Go somewhere more comfortable," he stated, his use of the word comfortable was a very obvious misnomer.

"What's more comfortable than this?" she had to supress a smile as she observed his ire. She was going to make him work for this and his reaction when he eventually understood what it was he had invested in, would be priceless.

"I've booked us somewhere more private," he told her.

Isobel looked around the room. Other than the two of them and the middle aged bar man at the far end of the counter, there was no one else here.

"I..." she began.

His face faltered and then flared, then he grabbed the hand that didn't have her drink in it, "I want to talk..." he said with meaning.

Bearing in mind his talk thus far had been cursory at best, he was on a sticky wicket, but Isobel decided to go along with his charade and see how he wanted things to pan out. She suspected that she already knew exactly what he had planned, not that things were going to go according to his plan this time.

"Oh, OK," she said meekly and she slipped from her bar stool and allowed herself to be walked to the room the rude man had booked.

When he got to the bedroom, he retrieved the key from his well-worn black suit jacket, a jacket that did not match the off-black trousers he was wearing. The key was on a large, plastic maroon fob with the number of the room cut into it. He fumbled with the key, trying to get it into the lock, too eager to get in through the door. He did not see the smirk on Isobel's face as she watched him. Neither did he see the hungry expression that she quickly masked as he turned to her, having succeeded in opening the door.

Once in the room. A room that was even more cheap, tired and worn than the rude man's suit, he pushed the door firmly shut and turned to her.

"I don't even know your..." she began, not getting to finish her sentence, enquiring as to what his name was before they got to any business. For this was strictly business for him, even if it wasn't for the other participant.

He had pressed himself against her and was mashing his lips against hers. She looked down at the diminutive man in an attempt to discern what exactly he was up to. For her, there was nothing enjoyable about what was happening and it certainly wasn't sexual, let alone sexy. He seemed to be enjoying himself though, which was, as far as he was

26

concerned, the point.

After a full minute of squashing himself against her and getting worked up, he stepped away, grabbed her and attempted to fling her onto the bed. A bed that had probably had fresh laundry placed upon it, but still managed to look both grubby and mangey anyway.

His first attempt at launching Isobel did not amount to much. He looked at her expectantly as he went for a second go. She telegraphed her comprehension at what he was trying to do and went along with it a second time, landing on the bed in a tangled heap which was helped by the soft, broken springed mattress that partially consumed her as she hit it.

She had to struggle in a very unladylike manner to free herself from the clutches of the mattress and even then she was not completely free of it. She could however see the rude man again and was treated to the sight of him unbuckling his trousers and dropping them around his ankles. The underpants that encased his now hard member had been white once, a long time ago. The colour they now were spoke of bad hygiene and a sad life.

"Get your knickers off," he growled.

She supposed that that was a sexy growl in his book, and that this was his attempt at the second half of his foreplay, following that one sided kiss of his. He stared at her aggressively, and while he waited for her to comply, he rooted around in his pants. It became clear what the rooting was for as his member emerged from the Y of his pants. This man was not only rude and selfish, he was all class.

"Off! Now!" he barked.

Isobel held herself in check and surprised herself as she bit her lower lip sexily and pulled her skirt upwards and said in a husky voiced whisper, "I'm not wearing any."

He growled and stepped to the edge of the bed, intending to climb onboard and work his own particular brand of magic. Isobel knew it would be a unique experience and that its uniqueness was the only good thing that could be said of it.

Quickly sitting up, she placed a hand on his chest. Noticing that his shirt looked off-white thanks to the mass of thick hair that she was now pressing her palm against.

"Wait," she said, staring meaningfully into his eyes.

She quickly snaked her free hand down between his legs, cupping his balls. This elicited a grunt of appreciation and allowed her the time and room to find her feet whilst keeping him firmly in hand.

"Did you book this room for the hour?" she asked, squeezing him playfully.

He nodded, "yes."

There was no sign of shame or notion that what he was doing

was wrong at all.

"Because you need to get back to work or your family?"

His thick brow knotted in response.

"Both!" she chuckled, "it's a family business, isn't it!? How delightful!"

"I..." he began.

She brought the hand she'd had on his chest up and placed a finger on his lips.

"Shhh! Don't ruin the moment!" she cautioned, "I bet you treat your wife badly too. Women aren't people to you are they?"

His eyes widened as she punctuated that last sentence by applying further pressure to his balls. Now he was uncomfortable and any game they might have been playing wasn't fun anymore. He pushed her, but this didn't have the desired effect, instead of her going backwards and sprawling again on the bed, on her back, where she belonged, with him in a position of dominance over her, instead of that outcome, he felt himself propelled backwards.

Isobel followed his movement and was right there in front of him as he partially sprawled against the dresser. That the dresser stood up to this sudden impact from the weight of the rude man was nothing short of a miracle.

The rude man's eyes widened with incomprehension, the catalyst for which was the further pressure that Isobel was applying to his balls. There was real pain there now and he was having none of it. She felt him tense and grit his teeth.

"Let go of me, you bitch!" he growled at her.

"So soon with the name calling?" she feigned a hurt expression.

"Screw you, you evil bitch!"

She applied yet more pressure, then eased off as he howled in pain.

Isobel gave the rude man a reproachful look, "there was no need for that, was there?"

"Fuck you," he scowled at her and in that look she saw the small boy he had been and still was.

"You just can't help yourself can you?"

She tugged downwards and he howled yet again.

"I suppose old habits are hard to break and your own mother taught you to be this way, didn't she?"

"Don't you speak of my mother you fucking whore!" he spat the words and she felt the flecks of his saliva on her face. There was something deeply unpleasant about having even such a small part of him on her. He really was a deeply unpleasant man.

"There you go, there are your true colours. You emotionally stunted rapist." She shook her head in disappointment and drew closer to him, whispering in his ear, "we're all whores aren't we? Except for your dear, sainted mother. She's the only woman you ever loved, in your twisted and broken way."

"Get off me!" he growled.

Isobel chuckled, "that's the closest you'll get to begging for your life. I suppose I should admire your stubborn determination. Or something like that…"

She drew her head back so they were facing each other, then she smiled a wicked and predatory smile which exposed her teeth and gave the rude man the first indication of what he was dealing with.

"What the fuck are you?" he said under his breath.

"The best woman, you never had, darling."

And now she laughed. She laughed as she took a step back and threw him around in an arc so that it was he who was laying sprawled on his back on that mattress. By rights, he should have screamed, but the shock of the sudden movement and the impossibility of it was almost debilitating, and then there was the pain. The excruciating pain. As he lay there he realised that something had torn and his hands had automatically gone to his crotch.

Isobel stood over him as he lay there broken, hurt and unable to understand what was happening to him. She stood over him, impossibly large and confident, smiling down at him with that predator's smile. He lifted one of his hands from his ruined crotch and instead of looking at the blood on his palm, he was showing it to her. In that action was a meekness she doubted he had ever experienced before.

She stared wantonly at the blood dripping from his palm and running down his wrist. Saw the pulse of his lifeblood on his wrist as it was cloaked in the plentiful blood.

"Now you know what it is like to lay powerless and at the mercy of a stronger being. Today, you get to play the part of the victim and I play the victor, and to the victor goes all the spoils. You just took what you wanted and you never showed any compassion did you?"

"No… please… I can change!" his chin was wobbling and tears streamed down his cheeks.

"Oh! You will change! There is no doubt of that!"

"What do you mean?" he said in a querulous voice.

"You really are an ignorant specimen aren't you?"

"Fuck you!" he moaned the words and there was a distinct lack of gusto to his protestations.

26

"Can't you feel it? There's no coming back from an injury like that. But still, you lived by the sword, so…"

"Oh no! No! No!"

Isobel's expression softened, "here, let Mummy kiss it better for you…"

And with that she climbed onto the bed and over him. The last thing the rude man saw was Isobel smiling up at him with those teeth bared and then the lowering of her head to his ruined and bleeding crotch.

She fed and this time the feeding was violent and painful. The rude man lingered for a long while in a well of terrible, pulsing pain. She figured he deserved that much.

27

After her fun and entertaining afternoon, putting the world to rights in her own way, Isobel freshened up and went for a walk. Finding a coffee shop with outdoor seating, she ordered a double espresso and savoured its aroma as she watched the world go by. From her bag, she retrieved a paperback and ensuring she held it the correct way up, she observed the passers-by and the other patrons of the small shop.

The vast majority of the interactions she observed were with screens. At the table but one to hers, there was a young woman staring intently at the screen of her laptop, tapping away at the keyboard in furious bouts of activity. Most of the rest of the people she observed were on their phones. She noticed the jealous looks and accompanying negative body language of the occasional person in tow, their place in the relationship relegated to a rung below the beloved electronic device and a selfish world beyond the glowing screen.

This was a pandemic, or perhaps a variation on a drug epidemic. That it had lasted for such a protracted time and looked

27

set to persist, fascinated Isobel. Very few people seemed all that bothered by it, yes they may moan and voice their concerns about how screens, social media and apps were affecting society, but it was always the consideration of *other*, it affected other people, not them. Humans were very bad at taking responsibility for themselves and their actions, let alone seeing beyond themselves and their selfishness to own the consequences of their actions.

Isobel did not fail to note the irony of what she saw and how that compared to what she was. She was a killer. Just like a tiger. And the inexorable march of the human population left little room for animals like her. If she was spotted and seen for what she was, they would either kill her or cage her.

Isobel smiled as she related her take on the passing traffic of humanity to the fun that she had had this afternoon. That had been a pleasant diversion and there was something deeply satisfying and empowering in doling out a small measure of justice and making the world a better place. The problem was that the nature of the world was so contrary. If that was the extent of the consequences of her targeting a bad person then it was obvious that she should select her meals with respect to their lack of goodness and the remote possibility of them redeeming themselves. She thought she remembered a time, long ago, when she had once roamed the night, taking her fill of cut throats and thieves, but this had come at a price.

There was always a price.

The downside of feeding on the evil and the damned was the

old adage of *you are what you eat,* and Isobel's weakness was the way that the living affected her. To feast on evil was to be drawn down into the very depths of evil itself. Maybe Isobel was deluded in thinking she was better than that, but it didn't change the fact that she did not want to be in that bad place by choice. Besides, it made her all the more dangerous and that led to recklessness and undue risk.

The other consideration here, and it was only a minor consideration, was that Isobel didn't always get it right. Not when the hunger took over. Her usually enhanced and incredible judgement, her ability to read a situation and in particular the people in it, was clouded so entirely that she had at times been blinded. That was when she took innocent lives and that had made her feel bad...

And yet, here she now was, skirting close to that eventuality because although she felt a pain at the moral wrongness of taking young, vibrant and at least partialy innocent lives, they filled her with a vitality and energy that nothing else could, and it hadn't escaped her that the better the quality of the kill, the sooner the hunger came around again. She almost urged it on in her eagerness to achieve yet another hit. She sighed as she considered this and that she was currently embarking on another double kill. She barely registered the coffee cup as she lifted it to her lips, but she did attend to it as the taste of the double espresso exploded in her mouth. That was good. Very good. Almost as good as... no, there was nothing that compared to the taste of a life being taken.

27

* * *

Another bar.

It amused Isobel that people took an age to get ready for a night out, preening and polishing until they looked nothing like their usual selves, then they congregated in dimly lit places and dimmed their senses with alcohol.

She had been watching Mr Dick Pic for a full ten minutes now. He was sitting at a table in the corner all by himself. He stuck out like a sore thumb and yet everyone ignored him. Occasionally, he would take out his phone and she watched as the blue light bathed his features. He wasn't bad looking and she spied strands of a tattoo coming from out of the sleeve of his shirt which added to her interest in him.

Isobel had expected a cocky man, and she had smiled at her unintended pun. Surely someone who had adopted a route one approach to the dating game had the confidence and the game play to back up that opening gambit? This guy though, he seemed nervous and didn't fit the profile she had conjured up in her mind.

Tattoos though. With a large tattoo poking out from his shirt, a conspicuous tattoo, this man was no shrinking violet. She guessed there would be more tattoos and the prospect of discovering them excited her. In her minds eye her finger was tracing their outline and her mouth following that path soon after. Her thoughts wandered to the time when those tattoos had been painted on his skin, the needle piercing his flesh again and again. Tiny beads of blood being drawn to the surface. Isobel didn't salivate, but this was enough for her to do so right now.

The last ten minutes had been well spent and she was enjoying the picture show in her mind so much she could well have doubled the time she spent observing him, but now he looked restless and already he had glanced at the door several times, not in anticipation of her arrival, but in consideration of his departure. He was becoming awkward and uncomfortable and second thoughts were beginning to make themselves known to him.

"Savannah?" he said her name gently and hopefully.

Savannah was the name she had chosen for herself online, but it almost wrongfooted her to hear it spoken for the very first time. Of course the rude man had not spoken her name, that would have been too intimate and he had intended to dehumanise her so he could fuck her and then move on, Mr Dick Pic was a world apart from the rude man, they could have been a different species entirely.

Isobel nodded, "hello Andy, I've only just spotted you. I was over there. It seems we were both sitting waiting like complete lemons and wondering whether maybe we'd been stood up!" She followed this up with a winning smile which he responded to immediately, returning the smile and standing.

"Please," he said, "take a pew. I'll get you a drink. What would

27

you like?"

He'd not only stood up, he'd moved around the table, pulled a chair out for her and helped her with it as she sat. Here was a man who had been brought up the right way by his mother, if you ignored his sending Isobel a photo of his cock that was.

"A whisky, please. Straight. No ice."

"Righto," Andy smiled again and nodded, "coming right up."

He dipped his body as he said this, then slunk over to the bar. The way he walked and conducted himself was... pleasant. He was polite and already Isobel thought he was kind. Nothing like the kind of guy who sent porn to women in the hope they could get straight down to creating some porn of their own.

When he returned from the bar with their drinks, Isobel was giving him a very obvious appraising look. She waited for him to settle in his seat, behind his drink of choice, which was a gin and tonic, not the lager or cider she had expected him to return with. She made sure he was aware that she was continuing to appraise him.

He smiled awkwardly, struggling to maintain eye contact, "what is it?" he asked, almost squirming in his seat as he did so.

"You're not in the habit of sending dick pics are you?" she asked. She already knew the answer, but was intrigued as to how he would field her question.

Even in the dim light of the bar, she saw him blush, "sorry, it was a bad idea…"

"I'm guessing it wasn't even your idea?" she smiled warmly.

Andy raised his drink, "too many of these… and…" his focus shifted to a middle distance as he went back to the fateful moment he had done the deed and sent the photo.

"And?" asked Isobel, bringing him back into the room.

He sighed, "It's not even my dick!"

"Who's is it then?"

"My friend's. We were drunk and although it didn't even seem like a good idea at the time between him and the drink I ended up thinking I'd got nothing to lose. I'd tried everything else and as my friend said, 'no one likes a nice guy', or something like that anyway."

"Nice guys always come second," suggested Isobel.

"Yeah, I think that might have been what he said," shrugged Andy.

Isobel leant forward and made meaningful eye contact with Andy, "you know that's a good thing, right?"

Andy blushed again.

27

Good boy, thought Isobel, he's not slow to pick up on the innuendo, nor the intent behind it. She smiled, she was genuinely enjoying herself and finding that she was in no hurry, her hunger sated earlier that day, it was good to be out and Andy had the potential to be good company.

"So, I take it you haven't been all that successful on the online dating front?" asked Isobel, taking a sip from her whisky as she awaited an answer.

"You could say that," Andy rolled his eyes, "and you'd be bang on the money. I was in a relationship for seven years. She walked out saying she wanted to find herself. She didn't finish that particular sentence… …find herself in bed with my best friend."

"Is that the guy who's photo…" ventured Isobel.

Andy nodded.

"You're still friends with him?!"

Andy shrugged, "what can I say? I've known him since I started school and friendship is important to me."

"Even though he slept with your girlfriend?"

"Yes, well that was awkward at first…" Andy shrugged again, "being best man at their wedding and god parent to their daughter was a surprise development."

Isobel formed an O with her mouth, "Wow. Are you in training for sainthood or something? I'd have disembowelled both of them and fed them each other's livers! And that would have been on a good day!"

"Well that did cross my mind in the early days," he laughed, "well, not the disembowelling thing. I think you might have some issues you need to work through there by the way. But if you were going to feed them a vital organ, surely it would be their black and betraying hearts?"

"There you go! You're not quite a saint after all!" Isobel chuckled, then got serious, "but of course you couldn't feed the second one the heart of their lover because they would have died. You have to think these things through." She arched an eyebrow and looked at him expectantly.

He burst out laughing, "Oh Savannah! You are funny!"

She smiled, she hadn't really been aiming for funny, but she found that, when the conversation entered an arena that would, between other parties turn awkward, her sheer presence led to a favourable rationalisation and at times like this, laughter as what she had said was not taken seriously. She could tell Andy exactly what she was going to do to him later tonight, when she got him on his own and he'd either laugh or get turned on by her words. Sometimes both. In some respects, it was too easy at times. Not that Isobel was complaining, she got results and managed to have some fun along the way, or rather, she was having fun on this new diet of hers. Old people?! What had she been thinking!?

27

"Penny for your thoughts?" asked Andy.

Isobel shook her head, "sorry, I was just thinking about how good people sometimes get dealt a shit hand..." she lied.

"Shit hand?" Andy pulled a face as he said this, he was confused and appalled in equal measure.

"Oh! No! I meant cards!" blustered Isobel.

"I know," winked Andy and with that he was back on his feet, "same again?"

Isobel raised her glass and realised it was empty, as was his G&T, "Yes, please." She said this almost automatically, finding that she was in no rush to leave the bar. That last drink had gone down quickly. She glanced at her watch only to discover that an hour had elapsed in the blink of an eye. Time. Sometimes it was reluctant to pass, sometimes it went so quickly it felt like it was stealing from you.

Andy returned with the drinks, "sorry! He put ice in despite me asking him not to. I thought I'd let you fish it out. Didn't want to stick my dirty fingers in your drink."

Isobel waited for him to sit before she reached into her glass and lifted the ice cubes out of her glass one by one, dropping them into her empty glass, "shame," she said as he watched her, "you missed out," and with that, she sucked her index finger clean of the whisky it was coated with and took great pleasure in seeing Andy flush.

"So," she said after a quiet and meaningful silence, "you lost in love. How long did you wait until you decided to get back on the horse?"

Andy looked upwards, counting the time down, "three years?"

"And how long have you been *on the hunt?*"

"Best part of two years," Andy shrugged self-deprecatingly.

"Two years?!" exclaimed Isobel, maybe a little too loudly.

"Yeah," sighed Andy, "it's been a nightmare. I have so many war stories, I could write a series of books that would go into double digits. The whole online thing has changed the dating scene for the worst."

"Why didn't you try more traditional methods then?"

"I did!" protested Andy, "but the online thing has poured it's pollutants into the real world."

"So, what's so wrong with it?"

"Have you got a week?" he shook his head, "there's so much that's wrong with it, but I suppose it's dialled into what was wrong with people in any case. People are insecure and online dating proves to them that the people they could potentially date are liars and cheats and deeply unpleasant, so they get defensive and play games to test you."

27

Isobel nodded, that made sense.

"Then there's the format. You're invited to tick boxes and select the attributes you want in your supposedly ideal match. How is that supposed to work!? Show me one person who truly understands what it is that they need in life. Need. Not want. Talk about unrealistic expectations!"

He took a big swig from his drink and looked apologetically at Isobel, "sorry, it's just got so combative out there. Whatever happened to two people spending time together and getting to know each other? You know, go in with an open mind and see how it goes? It's just all so loaded and expectations are all wrong and there's this anticipation that you're going to pull a fast one. No one is *real* anymore."

He sighed, considered his drink but decided not to take another big swig at it, instead he stared into it as though he could see the future through the slice of lemon floating atop the bubbling liquid.

"And yet, here we are…" the words were loaded.

Andy looked up and smiled, "yes. Here we are. Here you *still* are. I've ranted and moaned and proved to be far from an ideal match and definitely not what you would expect having responded to a photo of a dick that you now know isn't even mine…" he eyed Isobel with mock suspicion, "why *are* you still here, Savannah?"

"I'm new to all of this," said Isobel answering honestly,

"believe it or not, I have never received a dick pic before, let alone responded to one. I have to admit to being bored when I replied. It was a bit of fun. Then I was intrigued. I'm still intrigued. You've surprised me, Andy. You're not what I expected."

Andy gave her an appraising look, trying to work out what exactly she meant by that, "I'm guessing, for once in my dating career, that is a good thing. Which, if I'm right, should be a relief." He groaned, "it's not though."

"And why's that?" fished Isobel.

"Because, if you are for real, you're potentially the best thing that has ever threatened to happen to me."

Isobel clapped her hands in delight, "oh Andy! You are so sweet! I hope you're not judging the book by its cover though?"

Andy smiled uncertainly and glanced down, "the cover is superb. I'm not going to lie about that. What use is a good cover if the content is crap though? Honestly? I just wouldn't go there. More trouble than it's worth. You've got something about you Savannah, and I *like* you. You took a risk on meeting me and you're actually talking to me *and* listening. There aren't all these preconceptions getting in the way."

Isobel gave Andy an inscrutable look. He shrugged, "yeah, I know. I'm easily pleased. Talking. Listening. That'll do me," he raised his hands as though he were beseeching some higher

27

being, "they're so bloody rare though!"

By way of an answer, Isobel looked around the bar that they were sitting in and at the sea of faces bathed in the blue light of their phones, "I think you're right there."

"I've been on dates where, once I've bought my date a drink? They've got their phone out. It's chaperoned us throughout the rest of the date." He raised his eyebrows and shook his head.

"What about the sex?" asked Isobel.

"Yeah!" laughed Andy, "the phone was out during the whole two minutes!" he frowned, "I hope she wasn't filming us…"

It was Isobel's turn to frown.

"I was joking," Andy said in a serious voice, "I don't go on to shag someone if there's any doubt in my mind. That's not fair on either of us."

He paused.

"And…"

"How a…"

They both started at the same time.

"Go on," encouraged Isobel.

Andy looked about to try to wave her through, asking her to go first, but Isobel locked eyes with him and waited expectantly, "oh, I was just going to say that a gentlemen doesn't divulge that aspect of his life. But I think you may have sussed that I've not really had all that much between the sheets action of late. How about you, what were you going to say?"

Isobel smiled coyly, "take me somewhere quieter and I'll tell you."

Upon hearing this, Andy's mood changed, he looked defiant somehow, "OK, but I need you to know that I'm looking for something that goes way beyond tonight."

Isobel smiled demurely and nodded.

"We could go back to mine, if you're comfortable with that?" he said.

"As long as it's quieter than here," she smiled again.

"It can be as quiet as you want it, Savannah," he said returning her smile.

They left the bar less than a minute after that.

28

Andy hailed a taxi and when one stopped, he opened the door for Isobel and ushered her in. She smiled to herself, he was quite a nice guy and she liked him. She hoped he wasn't too nice and that his so-called friend had got him wrong.

In the taxi, she slipped her hand into his and leant into him.

"This is nice," she said.

"It is," he agreed.

She turned her head and whispered, "so, do you have any doubts about me?"

He looked down at her and smiled warmly, "just the one."

"Really? Do tell?" she lifted her head as she said this, turning in her seat so they were face to face.

He drew in a deep breath, looked about to tell her, then he

surprised her with a kiss. Actually surprised her. She knew he was about to voice a concern. She knew that much and then she felt his lips against hers. He hadn't lunged, instead it was gentle, a natural progression that she responded to without thinking. They kissed and the rest of the world faded away so that all that was left was the two of them and that initial contact. Exploring each other slowly and gently, feeling their way and feeling each other. Isobel felt light headed for the very first time, she never knew a kiss could be like this. Kissing had always been a means to an end for her. One of the things she did because she knew it was expected, that it was what you did as a precursor to sex and sex for her was the starter to her main course.

"Get a room you two!"

It was the taxi driver. The taxi had stopped and he had turned in his seat, awaiting his fare.

The interruption was disorienting and Isobel's head swam as though she'd just surfaced from too long underwater. She noticed that Andy was all fingers and thumbs as he paid the taxi driver, almost stumbling as he found his way out of the taxi and onto the pavement. He held the door and waited for her to climb out of the vehicle, taking care not to let his eyes linger on her long, shapely legs.

"Wow," was all he said as he shut the taxi door and it drove back into town.

His eyes were still misty from the kiss and he was enjoying the

28

afterglow.

"So it was as good for you as it was for me?" Isobel said as she slipped her hand back into his.

He nodded dumbly and smiled, "I don't think I've ever…"

"Me neither," Isobel agreed.

Andy realised that they were standing there on the pavement outside the house. His thoughts still entangled around the experience of that first kiss, "we should…" he nodded towards his house.

"This is nice," Isobel said as he led her through the hallway and into the kitchen. The kitchen was at the back of the house and led out onto the garden via a set of bi-fold doors which Andy was in the process of opening.

"Drink?" he asked her.

"Do you have whisky?"

He opened a cupboard full of bottles, "take your pick."

He watched her as she crouched down to look at the whiskies on the bottom shelf. She felt his eyes on her and she found herself liking the attention. "I'll have this one," she said handing him the bottle of Talisker.

"A fine choice," he said, turning to open a wall cupboard and retrieve two tumblers. He poured two generous measures and handed her her glass.

"Cheers," he said, watching her over the top of his glass as they chinked their glasses and took a sip.

She savoured the peaty taste of the liquid and took a moment to recalibrate herself. Stepping out onto the garden decking they both took in the night and drank a little more of their whisky. Isobel found she was enjoying the moment for what it was and she wasn't thinking all that much about her next step. Something was going to happen, she knew that and that was more than enough for her. The anticipation of something good happening and the very recent memory of that kiss were all good. They were enough and she was not seeking anything more right now.

She walked along the decking and spotted a wooden tub under a pergola, she pointed at it with the toe of her shoe, "what's that?"

"Oh that? That's my dirty sex pond," he said with a smile.

"Dirty sex pond?" repeated Isobel, baffled to what the over-sized barrel was.

"Sorry, bad joke," said Andy, "it's a hot tub."

He set his drink down and uncovered the tub revealing the water inside. Isobel could feel the warmth emanating from the water as the cover came away.

28

"The water's already warm?" she said, almost to herself.

She set her drink down besides Andy's and trailed a finger in the water.

"Yeah," said Andy, "I use it quite often. It relaxes me."

"I'm sure it does," Isobel was already kicking off her shoes, "I love the feeling of water on my skin."

Andy watched as she unselfconsciously unzipped her skirt and let it fall to the decking, then pulled her top over her head so she was left in her underwear. Her hand went to her stocking top and paused, she obviously thought better of it, left it where it was and instead took the steps at the side of the tub and stepped elegantly into the hot tub. Andy couldn't take his eyes from her as she lowered herself slowly and deliberately into the water. He looked a sight, open mouthed and transfixed at this development.

"Can you pass me my drink before you get in, please?" she said this as though what was happening was the most natural thing in the world and his joining her was a foregone conclusion. It was the best invitation Andy had had in a long, long while and he wasn't going to pass on it.

Isobel noticed his hand trembling as he passed her her whisky. He was still aquiver as he placed his drink within reach of the hot tub and set to work in unclothing himself. Now it was Isobel's turn to watch and she was not disappointed as he removed his shirt and revealed the extent of his tattoo. That more ink was revealed as he dropped his trousers was even better as far as Isobel was concerned. She had a dark moment as she saw his tight black boxers and thought back to the rude man's horrible underwear. That the memory of that odious creep had invaded and sullied this moment appalled her, but she quickly banished it as Andy finished undressing down to those boxers and climbed into the hot tub beside her.

"Well, I hadn't expected this," Isobel smiled and sipped her drink before placing her glass down. She trailed a finger along the surface of the water, describing something like a figure of eight. The size of the shape increasing on every pass until her finger brushed Andy's chest. Her finger continued its travels and Andy casually watched it, awaiting it's next pass. This time she kept her finger on his skin, lightly trailing her fingernail along the pattern of the tattoo on his chest.

"I like your body art," she was staring at his chest as she said this.

Tilting her finger so the pad was against his skin she drew the outline of the pattern. She liked the feel of the water, which made Andy's skin slick.

Suddenly, there erupted from the water a cascade of bubbles. This surprised and delighted Isobel and she bobbed around in the water enjoying the sensation of the bubbles and jets of water against her skin. Somewhere in the chaos was Andy and the motion of the water seemed to guide her to him. Her fingers returning to his chest, then her palms and as she drew closer, the follow up to that first, amazing kiss was inevitable.

28

She almost held herself back as it began to happen, the worry that nothing could compare to that kiss and the dark shadow of the potential disappointment of finding out for sure loomed large, but nothing and no one was going to stop this.

This kiss was different to the first, but no less special, supplemented as it was by their wet bodies. The sensation of contact in the water took things to a whole new level and although there was a familiarity here for Isobel, this was also unique. She had never been with someone in the water. The feel of wet and slick skin though was not new to her, it took her a while to place where she had partaken of such sensations and when it came to her a surge of sadness flowed through her. Blood. That was the lubricant she was familiar with. The times that she had feasted violently and abandoned any pretext of civility.

This was so completely different to that though and in exploring Andy, she was also exploring new territory. This felt so different and she was doing it entirely for the pleasure of it. That she liked Andy and already felt a connection was what made it so different.

She wanted this.

She wanted Andy.

And she wanted him in a way that she had never experienced before.

The kiss went on and on without end and they writhed against each other, moaning into each other's mouths, building to a crescendo of exploration that they lost themselves in. Isobel couldn't even remember the moment Andy had penetrated her. Nothing was a conscious effort. It just *was*. They moved against each other slowly and deliberately and she could not separate the gently undulating motion of the water in the hot tub to the building waves of pleasure within her. She could feel the pleasure, the water and Andy and they were all connected.

And then she was closing her eyes and abandoning herself to an orgasm that threatened not to end. As she came out the other end of the intensity of that orgasm she wondered if she had lost consciousness. She seemed to swim gradually back to the real world and as she did, she had a moment of panic. She hadn't been in control and when she lost control then something within her took over and...

Her eyes shot open in panic, expecting to see Andy ruined and lifeless beneath her. The relief she felt as he looked up at her and asked, "are you OK?" was almost overwhelming.

"Yes!" she gasped, and then she laughed, "that was bloody amazing!"

He smiled at her, stroking her back and an intense look on his face. She could feel him inside her still and he continued to fill her.

"So, it is true then?" she asked him.

"What's that?" he asked.

28

"That nice guys always come second..."

She began moving against him again and in the end, she disproved that theory. It was a dead heat that second time around.

29

"That was a first for me," she said softly as he held her where she was, still on top of him.

"You're not saying…" he began.

"No silly! Not that!" she laughed.

"The hot tub then?" he asked.

"Well, that was another first and it certainly added something. I've always loved the water, but I've never done anything like this in the water."

"So, what was a first for you, then?" then he looked like he'd twigged to where she was coming from, "ah… sex on the first date. I knew it! I wanted to wait! I really did…"

"No. Not that either," she saw his face fall, "I mean that wasn't what I meant, OK?"

He nodded and looked a little less crestfallen. She guessed that

29

he didn't want to think that maybe she made a habit of sex on the first date, which as he wasn't a proponent of launching in all guns blazing, made sense. Maybe that was why it had been so good...

"It's never felt like that before, Andy. Thank you..." she felt strange thanking him. Did people thank each other for great sex? She was in uncharted territory. Usually, there was no one to talk to at this point, so she'd never indulged in post sex small talk, nor had the opportunity to explore what it was that had just happened. At this point in the proceedings, she was essentially clearing the dishes and doing the washing up.

"It's me who should be thanking you," said Andy brushing his lips against her shoulder, "that was amazing. I didn't know it could be like that. It was almost like I've been waiting for you."

She leaned back so she could see his face, she wasn't sure why. She wasn't sure of anything in this moment. She had just indulged in sex for the sake of sex and nothing else and it had felt amazing, hadn't it? In the afterglow she could still feel it and she could feel something else. Some sort of affection for this man. She didn't just want to do this again. She wanted to spend time with him. It would have interested her and also scared her had she been made aware that she wasn't thinking of, or referencing her loneliness and the emptiness of her existence outside of hunting and feeding. This, right now, was independent of that and absolutely genuine. It had come from nowhere and they were both feeling it.

She wasn't even questioning the practicalities of spending time with Andy, the evident mismatch of two entirely different beings. There was something here and she wanted to keep a hold of it. As though hearing those words, Andy pulled her closer and wrapped his arms around her, his lips finding her shoulder and caressing it.

"You know, you've made a hypocrite of me tonight?"

"How so?" she said softly.

"I advise all of my friends never to sleep with someone on the first date…" he burst out laughing.

"What's so funny?" she asked, enjoying his embrace and barely responding to his outburst.

"I once had a mate crying on my shoulder because his dates never wanted to see him after the first time. Turned out he always shagged them on a first date. So I told him he should wait. Give some time and room for a relationship to develop. Next time I saw him, he was still glum. I asked him why, and he told me it was still going wrong in his love life, only now he wasn't getting a third date…"

"He was shagging them on the second date instead?" she whispered.

"You got it. Without fail."

"I don't think this makes you a hypocrite."

29

"Why not?"

"It's different," she thought a little more, "you're different."

"Hmmm... that's what people say when they're being hypocritical."

"True, but it's not what you say, it's how you mean it that counts."

He kissed her shoulder by way of a response, "we should get out of this sex pond before we go all wrinkly or grow gills."

She groaned in mock apathy and disagreement, but stood and stretched in any case. He climbed out of the hot tub and retrieved two large towels from just inside the house, obviously kept there for just such occasions.

"Two towels?" Isobel winked.

"There's a third there. I keep a stock of them as they have a habit of going upstairs with me," he pointed back from whence the towels had come. She'd already seen it but made the quip in any case, knowing full well that he was likely to bite.

She was about to make a quip about the lucky towels, but suddenly, her face clouded. The change was obvious and it was not restricted to her expression, her entire mood was altered and with it Andy's.

"What is it?" he asked.

She shook her head, her focus elsewhere. He stood watching her. It were as though she could hear something that he could not, and her early warning system was blaring at her. That she was no longer here, in their moment was upsetting and he saw it as a wider end. If this were so, he should have seen it coming. It was all of it too good to be true and he hadn't followed the correct script in any case. Crossing the lines he had spoken of always led to a swift end. If anything, Isobel's expression darkened further and this did not bode well. She looked seriously pissed off.

"I have to go," she said abruptly.

He silently watched as she dragged her clothes on. The transition from only a few minutes ago was so stark as to be startling, but he felt numb. She'd only been in his life for a matter of hours and now he was anticipating loss and worse still a hole in his life that would be nigh on impossible to fill. That thought was crazy and he sought to modify it, the loss of what could have been was what pained him. Tonight a door had opened and he'd seen inside, and now it was being closed firmly in his face. Yes, there would be other doors, but he'd had glimpses behind some of those before, and there was no comparison. Besides, the road to any of those doors was an utterly awful pain in the arse and he didn't know whether he had the stomach for it anymore.

And then she was walking away.

Andy expected her to go and for that to be an end to it, that she turned was approaching a miracle, "I'll drop you a line…

", then she stopped, made her mind up and came back. They embraced and kissed a kiss that didn't feel like a goodbye to Andy.

"Sorry," she said as she left his embrace, "I really have to go. I *will* be in touch." Her smile was pained, and then she turned and walked away, a clear purpose in her steps.

Andy watched her go. He stood there like a statue after she had gone, then he broke the spell, grabbed her discarded towel and his clothes and went inside.

* * *

"What are you doing here?" Isobel snarled as she came up on his blind side.

The figure froze, taken by surprise by her appearance.

"How..." said Quentin as he realised he'd been discovered.

"I'm quick," said Isobel by way of explanation.

Quentin eyed her warily. Isobel knew he was appraising her and she was not at all concerned with what he might glean. Her blood was up, he had intruded when he had no right to and his timing could not have been any worse. In this state, her senses were on red alert and it were almost like she could see right through him. She knew what made him tick and right now, what made him tick was fear. Fear would be her ally, and he was on his own and out of his depth.

"You've made a big mistake, Quentin," she said it matter-of-factly, in such a way that this could have been a work setting and a discussion of the promotion that he would miss out on.

"How do you know my name?" he was trying to sound confident and defiant, but falling well short. There were visible cracks in the façade. "It was you who took Camilla." He stated this last. It must have been, any alternatives only made for worse reading and this was as bad as it got.

Isobel smiled a cruel smile, "she also made a big mistake."

"So you killed her?"

"The choice was always hers. I merely made the best of her bad choices."

"You *fed* on her!?" he gasped, "but that is forbidden!"

"Forbidden? By who? You? Why would I listen to you?"

"No. Not by me. You... you don't know? Where have you been for the past..."

Quentin stopped, his already pale face took on a sickly grey hue. Isobel was past caring and guilty of at least a small dose of hubris. Her new existence had enlivened her and all she saw here was weakness. That and a nuisance that had

29

dared interrupt her in the midst of something that she was thoroughly enjoying. Quentin would pay and he would pay dearly for his impudence.

"I would say Camilla died well," she said cruelly, "but I don't think there is such a thing as dying well. That's just a myth humans tell each other to allay the fear of their ending."

Quentin raised a hand, "there is no n..."

He did not get to finish his sentence. The surprise of Isobel's speed was one thing, but her teeth piercing his neck and her arms encircling him in what felt like a contracting iron cage stunned him. He barely gasped as she penetrated his neck and there followed a protracted sigh as Isobel bit down further and drew his life blood from him.

Isobel very seldom fed like this, so swiftly and with no build up or preparation. That Quentin bucked and convulsed as she sucked against him was a revelation. He barely struggled and within a matter of moments, any struggle morphed into a strange kind of encouragement. He slipped his arms around her, returning her embrace and moaned softly as she fed, his moans matching hers. It turned out that her power over vampires was just as complete and overwhelming as her power over humans.

For all intents and purposes, they could have been lovers meeting secretly for a late night tryst and Isobel felt the familiar stirrings and building waves of pleasure as she fed and they both moved against each other. She was doing this, she knew. She took her victim so completely that she did more than break down their defences, she seduced them into accepting her completely. She was their fate and she expected them to go willingly.

They always did.

Once again, the blood of a vampire filled her and raised her being like nothing else could. She felt herself *growing* and becoming something more than she had ever been. She knew that most of this was a temporary fix, as every feeding was, but that something of Quentin and the vampire that he had been would remain within her. She supposed that this was the case every time that she fed, that she took something of her victim into herself, it was just so marked and powerful when it was another vampire.

Quentin started to buck violently and she knew he was close to the end. She could feel it and this encouraged her to suck harder against him and take everything that he had. She almost swooned at the end, feeling him let go. She broke away from him gasping for air and desperate to clear her vision and come back into the world. She felt dizzy and vulnerable even in her elated and heightened state. She stepped away from Quentin and let him drop to the ground, his dead form seemed much older, almost desiccated. It never ceased to amaze her, the transformation that took place when she took the life from a body, but when it was a vampire the difference was obscene.

She heard a slight noise and looked up from the corpse. There in front of her was an aghast figure. No one was supposed to

29

be out at this late hour and if they were, then she would know and she would act accordingly so that they never saw what she was about. That was what she did. That was what she always did.

Except this one time. This one unique time with that one unique person.

Andy.

"Savannah?"

Again, Isobel almost did not recognise the name as her own. What she did recognise was the meaning. One word conveying so much meaning. It was a thousand questions. It was recrimination. It was an infinite sadness that would haunt her for the rest of her days, a sadness that felt like it had always been there, but now it had a banner and it would be the bane of her existence.

It was the end.

"Andy," she said it softly and with something close to love, but she would never know love and having never known it, she could not understand it.

By rights, he should have said something. Anything. But she supposed that he did. The look in his eyes would never, ever leave her. The life inside him lingered beyond the point it had ever remained in any of the others as she snapped his neck and made their forever goodbye.

30

"I need to feed."

Isobel had taken to spending time in the dark front room with her companion. That was to say, she had slumped there and barely moved for what she thought might be days, but suspected was longer than that. Testament to that suspicion was her companion's announcement that she needed to feed.

She gave no response, instead she continued to stare into the dark and instead of seeing the nothingness and being filled with the nothingness she saw the memory of eyes and within those eyes was something worse than the darkness.

The companion said nothing for a long while and that suited Isobel just fine. She lay there slumped against the wall and allowed the darkness to wash over her. Laying passively in the dark did nothing to salve the pain she felt, the self-pity and the self-loathing. She could not even bring herself to sit up and she did not know how it was that she had come to this state, only that from sitting against the wall she had slid sideways

30

so that her cheek was against the bare floorboard.

Unblinking, she lay there and tried to give in. Any other creature could give up and die. She was not any other creature and dying did not appear to be an option for her. Options. Did she have any options other than to feed and exist? She recalled reading books on vampires, many of which were romanticised, but few of which depicted the hunger that overrode everything else. It was an addiction that expanded into a vampire's life and left room for precious little else. The brief respite afforded by feeding was overshadowed by the certainty that the hunger was ever present and would take control again soon enough.

The hunger was Isobel's jailer and she was trapped in the darkness by it. She had dared to think that she could be in the world and be a part of it and experience things other than the hunger, hunting and killing, but that was always a delusion. That it had gone so wrong even as she tasted forbidden fruit was how it had always been. Fleeting moments of hope for a better life rising up out of the pits of her existence, an existence so terrible she denied it in its entirety and in so doing, it clutched her all the more tightly, ripping into her mind and unhinging her.

She knew now why she did not remember all that much of her past, it was not only the weight of so many years past and her inability to comprehend the length of her existence, it was her refusal and denial to face what she truly was, and her holding on to a belief that she could choose. That she always had a choice. Now she was choosing to give up and give into it and even that wasn't working for her.

Outside, the light was fading on the Big House. That house was somehow altered. Darker and more ominous. As villagers passed they made a concerted effort not to look in its direction, nothing good would come of their paying it any attention. The stonework was darker as though chemical soaked mists had bathed it in poison. The windows had received similar attention and were no longer transparent. There was no further, outward sign of dilapidation, but the house was becoming a ruin, it were as though it had cancer and it was being eaten from the inside.

Despite this terrible degradation, the village of Brokmaster was oblivious to the spread of that cancer. The darkness was creeping forth from the Big House and a disease threatened all of the community. But then, that was so often how life ended, the darkness crept up on life and dulled it gradually day by day until one day it was too far gone not to acknowledge it anymore and by then, it was far too late.

"You know you cannot deny me, Angyal."

Isobel only blinked. There was that word again. Angel. She was no angel, not even a dark or fallen angel. She was cursed and twisted. A broken thing that corrupted all that she touched. She wasn't even Death. Death was an absolute and Death would not feel like this. If she were anything, she were the unliving embodiment of purgatory.

Lifting her hand she observed it in a detached manner. She was grey. Even the colour of her spoke of something *other* and something from the grave.

30

"Angyal, you need to feed too. We... cannot deny that which we are."

"And what are we?" Isobel breathed the words into the room.

"We are..." there was a pause as though even the companion did not know, "...hungry." She said that last in an almost drawn out and painful way.

Something compelled Isobel to find her feet and leave the room. Maybe it was that one word. She left the door open as left the front room and paused in the hallway looking at the stairs and the door to the kitchen. Instead of taking either of those options she stumbled around to face the front door, bracing herself against the wall for the moment and then she found a small reserve of resolve and made for the front door.

The front door had never been opened during her tenure here and the key begrudged being turned in its lock. It had settled where it was and the mechanism had almost forgotten what it was and what job it had to do. Likewise, the door refused to budge, the frame had moved sideways and trapped the door itself in a vice like grip. There was the laboured scrape of paint and wood as Isobel exerted her force of will on the door. A part of her hoped that the door was holding the structure of the old house up and that it would collapse, entombing her. The prospect of an eternity trapped under tons of stone and rubble did not concern her, and as she left the house she considered the woods and how easily she could dig and claw at the soft earth, digging deeper and deeper until the walls of the hole she had dug collapsed in on her and entombed her. Dying may not be an option, but she could still leave the world be.

As she walked through the village, she noticed that night had fallen and more time had elapsed than she had anticipated. The dark of the night suited her, but she was not sure of just how late it was and whether there would be anyone around. Gone was the careful Isobel. Nothing mattered anymore and she would take what she needed from the village and be done with it.

There were lights on in some of the houses and cottages that she past. Those lights were dim and appeared further away that they actually were. The street lights flickered and pulsed, as though they were fighting the darkness around them, and they were.

Only now did Isobel take in what she was seeing. Only now did she see it for what it really was. There were tendrils of darkness extending through the village. She turned slowly back to the Big House. The façade of the house like the top half of a dark face looking out across the village, it's mouth sunk deep into the village and drawing the very life out of it.

Brokmaster was slowly dying.

She walked back towards the Big House, finding a reserve of energy and resolve she hadn't expected to be there, as she drew closer to what she had laughingly considered her home, she realised that those houses closest to the Big House were in complete darkness, Isobel stopped, made up her mind and took the front path of the house nearest to her. She turned the

30

handle on the front door, so intent was she to see what was behind that door that she would never know whether the door was unlocked or whether she had broken it as she forced her way in. The entirety of this house was in darkness, but she could see well enough. She did not have to go far before she found what she was looking for.

On the armchair in the living room was an elderly woman. Isobel crouched down to look at her more closely. She was not dressed in the manner of an older woman and that told her all that she needed to know. The woman's skin was very wrinkled and looked dry, as though she were being drained. Isobel reached out a finger to touch the skin on the woman's cheek and as she did the dull eyes brightened just enough for Isobel to know that the woman was not yet dead.

A faint sound came from unmoving lips. Isobel leaned in in order to hear what the dying woman was saying...

"*Help me...*"

Isobel recoiled from the woman as though she'd been slapped. The words had shocked her. As she composed herself, she realised the sound had stopped and the woman's eyes had dimmed for the very last time.

Leaving that house, Isobel walked away from the Big House. It was some small consolation that the further that she walked away from the house, the thinner and less substantial the dark tendrils were. Walking away from the house became easier and easier and she felt as though a weight had lifted from her.

She knew what was happening, but the why of it eluded her. She could guess well enough, but did she know that this was even a possibility? That the effect she had on people could be this dire? Was this even her doing?

Her companion needed feeding, her thoughts came back to that. Address that first and then look into this further. Maybe feeding her companion would help in some way, she thought this and even as the thought formed in her mind it evaporated. There was more at play here and it was not something that would be easily addressed. She felt something like hope though, that maybe she could make this right. That she could stop whatever was happening and this took her out of herself and helped her go on.

She spotted a small cottage with a light on downstairs. She knew that the inhabitant of this dwelling lived on his own and was likely to have visited the pub earlier this evening. This, as far as Isobel was concerned was enough boxes ticked. She needed to act quickly and do this. Knocking on the door in an arhythmic pattern brought the middle aged man to the door quickly. He threw the door back to see what the emergency was and when he saw Isobel his mouth fell open at the sight of her. From his reaction, she knew that she was a sight to behold and that this was far from a good thing.

"What's happened to you?!" he exclaimed.

"I'm fine," she said and she quickly reached out and touched his hand. Once the connection was made, he forgot his worry and concern and a calm fell over him. The transformation was

30

instant and remarkable. She was weak from not feeding, but she could at least do this.

"Fine," he repeated. Then remembering himself, he invited her in.

"No, you need to come with me," Isobel told him.

"Fine," he repeated, and he did not provide any resistance as Isobel guided him by the hand, out of his house and along the path to the pavement and the Big House. He did not notice that he had left the front door of his house wide open and he did not seem to notice the insidious darkness that he was being lead into and Isobel supposed no one else but her could see it. They might feel it, a sudden chill passing through them and making them shiver and cross themselves, but mortals were oblivious to so much that this was just another thing that would pass them by.

As they entered the house, Isobel kicked the door partially shut. That was good enough, she doubted anyone would dare approach the Big House let alone enter it. She led the man past the front room and to the stairs, as they made their way up the stairs she could feel her companion stir.

Once they were in the bedroom, she undressed him. He stood and helped her to undo his trousers and as she pulled them down he lifted his jumper and shirt off over his head discarding them on the floor. He kicked his shoes off and she pushed him so he was seated on the bed. Kneeling before him she pulled the trousers off and then his socks so that now he was in his underpants.

"Lay back," she said this softly as she stood and helped him with a gentle push to the chest. She pulled his underpants off and then she climbed over him slowly. She could feel her companion approaching, but she would not be in the bedroom just yet.

Isobel's hands found the top of the man's arms and she slipped them slowly upwards until she reached his wrists. She leaned forwards a little more so she was pinning him. She was sat above his crotch and she could feel his arousal against the material of her skirt. Felt him growing hard against the cheek of her arse. She should have felt her own growing arousal and excitement, but instead she felt a strange detachment. She wanted this to happen, but that was the extent of it.

She leant forwards so her lips were tantalisingly close to his ear and she could feel his warmth, but her thoughts went no further. She did not consider the source of that warmth, the blood pulsing through his veins. She had no desire for it.

"Pleasure yourself," she whispered, letting go of his right wrist, she felt him lower his hand and use it to do exactly what she bade. She lifted her head so she could stare deep into his eyes, shifting her hands and weight so she now had a grip on his shoulders.

With his other hand free he slipped this down and stroked her arse with it. He groaned with pleasure as he began stroking her with his free hand, she could feel him pleasuring himself and moving against her as he did so.

"Take your time," she whispered, "that's it. Slower. I want you to hold yourself back, it'll be all the better for it."

Now her companion was entering the bedroom, but the man under Isobel did not notice, his eyes were glazed with lust and totally enraptured by Isobel. As her companion drew closer though, something in the room changed and for a moment the spell was broken. The man's face changed and suddenly he looked shocked.

"What's happened to you?!" he gasped and in that moment Isobel knew what he was seeing, she glanced down at her grey hands and knew that she had been too long, laying in the dark of that front room and having not fed her body had begun to decay. She may not be dying, but this body of hers was.

He snapped his head to the left towards the creeping darkness, "what the hell is that!?"

"Look at me!" she barked the order and grabbed his chin, turning his head back to face her.

"I...!" he began.

"Look at me!" she said firmly and this time his eyes held hers, "that's it. Focus only on my eyes and keep stroking. That's it. Keep going. That's good."

She moved against him, encouraging him with her body as

well as her voice and he kept going, she could feel him against her and she could feel his growing pleasure.

"Gah!"

His entire body tensed under her and the hand that had been stroking her behind pressed against her.

"It's OK," she whispered, "keep stroking yourself. That's it. Keep going."

She could feel him stroking, and his free hand slipped upwards and around her, pulling her closer.

"That's it," she said softly.

She could also feel her companion behind her, slipping up along the man's legs. His sudden reaction had been when she had joined them and the initial pain he had felt at her touch, now he was lost. There was no going back.

Her companion took her time, moving upwards and as she reached his inner thighs he began to tremble and buck under Isobel.

"Hold it back," she said softly over and over and she could feel him trying to.

As he came for the first time, she dug her nails into his shoulders and held him there. He thrashed and suddenly his eyes grew wide. He understood the danger he was in and he

30

tried in vain to break free. His movements lulled and she slipped sideways so she was next to him, stroking his chest and whispering in his ear as her companion moved up along his body taking her time and feeding upon him.

Not once was she tempted to lower her mouth to the prominent vein on his neck. She felt something as he slipped away, but what it was, she did not know. And she did not care. Now she *knew.* Maybe she did not know it all, but she knew that her companion had deceived her and had been deceiving her all along, and in knowing that, she thought perhaps there was a blessed end for her after all.

31

There was one other witness to the slaying of Quentin and the unfortunate passer-by. Not all vampires are alike and some have attributes that others do not. Uma had felt something happening. The feeling of an approaching storm, only darker and more ominous and she knew what it meant even before she cast eyes upon Isobel.

That the creature that had ended Quentin and likely ended Camilla also had not been aware of Uma was surprising to her, but also a relief. This blind spot in the powerful creature's armoury had allowed Uma to live another day. Now though, it was a curse. Uma knew of Isobel's existence and worse still, she knew that she had to do something about it, and not just because she had ended the only friends Uma had ever had and left her alone in this world.

Uma hadn't thought, she just knew to follow Isobel. She didn't want to let that creature out of her sight until she knew where she was headed. Then, and only then, once she had that vital information, could she let up and think about what she was to do next.

31

Twice she had almost lost sight of the unmarked van, but in both instances she quickly caught sight of it again. In those blind spots, she thought she could feel the presence of the creature and the van emerged both times exactly where Uma anticipated it, so she could in theory have tracked the creature at her leisure, but she dared not risk doing so because were she to lose the trail then the next time she encountered the creature was likely to be on its terms and when that happened, Uma's chances of surviving the encounter would be narrowed to a point of non-existence.

When the van turned down the track to Brokmaster, Uma was surprised to see the village itself emerge. There had been no sign of it on the road and indeed no signs for it. Once in the village itself, she had known exactly where the van would stop.

Then it was a case of waiting.

That wait had been long and arduous and she had had to withdraw a distance when the house itself had begun to change. She didn't know how often the creature would venture out, and the days had turned to weeks and the weeks had scrolled through to months, and still she waited, knowing that was the only sensible course of action open to her.

Weakened over such a protracted period, she had at last relented and found somewhere to feed. Uma did not kill if she could help it. She could control her feeding so that she could stop even if she remained ravenous. Drinking little and often during the course of a night or two would see her right, and it did.

The Broken Dragon was a good spot for her to feed, there was a dimly lit smoking shelter at the back of the pub and most of the smokers didn't bother to stand within its confines unless it was raining. There was also the back door of the kitchens a way along the back. Both of them out of sight of the other.

Uma picked a week night, but a relatively busy one to lurk in the shadows and await lone visitors to the back of the pub. The first was a man in muddy jeans, from his clothes and his physique, she guessed he was in the building trade.

"Hello," she said quietly as she emerged from the gloom behind him.

"Bloody hell!" he exclaimed, "you gave me a fright!"

"Sorry, let me make it up to you," she took his free hand and pulled him into the darkness silently.

"What..." he began as he felt her arms slipping around him and her cold lips on his neck. She felt him stiffen and he raised his arms to push her off him, but all of that changed as her fangs penetrated his skin and instead of those arms pushing against her, they wrapped around her. Both of them moaning in the darkness as she took her time and allowed his blood to pulse gently into her mouth.

That first one was the hardest to stop and she almost went too far, in fact she did go too far, leaving the man lightheaded and unable to walk in a straight line. She had to hold him up as she lapped at his neck and sealed the wound. Still, she had not ended his life and the venue she had chosen for her feeding meant that his erratic behaviour was not out of place.

He would not remember much of the encounter and anything he did remember he'd dismiss as a dream or a waking fantasy.

Feeling better for at least now having fed, but knowing that she needed more sustenance, she waited deeper in the shadows. Stronger and more confident, there was less urgency to what she was about now, which was just as well because as she began to move towards the young man smoking alone in the dark, the side door of the pub opened and a middle aged woman emerged, her heels click-clacking on the concrete as she approached.

Greetings were exchanged between the two. Uma, with her preternatural senses could hear it all, she could also read the chemistry between the married woman and the younger man. She was not surprised when the woman did not light up and instead pressed herself against the man.

"Not here, do you want us to get caught!?"

Although he said this, he had grabbed her behind and squeezed it through the leather skirt she was wearing. That said much more than his words and they both knew it.

"OK, over here then," said the woman and drew the man into the darkness, nearer to Uma.

Uma stayed exactly where she was, not concerned about being

discovered as the two lovers had eyes only for each other and this snatched and hurried moment.

"You're not wearing any…" the young man didn't finish this observation as he felt the buttons of his jeans being undone and fingers wrapping themselves around him, freeing him from the confines of his boxers and jeans.

"That's better," giggled the woman, "you like me wearing no knickers for you doncha?"

The young man grunted in response and for a short while there were only soft moans and sighs as they both stroked each other. This was short lived as the woman turned around and bent over, bracing herself against the wall of the pub and presenting her behind to the man. He took a half a step closer to her and she let out a low moan as he entered her. Reaching down to stroke herself as he fucked her. The sex was quick and frantic and a race to the end, the older woman knew this and sped up the movement of her fingers and increased the friction, her approaching orgasm sending him over the edge at the same time. He groaned a deep groan and she stifled her cries as her legs trembled with her orgasm.

Uma had to fight the urge to slips her arms around the young man as he entered her. She imagined what it would be like to feed on him and once they were done, switch her attentions to the woman. She was still hungry and there was something about the tableau presented to her that did more than turn her on. She was disappointed to see the man leave, she had had her sights on him and it felt like she'd lost out.

There was the woman however, and she was in the depths of the shadows, in an ideal spot to be taken. She had barely moved as the young man withdrew from her, buttoned up his jeans and returned to the pub. She was basking in the afterglow of her orgasm and in no rush to do much of anything else.

Uma slipped behind her and awaited the moment when the woman straightened up, slipping her arms around her waist and chest, she held the woman still facing the wall.

"Barry! I thought you'd gone inside!" she was about to giggle, but the sound was stifled and she let out a quiet gasp as Uma's hand slipped up from her chest and pulled her head to the side, her cool mouth eager against the woman's neck. Working against her to find the right spot. Uma tensed, realising her head had clouded as she had watched the couple fucking and her eagerness was too much, in that moment that she took to compose herself, the woman also tensed in anticipation in the exact way that she had as she had felt Barry behind her, only this time it was teeth that were penetrating her. She let out a low moan as she felt the teeth entering her and to Uma's surprise she responded to this development by moaning softly and rhythmically and encouraging Uma to suck harder.

Uma broke away and the woman groaned in disappointment. Turning, she extended her arms, "please..." she said softly, "...don't stop."

Uma took a step forward and as she did, the woman pulled her closer and tilted her head to the side exposing her neck, only this time, it was the other side, "bite me again," she said huskily.

Uma lowered her mouth and this time she took her time. Teasing the woman. In return, the woman stroked her hands up and down Uma's back, encouraging her and when the bite did not come, she slipped a hand downwards, finding the clasp on her trousers, unzipping them and then sliding her hand down her pubis and into her knickers. As the woman's fingers found her and began exploring her, Uma let out a groan against the woman's neck that sent a thrill through the woman.

"Fuck!" she hissed, and then she sighed as she felt Uma's teeth enter her. As the sigh ended she gasped, "Oh!" And Uma held her tightly as she felt the woman's body quiver and her legs tremble as she came again.

Soon afterwards she remembered herself and pulled away from the woman's neck. The woman took this as a cue and her fingers pressed harder as she stroked Uma and made her come.

As the woman straightened her skirt, she gave Uma her house number and street name. Somehow, she knew what Uma was and the thought of repeating this excited her. It excited Uma too. There were very few people who responded this way and wanted to do it again. That the woman had found Uma's spot and managed to give her an orgasm was also unusual, so Uma wasn't going to pass up the opportunity to do this again.

She fed twice more at the back of the Dragon on that night. She tried to convince herself she would be back here for a further

31

snack the following night, but she knew exactly where she was going to be and the thought of it excited her.

32

That first time that Isobel ventured out into the village itself to find food for her companion was the very next night that Uma went to feed. Sometimes the rules of the universe are perverse and they dictated that at the very moment Uma was being pleasantly distracted, Isobel would leave the Big House and walk the village right under Uma's nose.

Uma found the woman's house easily and saw her as she came around to the French doors at the back. Looking through the glass of those doors, she saw that the woman was on the sofa sat astride her husband. The scene looked planned, the woman was dressed in a see through nighty and stockings and had also made a point of wearing impossibly high heels. Uma guessed that this was all for her, and a pleasant bonus for the oblivious husband. She also knew that this deception would add another layer of excitement for the woman.

As the woman rode the man under her, she lifted her head from his neck. That she had been kissing his neck was a message and it thrilled Uma, that thrill heightened as the woman turned

32

her head and stared through the French doors, directly at Uma. Uma knew there was no way she could see her, but that she expected Uma to be there was enough. She bit her lower lip as she watched the woman continue to ride her husband whilst maintaining her gaze out into the darkness, only breaking that gaze as the man under her stiffened, this brought on the woman's orgasm and she buried her head in the man's neck as she came.

They remained that way for a while and Uma wondered whether the woman had been tempted to bite down on the man. She knew that she was. She had wanted to enter the house and join them there and then, but she knew that was not a good idea. She needed the man to leave the room, she was only there for the woman and that was more than enough for her.

The woman was now climbing off the man, she half turned and sprawled back across the sofa, facing those back doors. There was a brief conversation. The man was turning in as he had an early start, the woman grabbed the TV remote and said she would be up later. He didn't cast a backwards glance as he trudged out of the room and upstairs to bed.

Uma watched the light to the upstairs bathroom come on and barely two minutes later go back out. The same happened in the bedroom. The man's late night routine was evidently short and swift.

The French doors were already unlocked as Uma turned the handle, and as she stepped into the room the woman smiled and slipped the right strap of her nightdress down revealing her breast, then she sat back and raised her right arm. Uma joined her on the sofa, sitting to her left. The woman slipped her fingers to the back of Uma's head and guided her mouth to her breast. Uma was in no rush and planted gentle kisses on the flesh around the nipple, lapping at the nipple tantalisingly before returning to kissing. The woman threw her head back and moaned with pleasure and then she moaned as Uma slipped her hand down between her legs, feeling her heat and slipping two fingers into her wet hole. As those fingers penetrated her, the woman arched her back and Uma could not help but bite down on that luscious breast as it was offered to her.

Uma stopped feeding when the woman came. She was about to take her leave when the woman climbed from the sofa and stood before her. Then she knelt and pushed Uma's leg's apart. Kissing from her knee and along her inner thigh. Uma grabbed the back of her head and guided her movements as her lips and tongue reached the top of her inner thigh and she could wait no more. The woman pulling her knickers to one side and using her mouth and tongue expertly until Uma came.

Recovering from her own orgasm, she felt the woman slip onto the sofa, sitting in front of Uma, with her back to her and positioned between her legs, she leaned back and presented her shoulder and neck to Uma.

"Bite me," she whispered.

Uma could not resist. She slipped her arms around the woman

32

and her mouth found her neck as she explored her with her fingers.

Uma had not had anything like this for a long while and somehow it helped fill some of the hole that Quentin and Camilla had left. She had never slept with either of her friends, the three of them had been friends and nothing more, and yet they would always be more as they were her kind. This though. She had not done this in a long time and the intimacy and companionship was welcome. Being wanted was most welcome of all.

33

Somehow, Uma understood what had happened.

She was not clear on how she knew, but when she returned to her lookout post something was different. So, the following night, now no longer hungry and avoiding the temptation to visit her eager lover, she made a point of walking past the house, and that was when she saw it.

The front door was ajar.

She faltered for a beat before carrying on by the Big House and disappearing out of sight, but still the sight of that door lingered. Even when she put some more distance between herself and that house and it's slightly open door she could not budge the image of the door, or rather the gap in the door.

A sign.

And an invitation.

Uma had no plan. She hadn't even tried to devise a plan. She thought that something would present itself to her, and now it had. The ajar door told her that the creature had ventured forth when Uma had not been there and the creature was so complacent it had left the door open. What better than to go through that door and surprise the creature in its own lair and Uma would know exactly where the creature was. No blind exploration of room after room and the potential to be unsighted and surprised, no, Uma would go through that door and right to where the creature was and then she would…

That was the bit that was a blank for Uma. That was why she didn't have a plan. Anything that could despatch a vampire was not going to be easy to fight, let alone kill. And if the creature had ventured out of the house then it had fed and it was at its strongest.

Uma had not been this close to the house itself before and something was concerning her, without even thinking she doubled back and now, her attention was not on the Big House itself, as it had been ever since she'd tracked the creature here. Now she was taking in the area surrounding the Big House.

She had sensed the creature and the creature had filled her vision and her senses. The creature was a dark force, malevolent and evil and it sickened Uma to be anywhere near it. She felt unwell, even whilst separated by walls and distance. The stench the creature left had intensified as it had returned to its lair and Uma had had room for nothing other than the creature, had been blinded by it.

With a force of will, she tried to block at least some of that presence out, it took her a few attempts and everything she had, but as the creature itself receded what she saw shocked her. The creature was poisoning the village. Something of the creature was seeping outwards and already, in the nearest of the houses the life force of the occupants was being drained. Little by little, the diseased aura of the creature reached out further and further and once it touched a place the occupants remained indoors and allowed it to enter them. They were defenceless against it.

Now she could see what was happening and Uma ran up to the front door of a nearby house and banged on the wood of the door itself. No one stirred and no one answered. She ran around the back of the small dwelling and crashed through the back door. There on the kitchen floor were the desiccated remains of a man. Stepping over the corpse, she went into the living room to see what looked like an ancient lady and two miniature versions of the old man and woman. These had once, and very recently, been children. They looked like they were well preserved corpses of people who had lived thousands of years ago.

She could not help but reach out and touch the face of the little girl. She guessed she was seven or eight years old and only weeks ago would have been unable to sit still, so full of energy she would have been back then. Uma gasped as her outstretched finger met no resistance and kept on going through the child's cheek. She felt like she had violated the corpse and she gasped again, louder, as that violation led to the collapse of the face followed by the inward collapse of the body. Where there had once been a living breathing child, there was now only a pile of dust covered clothes.

How far and how deep had this contagion gone?

Uma ran from the house and walked briskly away from the Big House. By her reckoning, there were at least ten houses that had already fallen prey to the creature, and it was anyone's guess as to how much further that beast had reached out. She had to act now to prevent it going further and taking all of the rest of the village.

She stopped and looked about her, then she returned to the house with the dead family of four, she stood looking in through the broken back door of that house, seeing that her retreat past the fallen corpse of the man, or perhaps even the breeze through the ruined door had blown his remains away.

Dust.

That was all that remained of the creature's victims.

Back in the kitchen, she rooted through the drawers and retrieved a knife. That no one saw the knife wielding woman walk along the street and enter the Big House was no surprise. This area contained no one who would ever see again and without realising it, the surviving villagers were circumnavigating their fallen neighbours and turning blind eyes towards the creeping malevolence that was taking them one by one. The influence of the dark presence in the Big House doing its work and allowing them to sleepwalk to their ends.

34

The interior of the Big House was unsurprisingly oppressive. Uma shouldered the front door open and it squealed a complaint and a warning as she did. No wonder the door had not been closed, it felt like the weight of the house was sagging down upon it.

Or the weight of something within the house.

Uma felt like she was entering the maw of the beast itself, there was something alive about the house and yet nothing living could ever feel like this or be like this. She smelt corrupt flesh and as she walked further into the hallway the scant light from the doorway deserted her.

There was an unnatural darkness here and it felt like it was probing Uma, closing in on her and trying to find its way in. Her eyes watered and her head swam. It felt like something had found its way into her head.

She could barely breath and something made her head to the stairs, as she took the steps she felt some blessed release from

34

the atmosphere downstairs and she supressed her laughter as she realised that she didn't need to breathe, so how the hell had she been suffocating down there!?

Heading to the top of the stairs that foul smell of corrupt and decaying flesh grew stronger as did that presence she had followed back here all those months ago.

Only now she was here, there was something confusing about that presence. Something that was not right with any of this. Onwards she went, not wanting to stop, not wanting to lose her nerve. But then, at the bedroom door, she paused with her hand on the door knob. The creature was behind that door, she knew it. Raising the kitchen knife higher and tightening her grip on its handle she turned the door knob and strode into the bedroom.

She gagged with the foul stench of it and covered her mouth with her free hand. Her gaze fell towards the source of the smell and there, on the bed was the decaying corpse of the creature. A once beautiful woman, now corrupted and...

The eyelids flew open and fixed her with a stare.

Uma gasped, there was no way that this foul thing could still live. The animation of this corpse much be a trick or an illusion. Again her head swam and fought the ensuing dizziness. She had to end this right here and right now. Fighting against her urge to run from this place and never return she stepped forward and as she did, her knife hand raised in the air. She looked down upon the pitiful creature and as she was about to plunge the knife downwards, it raised its hands upwards, towards her in the same way as a lover would. Welcoming and beseeching.

She could pause no longer, gritting her teeth she brought the knife down and drove it into the creature again and again and again, not daring to stop, not wanting to give quarter. Knowing that she could not afford to lose this fight.

She did not know how long she went at her business, only that she could not stop. When eventually she came to her senses, she was sat against the bed crying. The knife laying on the floor before her. She could not look at her handiwork, she already knew that what she had left there on the bed was unrecognisable as the creature she had seen kill her friend Quentin. The remnants of a creature that had been so powerful and taken life so readily and easily, now broken and destroyed.

And yet now the creature was gone. She could feel the presence no longer. The room was empty of everything except herself and the remains on the bed.

So why did she feel so lost? And why did she feel so... scared?

There was something very wrong here.

In the end, it had all been too easy. Almost as though she had been led here and every move of hers scripted. That there was something else at play here and that she had been used. She had been led by the nose, because until she had witnessed the creature make easy work of Quentin she had led a charmed life

34

and had feared nothing other than discovery. Nothing could hurt or harm her and she had brought that with her here. She had remained arrogant and aloof and held onto her belief that whatever happened, she would prevail.

It felt like a trap and Uma had the growing certainty that it was a trap and a trap like nothing she could have possibly anticipated.

As her world shifted sideways and her certainty crumbled, Uma looked down towards the discarded knife, but she wasn't looking at the knife itself, she was looking at the floorboards, and the way that her focus was being affected as she looked down at them was disorienting and disconcerting. The gaps between the floorboards were growing more substantial, darker somehow. And then the darkness between the boards began to seep upwards and outwards filling the gaps and covering the boards. Covering the boards until she could no longer see them. Covering everything until Uma could no longer see the knife.

There was something truly terrifying about the disappearance of the knife, her weapon, her only chance, winking out of existence with a finality that spoke to her of her own fate.

The dark rose before her and she could feel it rear up behind her also, filling the room and surrounding her.

She was frozen to the spot and from that spot she felt the darkness against her, pulling her downwards. Holding her in a way she had never been held before. Any possibility of movement had been stolen from her.

"You are the creature," Uma struggled to form the words, and they felt alien to her as they escaped her lips.

"No, you killed the creature that you came to kill. It is done," said the dry, rasping voice of Isobel's one time companion, "and for that Uma, I thank you. Before our time is done here, I have more gratitude to bestow upon you. You have played your part better than I could have imagined."

"What do you mean?" Uma groaned with the effort of speaking.

"Oh! You know, dear. You already know my dear Angyal."

And there it was again, that word. Angel. There had been a great many angels and there would likely be more.

"You drew me here? Why? Are you going to kill me?"

"No, I am not going to kill you, although I do derive some satisfaction in ending your kind. You're all a bit dull and a waste of space."

"Then what are you going to do to me?"

"I have a use for you. I will use you, my Angyal..."

"But why?"

34

"You've seen it. I do not do well out in the world. It does not suit me. The creature you came here to kill. My Angyal. She failed me and would have starved me. You won't though. She was weak. Merely a human with a dark heart, whereas you my dear..."

"You tricked me! How! Why did I not see??"

"We all see what we want to see. Well, I say we. It's the flesh you see. It has its own needs and those needs get in the way. You were blind, just like all those blood sacks out there were. Didn't you think the willing victim you had your fun with was just a bit too... convenient?"

"You did that?!"

"No, Angyal. You did that. I just helped you along the way. Gave you what you wanted. Now I will get what I want and we're all square."

"You're like us?" gasped Uma as she tried to understand what was happening and what this thing was that had the abilities of a vampire but so much more power than she could comprehend.

There was no immediate answer. Instead there was a drawn out pause, and Uma thought the conversation was at an end, but then the dark companion spoke.

"I *am* you," said the rasping and dry voice, "only unconfined and unrestricted by that weak physical form of yours."

"But how is that possible?" asked Uma, but her mind was racing, she had seen what this thing was doing to the village and its inhabitants. The thing on the bed had only been a satellite to the true creature and that manifestation had been unimaginably powerful, it had ended Quentin effortlessly and feasted upon him.

There was a noise that approximated a chuckle and chilled Uma to the bone, "that is the problem with children, they think that they outgrow you. They strike out into the world and they become arrogant and disrespectful. Most of all, they forget so much in order to behave so badly to the parent they owe everything to."

"You are...?" Uma could not formulate the rest of the question.

"Where do you think you came from? You've wondered about your origins and what it is that you are all of your life, but in such a feeble and half hearted way. Deep down you knew, but you denied me and I indulged that. Now my patience is at an end, and now my children will return to the fold where they belong, whether they like it or not."

"You're going to kill us all?" asked Uma, incredulous at what she was hearing.

"Kill? Never! Nothing ever gets wasted, Angyal. I will draw all of my children to me and I will become stronger and stronger. I will grow and I will return to my former powers and I will regain my former glories, but here, in the world as it is now? It will be so much more fun!"

34

"How!" gasped Uma, "how will you do this terrible thing?"

"You my Angyal. You are one of them. They will never see you coming and they will not know what fate awaits them until they are already so far along the path there is no turning back. You are the perfect vessel for my... revenge."

Uma shook her head, trying to dislodge the pressure she felt inside it. The darkness was closing in on her. She could feel it at her temples and pressing down on her eyeballs. She didn't want to believe this creature, but somehow she knew that every word was true. She was home and in the embrace of her mother and her mother was never, ever going to let her go again.

"Wait! Promise me one thing..."

"You are in no position to ask anything of me, but speak and I may indulge you, my child."

"If you have me, you no longer need the villagers do you?"

"No, I do not need them," conceded the dry, ancient voice.

As Isobel's former, dark companion, Uma's mother, ceased speaking, an ominous silence fell upon the room and Uma felt this strange and awful sensation. The darkness closed in upon her and it did not stop. It entered her and she was crushed as the part of her that made her who she was pushed further inwards and deeper inside herself. The invasion was total and relentless and she barely had time to think a dissenting thought before she was banished from the vampire that had once been Uma.

As the new Angyal opened her eyes she thought that she heard something. She could have sworn that she heard…

I don't need them, no.

But I want them.

The words were barely heard and then they were gone, and then dark tendrils snaked out from the Big House, a darkness descending on all of Brokmaster, a darkness that would never truly leave it.

35

Brokmaster

The legend of Brokmaster would rival that of the Mary Celeste.

If anyone ever lived to tell the tale.

Of the former occupants of the houses in the village nothing is known. The village lies eerily silent. A shrine. A time capsule left there for the occasional, unfortunate explorer to pore over for a short while.

Not that Brokmaster gets many visitors.

You see, Brokmaster lies in a bowl within a bowl and is not overlooked by another living soul. It is not a case of blink and you'll miss it, you will never know that it was ever there.

And if you do?

Well, let's just say that your knowledge of the existence of

Brokmaster will be fleeting and closely followed with the knowledge of your existence blowing in the wind like a single mote of dust. Perhaps noted momentarily by a living being but never remarked upon and certainly not remembered.

The biggest consolation is that the chances of anyone ever encountering Brokmaster are so very remote. Nearly as remote as that encounter with an impossible creature that is sometimes dreamt about, but that we know we will never meet. That person that we see across a crowded room and in the moment of seeing them we just know that not only are they *the one,* but that they will make all of our dreams come true and life will never, ever be the same again as the life and the world we thought we knew shatter into a million pieces.

If you were ever to cross paths with Uma, or rather the vampire that became an angel? Well, you'd think it was worth it, more than worth it, whatever the cost. Even if the cost was everything that you owned and everything that you were...

* * *

Bonus Content

The following is a stand-alone, short story that explores just how the vampire Isobel came to be.

Isobel

35

She hated this time of year.

If she ever slowed down and stopped being so busy, she'd have to admit that she hated a long, long list of things. The list had been growing for so long she would be better writing a list of things that she didn't hate. If she ever came to write that list, it would shock her to discover the blank page before her. She'd been running from herself for so long she had run out of time to do anything other than be angry, and to hate everything.

She hated herself.

She mistook this hate and anger for passion, drive and determination, easily done when she ignored the world around her and failed to see the impact she was having. The reactions of those around her. She kept busy and she kept moving so she never had to see those things.

Isobel also hated mirrors and the mirrors she hated most of all were people.

This time of year was depressing.

Why was it so dark, and all of the time!?

Then there was the idiocy of Christmas. The earlier and earlier build up and fake excitement, only for it all to be over after a brief spell of paper tearing followed by a gluttonous meal that made people fat and guilty.

What was the point?

People were so easily led, and so stupid.

She turned the light on in her flat. It was cold. Isobel didn't use the heating unless she was there. She worked long hours and the idea of heating an empty space and incurring undue expense was repugnant to her.

The flat was cold and no amount of heating would change that. On first glance, it was a homage to the bleak and spartan eighties. A monochrome Yuppie flat with no soul. This place was the antithesis of lived-in and were Isobel to bring anyone back for sex they would read the flat's message loud and very clear: there was no room in Isobel's life for anyone else. Not that she entertained anyone here, if she were to feel the need to scratch that particular itch she would do it on neutral ground. Hotel rooms made the transaction a lot neater and discrete. Discrete as in there was a very certain beginning and ending, with little chance of a sequel.

A sigh of consternation preceded her entrance. This was an Isobel trademark and it filled all who heard it with dread. It was a prelude to an onslaught from her sharp tongue. Isobel was deeply analytical and could find the fault in everything, and attribute it highly effectively. Her speciality was to cut and slash and knock things into shape. A traumatised, much smaller shape, but the numbers always added up and investors were always, always happy.

That there was an aftermath to Isobel's work escaped investors and her alike. Any fallout was the fault of the loser who failed to pick up the baton and run with it. The *issues* that were sometimes mentioned in passing were communicated in a language Isobel could never understand, what the hell did morale have to do with selling and maintaining an effective cost base to give the necessary return on investment? No wonder businesses went south with all this soft, namby-pamby nonsense.

Today, she had been engaged on an assignment with the same business she'd rescued from the brink five years ago. The problem was, there were so few good execs. If she wanted a job done properly there was only one way to do it, fire the person cluttering that space and do it herself. Her mind was whirring with all the actions she was going to have to take over the rest of this week. She'd met the management team today and they'd brought her along to what they called their monthly Town Hall meeting. The world and her poodle had attended. There was actually a bloody poodle in attendance! The resulting meeting had been more like a cattle market and had lasted the entire day.

A day of stupid navel gazing!

Every now and then, a few of the managers had looked askance at her, as though they expected her to speak or something. She had glowered back at them and they had looked away. She wasn't going to speak! She was watching and assessing and working out what was to be done. It was so depressing for her to come so swiftly to the conclusion that she should sack the lot of them, barring the poodle. The poodle had grown on her and was the best thing in the room come the second hour of that horrendous meeting.

She had censured herself when she caught herself *looking for the good team members.* Good!? They were all woeful. Within the first hour, she had to revise her expectations downwards: who was the best of a really bad bunch? Who would she save from the impending cull?

As she stepped into her open plan flat, she was forming her very first tangible action, she would find the building maintenance guy in the morning and take him to the meeting room she had endured an entire day of nonsense in, and she would have him take down the walls. There would never, ever be a meeting such as that again.

Meetings cultures were poison and a visible sacrifice would be made right from the very start. The room would go and then all those empty vessels would be on notice. Most of them would be without a job in a matter of days. She would push HR and override their procrastination and obstacle-making and if any of them didn't get it and didn't tow her line, then they would be made to add their name to that first list of fires. That usually got the point over, loud and clear. Forget procedure and process and do some bloody work!

The lights went out.

Isobel had taken three steps into her flat, she stopped and expelled a violent gust of air. By rights, the lights should have come straight back on in response to that breath of hers. Instead, the door that she had walked through closed itself, firmly. This should not have startled the unflappable Isobel. The door was after all, on a spring and self-closing, but the

35

timing of its shutting seemed to punctuate a moment in time.

It also removed the light from the outer hallway and the flat was plunged into almost total darkness save for the thin and inconsequential light from the outside that was filtered by the tinted windows.

Isobel stood there for longer than she should have. The flat was colder than it should have been and something felt out of kilter. She found that she was craning her neck and focusing on the faint sounds of the space around her. The gentle whir of the fridge, the almost imperceptible ticking of an analogue wall clock. Listening for the other sound that she expected to hear, but was not there. She waited a full minute longer, was there someone in her flat? Or was it that someone had been in her flat and left something of themselves on the air itself?

She shook her head as though to clear it of these childish thoughts. Something had obviously tripped the main light. A bulb had gone, was the mostly likely explanation. She nodded to herself and then clapped her hands.

The sound of the clap rang around the sparse flat, impossibly loud. Nothing happened. The side lights, standing light and table lamp should have come on. Even at this distance, with that resounding clap, lights in the bedroom should have come on.

They hadn't.

Isobel's heart skipped one beat and that was enough to spook her. She took a deep breath and it frightened her to feel it tremulous in her chest, a barely contained sob pressing upon her and fighting to free itself. She closed her eyes, even in the darkness, and composed herself.

This was ridiculous! She was acting like a child, it was just a simple power cut! A cold chill ran down her spine and tested the resolve of her legs.

Then why were the lights on in the hall and why were there lights on outside the flat?

She reached into her handbag and fumbled around, an unaccustomed clumsiness to her movements. She gasped as she managed to snag something under her finger nail. Gritting her teeth she redoubled her efforts and was rewarded as her finger found the familiar, smooth rectangle of her phone.

She almost cried with rage and frustration as she lifted it from her handbag and she saw that it remained dull. It nearly always lit up as she retrieved it, anticipating its use to her. Even before her finger found the circular button at the base of the screen she knew it was dead. She stared at the dull shape in her hand. She knew it was almost fully charged when she had used it on her way here, so why had it picked this moment to desert her and leave her in the dark? She had to fight the urge to sling it across the room and experience the immediate satisfaction of destroying the impertinent phone for its defiance.

The phone remained in her hand as she carefully walked the length of the dark flat to her bedroom, hoping against hope

35

that there was a working light in there or in the en suite. If not, she would use the phone on her bedside table to phone the concierge and get someone to fix the fault.

There, that was it. She now had a plan. Always have a plan, she thought to herself. She was unstoppable when she had a plan. Execution was her thing.

The index finger of her left hand found the light switch and pressed it slowly but deliberately.

Nothing.

Had she expected anything else?

She made the two steps to the en suite door and opened it. The lights in here came on automatically as the door opened. When they didn't, she walked in and waved her dead phone in the air like one of those brain dead girls at a boy band concert.

"I love you Bobbie," she said very quietly to her herself using a high pitch and saccharine voice dripping with contempt.

What the hell was going on, she thought to herself. She didn't have time for this! She left the en suite and walked carefully to her bed. The bedroom was almost pitch black. She never opened the thick, lined curtains. Her bedroom was for sleep and she was up and out in a matter of moments, and what was the point in opening curtains to a succession of dark days anyway?

She reached her hand out carefully towards the bedside table and patted the air several times, each time recalibrating the position of her hand to where she thought the bedside table should be. It pained her to get it wrong three times in a row, and even when she hit paydirt, she was way off the phone itself. As soon as she felt the shape of the phone, she slipped her fingers around the handset and lifted it to her ear. She was wondering how she'd find the zero button, but recalled the handset was old school and she'd find it on the fourth row below the grid of nine other numbers. She'd barely finished this thought and experienced the tiny slither of relief of her simple problem solving, when she attended to the phone at her ear.

Dead.

This wasn't right. Someone had done this and she had walked right into her flat. Was this a trap and if so, who would do this? She had plenty of low-level enemies. People needed to project their inadequacies on someone better than them, she got that. None of those people had the gumption and abilities to do this. None of them knew where she lived.

She listened again for a moment, but was greeted yet again with complete silence. She turned and felt for the edge of the bed with the backs of her legs, then she sat down.

That was when she screamed.

That was when she let go of any semblance of composure and self-restraint.

35

It turned out that she was a flight sort of a gal. She'd convinced herself that she was fight, fight, fight all the way, but in this particular set of circumstances? Yeah, she was all about getting the hell out of Dodge.

She launched herself from the bed and she lunged for the doorway. She caught the corner of the en suite wall with her shoulder and careened sideways, hitting the opposite wall and hearing the crack as she caught a picture frame. It crashed down behind her as she sought the doorway, the sound of it propelling her out of the room. She barely made it out through the doorway without hitting it. Had she have done that, all bets were off, she was going full tilt and like to do herself an injury.

She broke through into the main living space of the flat and abruptly slid and slipped to a halt. The physics of this manoeuvre did not work well for her and there was a snap. For a moment she dared to hope that it was only her heel that had failed as she felt it break under her foot, but then a spike of terrible pain shot up from her ankle and she collapsed almost soundlessly, grabbing the arm of the sofa to break her fall, she ended up in an awkward crouch, sobbing and biting her lip as the pain wracked her body and her head swam.

"You found my leftovers then?"

Despite her predicament, Isobel's head shot up and around at the sound of the voice. There, sat at the kitchen on one of the two barstools was a figure. Indistinct in the dark, but the voice was that of a woman of a similar age to Isobel.

Isobel opened her mouth to speak, to challenge this intruder but instead a low groan escaped her lips. Her ankle, it must be broken. Her eyes closed automatically as the pain rolled over her and she squeezed them tighter shut as she rode the wave. Her fists clenched and she dug her nails into her palms. A small, secondary gout of pain went almost unnoticed as her buckled nail gave out further and tore away from her finger.

She fought to clear her mind of whirls of confusion. Something had happened as she came into this room. Some thing. She had known there was something terrible here and she'd panicked, trying to halt her progress and get away from it, but then the pain had undone her and thrown that thing to one side, now there was a woman sat at her kitchen, only she didn't think it was a woman. Not exactly. She didn't stop to think about where she had come from. That surely she couldn't have missed her presence as she had entered the flat...

"What are you doing here?" Isobel breathed out the words as the pain wracked her body.

"Daniel brought me here."

Isobel flinched. The voice was closer now. She opened her eyes and the figure was standing over her. Still shrouded in darkness, her inability to see the intruder frightened her even further, as did the power imbalance between them. This standing over a weaker person thing was a trick right out of Isobel's book.

She grit her teeth and looked up into the place where the

figure's face would be, "Daniel? How the hell...?"

But of course, she knew, the toe rag had kept the key card she had given him. The one exception to her rule of not bringing anyone back here. Her one attempt at a so-called steady relationship and he'd lied when he'd said he'd lost the key to her flat. That wasn't the only lie he had told, but what had she expected from him, really?

"Is he...?" she asked the question automatically, and the sound of it surprised her. She did not want to know the answer to this question and it should have appalled her that she didn't care. Not really, Daniel didn't mean that much to her, never had. Nothing meant all that much, just her, and right now, her pain.

"Any good?" the voice carried a lilting tone that taunted Isobel, "you'd know better than me on that score. I'd give him a seven out of ten for effort, but his technique was somewhat lacking."

"I didn't mean that!" Isobel snapped despite her discomfort.

The initial pain had become a constant throbbing and she felt nauseous and despite the darkness, her eyes were swimming. It was more the sensation of dizziness that seemed to be coming through her eyes and rolling her head this way and that.

"That's the spirit! That's more like the Isobel that Daniel knew and loved!"

"Loved...?" she said it quietly, uncertain that she had heard right and even if she had, it couldn't have been meant that way.

The figure laughed and clapped her hands in glee, "you didn't know! Of course you didn't! Oh how exquisite you creatures are! Denying what you are. Denying what you see right in front of your very eyes. Denying that which you need."

Isobel growled in response.

The figure crouched down and reached a finger out to her chin, lifting her head, "and you... you are filled brim-full with denial. Anger and denial. You might just be the most blinded specimen I have ever encountered."

Blind.

Isobel was face to face with the figure now, and even in the dim light struggling to creep inside the confines of the flat, she should have been able to make out the features of that face and seen the eyes that she could feel boring into her, analysing her, assessing her. Measuring her up.

The finger under her chin was cold. The nail at its tip was very sharp, and it was incredibly strong. Isobel pressed her chin downwards and the finger did not budge, but the nail threatened to pierce her flesh, so she eased off a little. Only a little. Isobel wasn't used to backing down.

"What are you?" Isobel hissed the words.

A natural question and another question that Isobel didn't want the answer to, but it was there between them and she had to ask it.

The figure leaned closer, "tell me, what do you see?"

Isobel felt the cold words on her face and breathed in the breath of the creature before her, she smelt something ruined and ripe and fought her gagging reflex as the stench assailed her. She wanted to close her eyes and wish all of this away, but knew that she couldn't. That she wouldn't. She might have run when she felt that cold, dead body laying behind her in her own bed, but now that was not an option. Now she would fight or at least defy this thing and in that find at least a little redemption.

The thing in front of her chuckled and whispered, "that's the spirit! I like a fighter..."

A cold fist of ice clenched in her guts and twisted, her bladder threatened to let go. Was this thing really able to read minds? For a moment there, it felt...

"Tell me," more insistent now, "what do you see?"

"Nothing," replied Isobel.

"More," it snapped, "you can do better than that."

"Darkness and nothingness. You're cold and... there's an absence that..."

"Yes?"

"Terrifies me."

"Good, good!" the figure stood again, "with acceptance comes healing!"

Isobel shook her head, "what the hell do you mean?"

The figure merely shook it's head in reply, "get up, take the weight off, you look uncomfortable sitting like that."

"I can't!" shrieked Isobel.

"That word is banned in this house!" her father's voice boomed from the figure and Isobel, eyes wide with shock instantly scrabbled behind her and lifted her weight onto the sofa. She sat primly and properly, just the way she had been taught to behave. Her father's word was law and this was a habit that would never be broken.

"Good," said the figure, returning to it's almost generic, thirty something, female voice. It was a seemingly pleasant voice made for voice over work, there was nothing offensive about it, but then there was nothing of substance to it either. It promised nothing.

The figure took a seat beside her, Isobel did not fail to notice the absence of weight pushing down on the seat beside her as the figure took its place.

35

They sat like that for a while. In the dark. A tangible and brooding silence between them. Isobel remained sitting to attention, just as she had been taught. Her hands placed neatly on her lap.

"Ah!" said the figure, making Isobel jump and wince with the movement on her ankle, "I forget. I have forgotten many things. You do you know, when you're as old as I am."

Isobel sat quietly, not wanting to ask this thing how old it was. It had used her Father's voice and it *knew*. There was a place beyond fear and she was there now. She felt detached from herself and what was happening, even the pain was blurred and of no real consequence. She was fine where she was right now and she did not want to do anything that would snap her right back into that fear and confusion she had experienced. Maybe this wasn't real. Maybe she had finally lost it, just exactly how her father had predicted. Snapped and lost her mind, just like her mother had all those years ago when Isobel had been too young to remember.

"Oh no! Do you still think that?" the figure chuckled, "but of course you do! Daddy's Little Girl aren't you!"

Isobel turned her head towards the figure, incomprehension shrouding her features.

"Your mother was never crazy, far from it. Maybe if she'd found a seam of crazy and embraced it she wouldn't have been driven to her death by *him*."

Isobel's brow knotted and her mouth fell open.

"He killed her as sure as eggs is eggs, my dear."

A single tear fell from her right eye. She felt it travel down her cheek and wondered at this strange detachment she was feeling. She felt almost… anaesthetised. A small voice deep within her was shouting, but she could barely hear it. Something about danger and that it was doing this. That thing. It's what it does…

"But of course," the figure continued, "you always knew that. You saw it all, and then you had years and years of him showing what a cold-hearted and loathsome bastard he really was. No one could survive that…" the figure pointed a finger at her and jabbed the next words at her, "except… you… did!"

"This isn't happening…" whispered Isobel.

"Well, that is one option you could take. Pretend it isn't happening. Just like the worst of the people you crush under your corporate heel. They really are the worst of them, aren't they? I have to agree, and I'm not just saying that, because, you know…"

The figure waved an encompassing hand at itself and then at Isobel.

"Are you saying that you're me?" asked Isobel.

The figure clapped, "there you go! You're on the money!

Kinda..."

Isobel shook her head.

The figure tilted its own head, "Hmmmm... we'll come back to that in good time, for now, less about you and more about me. I don't get to talk about myself very often at all. Can't remember the last time. It's the hunger you see, once I go beyond a certain point I lose a degree of self-control and it takes over. So, I shouldn't pass up this wonderful opportunity should I?" The figure shrugged, "where to begin," it said in a deep, Scottish male voice, "not there," it said in an urbane man's voice, "or there," in a Welsh woman's voice.

The figure paused and looked at Isobel, "I should lose the voices shouldn't I?"

"Why don't you use your own voice?" asked Isobel. The voice deep inside screamed at her, but she either couldn't hear it, or was ignoring it, she was in a different place and beyond help now.

"I don't..." the generic female voice had returned, "you haven't guessed the half of it, have you?"

Isobel shook her head. She was astute, but this was too much of a reach, even for her. Besides, her imagination had been boxed up and locked away very early on in her childhood.

"Let me tell you a little about myself. What little I can remember anyway..." the voice became Isobel's voice and

Isobel shuddered at the theft of a part of herself.

"My self is a difficulty I'm afraid. It escapes even me. Sometimes I wonder whether all I am is that overriding hunger... I am a reflection. A mirror. Only people see what they want to see and for my part, I let them see what they want to see. The more that they gaze upon me, the more lost and enmeshed they become. Invisible and impossibly thin threads entwine them and in time they shroud themselves in those threads and present themselves to me. And my hunger. They are unaware of any of this, and yet they always know. People were built to know in order to survive, but they have got so good at denying, that my work is made easy.

"Mostly, people see someone they dream of meeting. A unicorn of a person who will save them and make their lives whole. They want happiness, as though happiness were a destination or a permanent state of being. Some focus upon a single person from their past, someone they have made unreal over time. Others create amalgams of loves past and loves lost. The ones that got away. Others have a little more imagination and create their own object of desire almost from scratch.

"I have lapsed of late into a terrible drudgery and mostly I have feasted upon the elderly. I say feasted... they're like a Chinese take away, I'm hungry five minutes later. They are so close to death, the pickings are slim. Some of them have such a pending immediacy with death that that is the object of their desire. Always the same. Skeleton in a hooded cloak. No imagination when it comes to death. Then again, I've tried to come up with some alternatives and whoever designed that version of death managed to add that tip-of-the-tongue or ear-worm attribute, so that once you have skeleton death, nothing can replace it. Other than nothingness of course, which is what death is.

"You are a bit different, my dear. Not unique. So many of you out there and so few combinations and permutations when you grind it all down in a mincer. You see almost nothing. You see yourself, except you're dark and at the same time, not there...

"You got issues, girl! So much hate and anger! He really did a number on you your dad, didn't he? Ah well, never mind..."

"So, what are you?" asked Isobel as she glanced towards where she knew the door to freedom to be. Keep this thing talking and pick a moment, she thought to herself. Listen, act natural and find that moment. The diatribe it had launched into had seemed to have weakened its hold on her and already Isobel was dismissing that episode as the shock caused by the injury to her ankle. Now she had hope and she thought she still had a chance.

"Still not got it?" the figure shrugged, "I suppose not. The legends of my kind are close, but no cigar I'm afraid. The problem is that no one has ever met me and lived to tell the tale. That's how I roll. I take my time to get to know a person and then I just can't help myself I'm afraid. I go to all of the bases and beyond and there is never, ever a second date. Nothing left to have a second date with if you're nit picking."

Isobel nodded at the figure, urging it to go on. Wanting it to go on so she could find her moment.

"Blood, I drink blood."

"You're a vampire?"

"That's the one! Got there in the end didn't we?"

"But I thought…"

"Sparkles? Can't go out in daylight? Garlic? Crosses? Enduring romance laced with erotic danger?" the figure leant in, "think about it, you're a bright woman. How does any of that stack up with a cold, heartless apex predator? This is the first time I've had a proper conversation with anyone in as long as I can remember. It's quite liberating really. I should do it more often. And I will. Thanks to you."

"Am I meal or are you going to turn me?" asked Isobel.

"Straight down to business! I like it! And you are, no doubt, taking into account that I have just recently eaten. However, there are facts that you are not in possession of. How much do I need to eat? I may still be hungry, in which case, you are on the menu. But if not…

"Let me dissuade you of something right now. Turning isn't an option. How would that work? Seen any precedents for it?"

Isobel shook her head.

35

"No, I don't turn people. They're food."

"Then how do you…" Isobel eyed the door again and the space between her and where the handle should be. She needed a distraction. She needed to get through that door and into the light and then she would stand a chance. She could make a noise and get help. From here though? No one would hear her and she did not doubt that this thing would shut her up swiftly and very finally if she tried anything in close proximity to it.

"Procreate?"

Isobel nodded.

"We live for a very long time, some say forever. That's enough for me. I dare say we could mate, just the same as the birds and the bees do. Why bother?"

"So, you're a vampire. You show people what they want and do it in such a way that they willingly let you bite their necks and feed?"

"That's the short and tall of it. Only, I don't often go the whole hog, I give people enough of a fighting chance that they can still put up a bit of a fight. It's more fun that way. The final struggle. There's something thrilling in that. And it sates the hunger no end."

"But no one has ever fought you and won?"

"No… I like my meals hot. I want that blood pumping!"

"Do you ever... you know?"

The figure chuckled, "sex and death? Of course I do. Actually, I don't have a choice more often than not, there's something in the way people respond to me and their impending end, and if it works for them, then it works for me. If you know what I mean."

Unfortunately, Isobel thought she knew exactly what this figure meant.

"What about me?" Isobel placed a hand on the figure's thigh and tried her best not wince at the way it felt, cold and somehow... dead.

The figure's head bowed as it looked at her hand and that was all Isobel needed, she pushed up from the sofa and put her best foot forward. Ragged pain shot up her leg from her ruined ankle but she carried on through the pain. She had slipped her heels off as they spoke and she used her good leg to propel her forwards as far as she could with each step on that foot, her bad ankle was slowing her down, but there were only a matter of a few steps across the flat to that outer door. As she neared the door she stretched her arm out and leaned forwards as though she were seeking the finishing tape. Her hand closed on the door handle and she felt a wave of elation as she turned the handle and pulled.

The door did not open.

"You ran," said a voice directly behind her.

35

Isobel tensed and at the sound of it. Her mouth set. Determined not to show any sign of defeat or weakness.

The figure moved up close behind her. Almost, but not quite pinning her to the door.

"I knew you were different," it said in her ear.

Isobel shuddered at the voice and the way it stroked her ear.

"Turn around."

"My ankle," she said by way of an excuse not to turn.

"Will soon be of no concern to either of us. Turn around," the voice was not her father's. Not quite, but it would not be defied.

Isobel turned, avoiding contact with the body of the figure hemming her against the door, but feeling it all the same.

"What are you going to do to me?" she asked, struggling not to let her voice break with the terror that was rising up inside her.

"Do? Now that is an interesting question. Let's couch it in terms you will be familiar with. I'm taking over your firm. This is an aggressive takeover bid and from now on in, I will be in charge."

The figure's head drew close, almost nose to nose, and gradually, like the dawning of a new day, the darkness on the face drew back to reveal a face familiar to Isobel.

Her own.

Isobel gasped.

"I'm going to *be* you," said the figure and with that, her mouth closed on Isobel's and she took her in an embrace that was so encompassing she could not move at all. She felt that cold fetid breath enter her mouth and go down, down, down filling her. Her head swam and a scream climbed up inside her, but could not escape and with it, her breath was stilled in her body. Her eyes went wide and all they would see were her own, intense eyes staring back at her.

Then nothingness.

* * *

Isobel awoke sometime later on the cold, hard floor of her apartment. She lay there motionless and eyes still closed, disoriented by the strange dream that she had as she lay unconscious. She supposed that she must have passed out. Overdoing her working hours had eventually caught up with her.

She opened her eyes cautiously and let out an involuntary yelp.

35

The last thing she had experienced in that strange and frightening dream was the first thing she saw now. Her over large eyes staring back at her.

Then she laughed.

She had collapsed at the base of the full length mirror by the front door of her apartment.

The cold, hard floor and the reflection of her eyes had somehow been incorporated in her dream. However, the lights were on and it was still dark outside, she was relieved that this was so. She had passed out, had a bad dream and now she was back in the land of the living. This was a dream she was not going to share with anyone. A therapist would have a field day with a dream like that!

She moved to get up from the cold, tiled floor and let out a wail of pain, grabbing her swollen ankle as she remained seated and rocking to and fro in time with the waves of pain. Her mouth fell open, and this time she didn't rationalise the damage to her ankle away, because she was looking over at the sofa and the heels laying there on the floor beside it, one of the shoes was missing a heel.

Surely it wasn't…

Real?

Her head whipped around frantically for a sign of the shadowy figure and when there was none she did not relax. Could not relax, because there was this strange sensation coming from inside her. A building from her core and a corresponding growing sensation from within her head.

"No…" was all she managed to breath from her body as something grew and pushed and writhed within her.

I'm going to be you.

* * *

A man with blood shot, weary eyes and a hang dog expression, lifted the police tape and rolled his eyes theatrically at the constable who was standing guard and fielding questions from nosey neighbours feigning concern.

The expression said it all and there was a shared moment, neither of them would willingly swap places with the other.

The DI took the lift to the top floor of the apartment block and walked to the only open flat door, that it was flanked by two more constables gave the location of the crime scene away. He nodded at the man and woman standing with their backs to the action then he looked through the door and immediately covered his mouth, swallowing at the rising acid threatening to come all the way up and out of him. He was glad he'd not had time for his customary black coffee, let alone breakfast.

"Hell!" he gasped at the sight before him.

35

He could feel slight acknowledgements from both constables. They were glad to be facing away from this particular scene.

DS Tadcastle had heard the arrival of her boss, DI Burke, and she was now at the door. Burke backed up, encouraging her to come out of the flat so he could calm himself and process what he had just been so rudely confronted with.

"What have we got?" he said in as business-like manner as possible.

"Man dead in the bedroom, possibly a sex game gone wrong," she started with the most straightforward aspect of the crime scene.

"What about that in the living room? Don't tell me that was a sex game?"

Tadcastle shook her head, "No boss. The Professor took one look at it and asked where the Pharoah was."

"Come again?"

"You know how they used to pull the brains out through their nostrils and..."

The DI raised a hand, his gorge rising again. Best part of thirty years in the force and this was the first time he'd gotten squeamish. He took a breath and steadied himself.

"You're saying someone removed his insides?"

"Not his, someone else's. Possibly the lady who owned the flat."

"Where's the rest of the body then?"

"Damned if I know…" shrugged Tadcastle, "It's weird. It's as though it got up of its own accord and walked away."

About the Author

Jed writes about people. It doesn't matter who or what the people are, nor where they are, it is all about what they do and how they react and behave, when life happens to them.

Jed does his very best not to take himself too seriously. There was a point in his former life where he lost his inner child, having left it in an umbrella rack in the foyer of an office near Liverpool Street Station. He is still doing his best to make amends for that unfortunate oversight and his inner child is not letting it go any time soon.

Jed Cope is the author of seven Ben and Thom books. He has also penned nine further books and a collection of short stories. He is working industriously to add to that number in the mistaken belief that he will be given a day off from writing once he's written his twentieth novel. Unfortunately, his captors got distracted by an ice cream van that had been converted into a travelling pub and completely forgot about

Jed. Still, I'm sure it'll all turn out fine in the end. Usually does in circumstances such as these.

The eight books that aren't set in Ben and Thom's universes cover such genres as crime, supernatural and horror. Jed writes as he reads, across a variety of genres. Maybe he likes variety, noting that it is the spice of life, or perhaps he is hedging his bets. Whatever the case may be, he likes to write stories that have a twist or two along the way…

As well as gullible and well-meaning, Jed is a charismatic, enigmatic and pneumatic sort. Having retired from a successful career as a secret multiple F1 Champion, octopus whisperer and technology trillionaire, Jed was abducted from his underground shed where he was working on the next generation of psychic begonias, to do what he does best; make things up.

You can connect with me on:
- https://twitter.com/jed_cope
- https://www.facebook.com/jedcopeauthor

Also by Jed Cope

The Village - A Vampire To Die For, is Jed's seventeenth book.

He has another horror title - The Pipe, if you've enjoyed reading about the vampire Isobel, why not try The Pipe next?

So far, there are seven Ben and Thom Books:
　　The Chair Who Loved Me
　　Are Bunnies Electric?
　　Smell My Cheese!
　　Death and Taxis
　　Oh Ben and Thom, Where Art Thou?
　　Something Merkin This Way Comes
　　Mrs Ben's Boys

Book Eight is a twinkle in the author's eye, but that twinkle is a determined wee beggar and it has a habit of making its way out into the world, so watch this space! The title may even include the word Twinkle...!

There's a children's Ben and Thom Book:
　　If Only... The Adventures of an Intergalactic Chair

And seven further books that have nothing whatsoever to do with Ben and Thom:
　　The Pipe
　　The Entrepreneur's Club
　　Two for the Show
　　The Rules of Life

Dear Kids
Do You Remember?
Lola's Path
The Village – A Vampire To Die For

And a collection of short stories:
   Locked, Down and Short

Jed intends to add to the list before you've finished reading this one. It's what he does.

Printed in Great Britain
by Amazon